Ruby's Story

A Novel

Bill Cronin

Printed in the United States of America
ISBN: 978-0-9908381-2-8
Library of Congress Cataloging-In-
Publication Data
Library of Congress Control Number
2016910501

Dedication:
For Linda, the person I write for.

1

The sun breached the horizon and bled out on the still water of the lake. Wisps of fog formed by frozen air and warm lake water drifted across the path of the sun and diffused its brilliance into opaque yellows and oranges. Through the misty vapor, the Lakeside Inn across the water appeared to be on fire as the sun rose directly behind it.

I stood on the end of the sixty-foot, T-shaped, frost covered dock, my beloved Lake Dora laid resplendent before me. To my left, the city of Mount Dora was a silhouette on the horizon. To my right the shoreline wended westward in an arc to a point beyond which darkness still lay on the lake in slumber. Immediately in front of me, on the bottom of the lake, with only the windshield breaking the water was our ski boat, neglected and abandoned. Weathered nylon rope still tied off to cleats on the dock led to frayed breaks where the weight of the sinking boat had broken the tethers fore and aft.

The dock on which I stood was once a point of pride. Now, its treated-pine decking, posts and rails were a collection of warped, rotted and nail-exposed hazards slick with frost. I stood in flannel pajamas, a fleece bathrobe and flip-flops, my uniform over the past forty-something days, I hugged myself, shivered, wanted to tip-toe my way back to the safety of shore, but held on to the rickety structure by the importance of the moment and the significance of this particular setting.

Em and I brought a bottle of Chardonnay in a bucket of ice with two glasses to this very site and toasted the completion of the draft of every new novel. In addition, with the toast, my work would end and hers would begin. It was a ceremony during which the bottle was emptied, the baton was passed, and on most occasions lovemaking followed. Em was not only my wife of eight years she was my manager, and my editor. She was still, technically, my wife. This morning there will be no wine, no Em and definitely no lovemaking. Em left me more than a month ago. Out of compassion for my state of mind, she would not file divorce papers until I was in a more stable emotional state. She finally realized that she could no more raise me from the bottom of the pit I was in than I could single-handedly raise the boat whose waterlogged, rotted remains lay on the bottom of Lake Dora. Her efforts were courageous and selfless. Despite her hardened steel will and relentless drive to lift my spirits, she failed, lost hope and finally gave up.

The boat was emblematic of my life over the past three years. While the process of sinking took a while, multiple projectiles to the hull of my life slammed it to the bottom in a matter of hours. Although my life was shredded months earlier, the events of November 14, 1995 tipped it into the emotional abyss.

It has been forty-one days since my publisher threatened to cancel a million dollar contract if I did not complete a draft of a long overdue novel. Forty-one days ago, my publisher Reynolds and Ryan summoned me to New York and threatened me with a breach of contract if I did not deliver a draft of the second of three novels by December 27. On my return from Gotham, Emily had backed a truck up to the door of our home in my absence and emptied it of her belongings after eight years of my mercurial personality. Em told me she was finished watching depression ruin my life and career and wanted out before it ruined hers. It was less than ten minutes following her announced departure that I sat on the side of the road and reached for a Glock 9mm handgun that I kept in the glove box of my car with the intention of ending what little life I had left. Her rejection was the final indignity, the last grain of despair that could be poured into my desperate life. Only a state trooper, curious about a car parked on the side of a major highway in the fog of early morning, intervened and disrupted my hastily conceived exit plan.

At the very moment the trooper rapped his knuckles on the window of my car, as I reached for the gun in my glove box, I felt my life crash to the bottom of the pit I had been freefalling in for the three years. It had been forty-one days since the state trooper told me to "move on." The weight of that command carried more meaning than I wanted to admit to myself then. Now it seemed so clear. The young kid with the Smokey-the-Bear hat was an angel unaware. From the grimy bottom of the darkest place I had ever been his knock on the window of my car was a good-Samaritan, last second grab at a man who had jumped from a building. It was only a moment but so much happened in that wisp of time.

The weight of my life crushed me; it broke me into nothingness. Never had I ever felt so insignificant, helpless and fearful. Everything that I loved had been taken away from me. I was nothing and had nothing. I cried out to God. "Help me." I had no solutions for any of my problems. I had no direction. The horror of it, the memory of having nearly lost my mind and the cold, dark loneliness frightened me beyond description. Something in me changed. In the very core of me, my "want-to" was transformed. There were two things I knew in that instant: first, I wanted to live and, second, I wanted out of the darkness and never wanted to return to that miserable God-forsaken place.

There was the faintest of light at the top of the long black tunnel above me; only visible with great effort and concentration - but light none-the-less. As the trooper extinguished his flashing blue lights, pulled around me and accelerated on to highway 441, it marked the point at which I began to make a conscious effort to climb out of the pit I had excavated for myself. Until then, writing was just out of the question. It required energies from sources in me that my problems had long ago extinguished. I looked at my submerged boat in front of me and realized that it was on the bottom because I lost interest in it - I did not care whether it survived or not. Forty-one days ago, I did not give a rip about anything in my life including me. However, in that instant, when I realized how close I had come to the end my life, the wind changed. In the days that followed, with help from my sister Billie and my childhood sweetheart, Jody, I began to write again and with the writing came hope.

I do not know how long I stood on the end of the dock before the numbing cold registered. It was Christmas morning. While I could celebrate the completion of my novel, there was still the collateral damage of the emotional destruction I had caused those around me - Em in particular. Selfishly, I had a book that needed editing. I had no doubt in my mind that as soon as I delivered the draft of this book to my agent, Lisa Catera, Reynolds and Ryan, my publisher, would demand the final installment with the same threats and intimidation of forty-one days ago. Normally it took three to four months to write a novel and that with my full focus. Usually, my publisher was happy to get two completed works a year. This gave me three to four months to rest, fill my creative tanks, research and think through future projects. To get another novel written in forty-five days or less would mean writing ten hours-a-day, seven days-a-week. To finish this novel, I had been chained to a keyboard day and night for the last month. While I had been a slave to my writing, it had done more than any counselor had or therapist could have done to extract me from my funk. *Death in the Desert*, was more than just another novel in a string of action/adventure tales. It was the gear I needed to break out of my emotional prison. Yes, it was an escape, as my writing had always been — a departure from the realities of life that were often more than I could handle. However, while I was deep in the imaginary Sahara Desert, ready to coax a fifty-year old B-24 Liberator bomber into flight, I worked through all the emotional issues that had sandbagged my life and had brought my writing career to a dead stop. In the long hours hunched over my keyboard, I mourned Em's irreconcilable departure, wrapped my mind around the reintroduction of

6

my half-sister Billie into my life after nearly a thirty year absence, forgave myself for a long misplaced feud I had had with my long-deceased mother and gave recognition to new wounds I had created with my father. Writing had always been therapy until depression sapped my energy, the words disappeared and then the spiral downward began in earnest. Writing had always been my interface with the world around me. When the words ran out so did my ability to cope. Once I understood that which held me captive emotionally, and I moved past it, only then did the words pour from me as they had for so many years.

The sun stretched out in the sky and drew the yellow and orange mist hovering on Lake Dora away like one would pull a curtain from a window to let light fill a darkened room. Bass cleared the surface of the water nearby with a slosh. A gaggle of black and white headed Canadian geese splash landed on the glassy water, formed a line near the dock and headed off into what was left of the fog. Even in the depths of my depression, early mornings on this most hallowed dock kept me from falling off the edge of sanity. From this very spot when there was not an emotional drop of water left in my life, I found a canteen here even among the ruins of my boat and this beloved structure.

I wanted to call Em. It was not because I needed her professionally, every bone in my body ached for her. I wanted to tell her that my life was on the mend and ask her for another chance. I had done that and she rejected that option out of hand just over a month ago and I had not called her since. I wanted to tell her that, despite my loneliness, I felt better than I had felt for a long time. I wanted to share with her the good news that I had completed my story in record time and strategize my next novel as we had done on my previous sixteen books. Em told me when I talked to her last, that despite the fact she could not live with me anymore, she would continue to work for me if I felt like I could handle it. That was the rub; could I handle it? Probably not. Aside from her professional competence, she was one of the most desirable women I had ever been around. She was, until I destroyed it, one of the best friends I had ever known. I do not think I could be with her without the total oneness we had enjoyed together.

I needed to call Lisa Catera. Lisa was more than an agent. For the past twenty years, she had been a friend, confidant and champion of my career. Em and Lisa had been closer than sisters. Lisa, however, was also a pile driver of a boss. As soon as I called her to let her know that *Death in the Desert* was finished, she would begin to pressure me to complete the next one.

The cold finally penetrated. I knew I wanted Em back in my life. I knew the odds were long, but

I had to try. I needed to find an editor. I did not want to ask Em to do it unless I could have all of her back and I knew that would take time, perhaps a lot of time and I needed an editor now. Before I turned to go to the warmth of my home and studio, I looked at the dock and pledged to myself that I would have my boat raised, replace it and my dock rebuilt as soon as businesses reopened after the holidays.

2

Lakeshore Drive separated many of the homes along Lake Dora from the water. Owners took advantage of Riparian Rights that gave them deeded access to the lake. They constructed docks or boathouses on the water directly across the street from their homes. While some felt it an odd arrangement, I valued the southern exposure and views of the lake from my studio.

I walked across the street to the redbrick structure I called home. The house was the shape of a square C with the open end tilted slightly toward the lake. The main house was located in the lower leg of the C and my studio in the upper where a plate glass window gave me an unobstructed view of the lake. By day, the many angles of the sun gave life to the water, and by night, the lights from Mount Dora brought atmosphere to my secluded workspace. During the worst of my depression, I had never left my studio. I would sleep in it for days on end, doors locked, and cellphone off. When I first bought the place, cellphones still looked like bricks with an antenna and wired phones were still a necessity. I did not want a phone in my studio, so I installed an intercom system between the house and the studio. When I was writing, Em would save me from the phone and only signal me if a call was crucial. When I could not write, she would plead with me over the intercom to come into the house and eat, or to get out of the "hole" for a while, her name for the studio.

One afternoon she had an accident in her car and could not get through to me. She demanded that we install a second line that had an extension in my office. There was no bell to ring, only a red light would flash then stay red if a call had come through. Since Em was the only one with the number, it was always her and she would only call with something important. Then cellphones came into vogue, became irreplaceable and she made sure I had it at all times

When I approached the door to the studio, through the reflection of Lake Dora on the plate glass window, the red light blazed on the old telephone set that sat on my desk.

"Em, is everything okay?"

"Merry Christmas to you too, Scrooge."

"Merry Christmas, it has been so long since you used this line. I just thought there was a problem."

She said, "I tried your cell but it went straight to voice mail. You must have it turned off. I decided to try the old landline. Guess it still works."

I pulled the cellphone from the pocket of my robe, checked it and the phone was dead. I tried to turn it on without success. "The battery must have died."

"When did you use it last?"

"I can't remember. I've been too busy. Maybe a week ago, I really don't know."

"Your aunt has been trying to reach you. How she got my number I've no idea, but she has been trying to call you for several days."

"Em, I haven't been in the main house to check messages for days. Anything serious?" Ruby never called me. Never. I tried to call her at least once a month and Em and I tried to see her two to three times a year. Ruby and Glory Jean were my mother's sisters and on opposite ends of the personality spectrum. Glory Jean was an irreverent, non-conformed, wild woman. Ruby was deeply religious, serious and gracious down to every fiber of her southern roots.

"Actually, it was St. Vincent's Hospital in Jacksonville. Someone in administration called for her. Apparently, she's there and is asking for you. They wouldn't tell me anything other than that. I hope it isn't serious." Em's concern was genuine. She had grown close to Aunt Ruby over the past eight years and they connected at a level that I did not comprehend.

My Tabby, polydactyl cat, Hemingway, jumped up on the desk and surveyed his vast domain then inched his way across the desk and nudged my hand for attention.

"I hope nothing is wrong as well. As soon as we get off, I'll call the hospital." I had resisted calling Em as I neared the end of my story. Part of it was stubborn anger that she had left me, rejected me even. The other part; I found it difficult to juggle all the emotions regarding the enormous role she had played in my work and life. Even though Em had told me that she was finished with me, I had held out a sliver of hope that I could still piece together my relationship with her. I was afraid that if my conversation with her drifted much past hello that I would learn that my hope was displaced. No sooner had the words, "I finished the bomber story" left my lips, I regretted it.

"That's marvelous," she cooed. "When did you finish it?"

"This morning, actually an hour ago. I wanted to call you and share the good news." There was awkward dead air.

"My offer to continue to edit for you still stands . . . that's if you still need me . . . if you still want me to."

We came instantly to the place that I did not want to go.

"Em, I need to ask you something." My stomach felt like a caldron into which someone had just poured a pot full of hot pasta. I wanted Em around me very much, I wanted to see her, smell her and be absorbed into the warmth of her being. However, I knew that if I were around her or had constant interaction with her, it would irritate the open wound she created when she left me. I barely hung on emotionally as it was. I needed to protect the fresh coat of paint I had applied to my life.

"Shoot," she said. I could picture her perfectly made up mouth as she said the words.

"I'm much better. I'm writing and enjoy it. I feel good. I know you had to leave to get away from me. I needed to get away from me. If I continue to progress as I have for the past month or so, I'll be back to my old self . . ."

"Jack, I know where this is headed and I don't want to go there. In fact, I had planned to wait until after the first of the year to send the divorce papers to you. I promised I would give you some time. You're writing, doing better and I'm proud of you. And I'm willing to help as long as you need me."

"But getting back together?" I hung the question in the air like the blade of a guillotine.

"No, Jack. That won't happen. I'm sorry."

"Em, I don't think I could handle working with you right now. It would be too hard. I'm still in love with you."

I could hear her breathe into her cellphone. "I understand, Jack. We all have to do what we need to do. Let me know what's going on with Ruby. I want to call her or send her flowers. I'll let you go now."

"Bye, Em." I laid the antique phone onto the receiver base, scratched Hemingway behind his ears and considered whether this was the final nail in the coffin of our marriage.

I looked around my studio. The sleeper-sofa against the wall that I used as a bed stood disheveled. I had not changed the linens in two weeks. Books, magazines and printed-paper from the Internet and remnants of fast-food meals warred with each other for control of top of the desk in front of me. I had piled dirty clothes on the guest chairs in front of the desk. The single counter kitchenette was overrun with dirty dishes. Burned coffee covered the bottom of an overworked and under-cleaned coffee pot; the smell contaminating the air. Dust covered everything else. Dust motes swirled in the air as the sun fought its way into my corner of the world.

I could feel myself backslide into darkness and my resolve not to call Lisa dissolved. I thought about calling her on the old landline, but I knew she would not recognize the number on caller I.D. and there was no chance she would take the call at home. I pulled my cellphone from my pocket, reached for the charging cord that had fallen on the floor, plugged in the phone and called her New York number. I did not want to call her, but I needed to talk with someone.

"Lisa! Merry Christmas!" I thought I sounded desperate, lonely.

"Jack, do you realize what time it is?" Her voice was filled with sleep, and her groans equal to the effort the sun made as it struggled to rise above the fog on the lake.

"I just wanted to share the good news. I finished the book this morning."

"That's wonderful," she said and yawned. "I talked to Em the other day and she's ready to edit as soon as you're finished."

Lisa Catera was my friend. When nothing else had gone right in my life, she had been there for me. She also worked for me and made a handsome living as my agent. There was no question in my mind that she was my agent first and my friend second. I had always wondered how long our relationship would last if our business dealings ended. I did not have that many friends that I could be meticulous. It was comments like these that reminded me of her place in my life. Despite the glamour that goes along with the profession of a novelist, it was very solitary work. I spent hours huddled over a keyboard. You have to be somewhat introverted to endure the seclusion. I have relationships with other writers, but I have not reached out to them in a while. Depression had so isolated me I had cut myself off from just about everyone. Lisa was one of the few people I let in.

"That's why I called, Lisa. Em and I just got off the phone. I don't want to use her. In fact, I can't. It would be too hard."

"Jack, we're up against it. I get daily threatening calls from Reynolds on your progress. You know they're going to tap dance on my head for the next novel as soon as we meet their deadline. They want a draft of the third and final novel by February fifteenth. We just don't have time to look for someone else."

I considered the dilemma. "If I start right now and do all-nighters for the next month and a half, I might, just might, meet their deadline. I don't have time to find another editor and I'm not going to use Emily." I stopped short of saying something like, 'earn a little of the ten percent you get and find one for me,' but I held my tongue.

Lisa breathed heavily into the phone. "Jack, these are the holidays. How can I find someone now?"

"Lisa . . ."

"Alright. Alright! I'll take care of it." More breathing, less labored. "How are you and Em?"

"That's the point, Lisa. We aren't. Em has no interest in reconciliation. None. She'll serve me papers any day now. She would've done it six weeks ago if I hadn't asked her for a little time. She told me then that there was no chance. I wasn't ready to hear it. It's done." The finality of the words hit me hard, unexpectedly hard.

"I was afraid of that. I feel bad, Jack, for both of you."

We finished our conversation. She wished me a Merry Christmas and said that she would get to work on an editor. Those would be big shoes to fill. I could not worry about it. It was in Lisa's hands.

3

I turned my attention to the scribbled telephone number of the hospital in Jacksonville. I called and talked to a social worker assigned to my aunt's case. She relayed the same message she had given Em; that Ruby was asking for me. She said she wanted to meet with me when I came but was evasive about the nature of the discussion. I had to write another novel by the middle of February. As much as I loved Ruby, I just did not have time for this.

Late in the morning of Christmas day, the lobby of St. Vincent's was sparsely populated and heavily decorated for Christmas. Tinsel hung and Christmas music played softly in the elevator and the nurse's station on the third floor had a North Pole appearance. The door to room 301 was ajar. I poked my head in. A curtain had been pulled around the far bed in the semi-private room.

"Oh, honey, I'm so grateful for this. A woman has to smell pretty to feel pretty."

A nurse's aide looked out from behind the curtain. "I'm sorry sir, but you'll have to wait in the hall until I'm finished with Mrs. Johnson's bath."

From behind the curtain, "Is that you, Jackie?"

I answered, "Yes, ma'am."

"The nurse won't be long. Besides, you don't want to see an old woman in her all-together."

"I'll just be out in the hall." To the aide I said, "Take your time. I'm in no hurry." On the outside, I may have given the appearance of calm. On the inside, my stomach roiled and all I could think about was the plot to the next novel and all I had was the kernel of an idea.

Ruby's hospitalization was an untimely and unfair intrusion into the madness of my life. She was eighty-five.

Ruby's voice echoed off tiled walls and found its way into the hall. The banter between Ruby and the nurse's aide was comfortable and casual, as if they were sipping iced mint-tea together on an open porch. That was the place all of Ruby's conversations ended, a waltz of words where she made her guests feel uniquely special. As the aide bathed her, the aide had become a guest in Ruby's room.

Light footsteps from behind approached. I turned and caught the doctor before she entered Ruby's room.

"Excuse me. Are you Mrs. Johnson's doctor?"

The small elderly woman in the white smock and the name badge that read, "Alicia Sommers, MD," stopped. She asked, "Are you a relative of Mrs. Johnson's?"

"Nephew. But we're very close."

"Well, she's been through a lot. Doing quite well, though."

"What's the prognosis?"

"You mean from the surgery?"

"I just wondered if you were able to get all of the cancer."

"And your name is?"

"I'm sorry. Excuse my manners. Jack McNamara." I extended my hand and enfolded her small delicate hand. "I'm her health surrogate."

"Ah, you must be the author she talks about all the time. She's quite a fan of yours I'd say."

"Ruby's a character."

"That she is." She paused, and looked distracted. "I usually get a cup of coffee after rounds. Would you meet me in the cafeteria in about thirty minutes? I'd like to talk to you about Ruby and some options about her care."

"That would be great."

She patted me on the arm, gave me a warm look and then disappeared into Ruby's room.

Ruby lived in Jacksonville, Florida. Ruby and her sister Glory Jean were not terribly close. Had I moved Ruby to Savannah to live near Glory Jean, it would have been more difficult for Em and me to be involved in her care.

Ruby said behind the curtain "Oh, thank you, Juanita. You're such an angel, the bath was marvelous."

"The doctor will be finished in just a moment," the petite Hispanic aide said to me as she came through the door into the hall.

I could hear the muffled tones of the doctor's conversation with Ruby, but none of the words. Dr. Sommers appeared in the doorway. Her eyes narrowed over granny reading glasses. "It's good you're here." She reached up and squeezed my shoulder with her small hand. "She'll need your support now more than ever." She looked down at Ruby's chart, flipped through some pages, then briefly looked up at me. "We will talk more in the cafeteria." She let loose of my arm, patted it and then departed down the hall. Her touch of my arm communicated warmth in a way that words could not.

When I walked into the room, the doctor had opened the curtain and furled it against the wall. The room was on fire with orange and red Gladiolas Em had sent her last night. Ruby had her head turned toward the window and was startled by my entrance as though she had forgotten I was there.

Her face brightened. Her tightly curled grey hair surrounded her round fleshy countenance. Reluctantly, her lips formed a crooked smile. "Oh, Jackie, honey. Come give your Aunt Ruby a hug."

I slipped my hand under her neck and shoulders, bent over and kissed her on the cheek. She trembled at my touch and began to cry, first softly, then with abandon. I held my embrace until she gently pushed me away. "You're so precious to me.

24

The last thing you need is an old woman blubbering all over you." She patted her hair down, wiped her wet cheeks, and tried to sit up in bed, but the pain from her surgery blocked her. "Jackie, honey, find the switch on this contraption that raises my head, will you?" she said through clenched teeth. "I've got enough stitches in my stomach to open a quilting store." She made a significant effort to smile at her own joke.

I found the bed control just out of her reach and raised the top half of the bed to a half-sitting position. "You O.K.?" I took her hand and put it between mine. Rheumatoid arthritis had gnarled her fingers.

"It'll take more than a little surgery to get this old gal down. Remember, you're talking to the Bionic Woman."

Doctors had replaced both of her hips and one of her knees to counter the ravaging effects of her crippling disease. Bionic Woman is a title no doubt given to many patients who have undergone joint replacement. The honorary title stuck with Ruby, who wore the moniker with pride.

"What did the doctor say? You seemed pretty upset when I came in?"

"Isn't Doctor Sommers a jewel? I don't think I've ever met a doctor with the sensitivity she has. She cares so much about her patients. Always takes the time to explain things so that even I can understand. I just love her." With difficulty, she pulled tissue from a box on the rollaway table next to her bed and mopped up her eyes. "I want to talk to you about our story."

I had no idea what 'our story' was — there were so many of them. "O.K., let's talk about it."

I always found it of interest the vein of artistry that had woven its way through my mother's family. Ruby was an accomplished artist. Her oil painting skills blossomed late in life, oddly enough after arthritis had rendered her hands and fingers useless for anything more than the most rudimentary endeavors, one of which was to sketch and paint. Her favorite subjects were floral scenes painted to perfection with her unusual sense of color, eye for composition, exacting detail and subtle emotion.

Whenever I visited her, she had a slew of ideas for stories. She stubbornly refused to let me leave her company until I promised to use one of her ideas in a short story or novel. She would have written them herself, she told me many times, but found it difficult to write or type with her hands. Many of her ideas were good. Unfortunately, none of them lined up with material publishers felt had

26

any commercial value. I did not have the heart to tell her that I could not or would not use them. Therefore, I was not surprised when she wanted to talk about 'our' story.

For a writer to use the ideas of others is a mortal sin. The last thing a novelist needs is a lawsuit from someone who claims you have used one of their notions and then have to share royalties. In fact, at the end of every one of my books was a statement that, "I don't want story ideas from anyone and all the material I write is my own." She leaned forward and whispered to me. "I've got an idea for a novel you'll love. I know every time we get on this subject you think I have diarrhea of the mouth, but this is different. This story has been in me for a long time. I've got the whole thing written in my head. I want you to have it. But I want it to be ours."

"I'm always open to a blockbuster idea," I lied.

"Jackie, I'm serious about this one. I want this to be a legacy, my swan song. I am asking a lot, I know, but you're the only one I can turn to. I want you to promise me you'll write this story."

"You know I will," I lied again.

"No, Jackie, I mean for real. I want you to promise me."

"Publishing a story isn't always easy. It depends on the topic and whether a publisher will go for it."

"They'll go for this. I've no doubt. God gave it to me."

"God gave it to you?" Ruby had told me many times that she and God talked to each other. I understood the prayer part; it was the God-talking-back part that made me wonder about my bible-thumping aunt.

"Every detail. The whole story came to me as a single thought. Sugar, it's all here. Every line." She tapped the side of her head with a twisted finger.

"What's the story about?"

The Hispanic aide who gave Ruby her bath flew through the door. "Well Mrs. Johnson, you ready go? These two good-looking gentlemen will escort you to MRI. Doc wants pictures for your photo album. She says a beauty like you needs be photographed." The aide and the two attendants rattled around Ruby's bed and prepared to move her.

"Do we have to do this now? Jackie, my nephew, has come a long way to see me. Juanita, this is my nephew, Jackie, I mean Jack McNamara."

"It's nice to meet you." (You came out "jew.") She shook my hand. "This machine cost a lotta money and when people no show up, they get crazy. Maybe Jack will wait until you be done. No take long."

The attendants moved the IV fluids to the pole on her bed, unlocked the wheels and prepared to wheel her out of the room.

"Jack, please wait for me. We've so much to talk about."

"Mr. Jack, we have a waiting room down the hall. You could be there if you want." The nurse pointed at the wall in the direction of the waiting area.

Juanita smoothed out the sheets that covered Ruby and signaled the attendants and they maneuvered her through the door then down the hallway.

The crowded cafeteria on the first floor bustled with hospital staff and visitors who queued up on two food lines. Patrons talked loudly over the din and I wondered when the doctor came if we would be able to hear one another. It was nearly eleven when I went through the line, and found a quieter table in a distant corner of the room. I loved the smell of fresh coffee. The aroma wafted from the large Styrofoam cup on the table. Ruby's emotional reaction to her discussion with the doctor did not bode well. While Ruby had always been emotional, she would tear up at the slightest joyful provocation; she seldom wore her troubles on her sleeve. She would cry when she saw you for the first time in a while. She would tear up when someone showed her a kindness, or when something from nature moved her as particularly beautiful. She had always been a fountain of joyfulness and her tears had always been an expression of the overflow. It was rare to see her cry from hurt or sadness.

As a child, my father all but cut us off from my mother's family. My aunt Glory Jean speculated that my father could not tolerate my mother's redneck relations, all of whom hailed from Georgia and South Carolina. As I grew older and my mother's health declined, I came to appreciate my mother's family.

Since Ruby's husband died, she had lived alone in a large antique frame home in the center of Jacksonville. Her deceased husband, who sold life and health insurance, had left her without any insurance save a small burial policy. A small, dwindled savings account and social security were not enough to rescue her from her submerged financial situation. Four years ago, I helped her sell her home and possessions and moved her into a small, well-lit apartment so she could paint, see her friends and most importantly to continue to attend her church. Thus began my stewardship of her affairs and my three to four trips a year to see her. Then her stomach pains began.

After several visits to the doctor, tests at the hospital and the loss of a very close friend who cared for her, I convinced her to let me move her to an assisted living facility. She insisted it be in Jacksonville near her church. That was a year ago. Actually, Em handled much of this since my bouts with depression were in full bloom and her miseries, added to my own, made my life a challenge. As I tried to remember the last time I had visited Ruby, I noticed Dr. Sommers as she stood in line and filled her coffee cup. A doctor was not going take this kind of time to discuss a patient's condition unless it was serious. I knew when she asked to meet me here that the news was not good.

4

"Mr. McNamara?" Dr. Sommers placed her large Florida Gators coffee cup on the table and took the seat directly opposite from me her back to the rest of the room.

"Doctor."

"I only have a few moments, so I'll get right to it." She looked at me over the top of her glasses for an O.K. to begin. She brushed a spray of gray hair off her forehead, and smoothed back her short, cropped hair. Her kind, light brown eyes and the friendliness of her voice softened her abrupt approach.

"Alright. I gather from Ruby's reaction to your visit in her room that the news isn't good."

"I didn't feel I could discuss her situation with you until I'd talked to her first. No, the news isn't good. The cancer we found in her colon, we found late. It has spread to her liver and pancreas.

Actually, it has spread all over her body. Given the extent of the liver and pancreas damage, her age, and recovery from major surgery, I don't think we should intervene any further."

"Is she terminally ill?"

"The surgery we performed on her colon will buy her some time, but the main reason for the surgery was to make her more comfortable. I estimate a couple of weeks or so at the most and probably less. I'd hoped we would have better news. But this is why I wanted to talk to you."

She lifted the large mug on which the Florida Gator's mascot stood defiantly and studied my face. Even though I suspected this news, to hear it officially hit me harder than expected. "What could be worse than Ruby being terminally ill?"

"I know this is hard. Facing death can be a difficult proposition. Your aunt has a very strong faith in God, so, down where it counts, she's as prepared as any patient I've ever had. But emotionally prepared and physically prepared are two different things."

"How can you be physically prepared?"

She leaned forward, and rested her elbows on the table. "People your aunt's age have prepared for death for some time. That doesn't mean that they're ready for it, or will even accept it. It just means that they expect it. They've made the mental and emotional preparations. They fear two things: loss of control, and the pain.

"I understand the pain part, but loss of control?"

"For most people, we spend our entire lives the captain of our own ship. We're independent, make decisions on an hourly basis about how we will spend our lives and our time. When patients think about the approach of death, they worry about the loss of that basic control."

My confused look told her I still did not understand.

She reached across the table and patted my hand. "Have you ever been in a hospital before?"

"Hernia surgery, age twenty-two."

"And who made decisions about your care, your medications, and the date you would be released from the hospital?"

"The doctor."

"And what do you remember about the experience?"

"Well, if I recall, I wanted to be home to watch the World Series on television, but the doctor wouldn't release me from the hospital. It felt like I was a prisoner. I wasn't in control."

"Very often when terminal patients reach the final stages of life, everyone makes decisions for them. I remember the first time I became aware of this as a young physician. I'll never forget George Daly. He was seventy-five, dying from lung cancer in my care. His wife and I were discussing his medication. 'Hey, I'm not dead yet. You guys talk about all this stuff as if I'm not here. I may be dying, but I can still make decisions for myself.' I'll never forget those words. They changed the way I handled terminally ill patients.

"As doctors we're trained to find cures. Our mindset is to heal, and many in our profession consider it a failure when all of our training and experience is unsuccessful in saving a patient's life. Death is as natural a stage in the life cycle as birth. I've come to understand that doctors must feel just as comfortable with the process of death, as they do with the process of life. Unfortunately, many doctors and hospitals don't understand the process of dying. They're in the business to save lives not admit that they've lost the battle. As a result, they miss the opportunity to prepare their patients for the dying process. They don't understand that the process of dying can be just as important and fulfilling as other phases of life.

"I know I've thrown a lot at you all at once. My point is this. Ruby has reached that stage in life where medical options won't prolong her life. Intervention to try to extend her life will only make the final stages of dying more painful. I recommended to her and to you that we switch gears in her care. We should help her make the physical preparations for death in a way that places her in control of how she would like to spend the remaining time that she has."

Dr. Sommers sipped her coffee as I pondered her recommendation.

"Have you had this discussion with Ruby?" I asked.

She nodded. "Not in the depth that we discussed it, but, yes, I've told her that she has a few weeks to live at the most, and that I want her input on how she wants to spend her remaining time. You and she should discuss this at length if you want to be her caregiver."

"Caregiver? Whoa, now. I haven't agreed to anything like that. I'm up to my eyeballs in work I can't possibly finish. I agreed to be her surrogate and make medical decisions for her if she were unable to make them on her own. But I didn't sign on for caregiver duty."

"Well, I don't know what her financial circumstances are or yours for that matter, but the quality of the end of her life will depend on the care available."

"What did you have in mind?"

"Ideally, I would like her to spend some time in our Palliative Care Unit."

"Pall . . .?

"Palliative Care. Some time ago, we recognized that managing pain and making a terminal patient feel comfortable were just as important as healing healthy patients. Dying doesn't have to be the painful ordeal you fear. With the use of drugs, we give the dying a more comfortable quality of life. We have a unit here in the hospital that specializes in providing this type of care."

"Doesn't administering drugs to a patient remove quality of life?"

"In the late stages your aunt is in, she'll require morphine to deal with pain. As the cancer continues to spread and her organs deteriorate, the pain will increase, and so will the levels of medication. Even with meds, the pain may be more than she can handle in a conscious state. Then we will sedate the patient into a comfortable sleep. The amount of morphine will depend on her circumstances, the progression of the disease, and the rate of her deterioration. Your aunt is lucky. She has had time to prepare and the option to make decisions on how she would like to face it. She has access to one of the best Palliative Care units in the country.

"I would like them to evaluate her, and begin a program of follow-up care as an out-patient or she could be enrolled in hospice care. She could go back to her assisted living facility, but I believe that such a move would be short lived, as she'll need much more attentive care than they can provide. A hospice is an organization that cares for terminally ill patients. They're equipped and trained to provide comfort and care to the dying in either your home or one of their facilities. There will come a time, very soon, where she'll need significant personal care that can only be provided by relatives, a nursing facility, or through hired, full time, round-the-clock professionals to care for her."

"I don't think she can afford a professional staff."

"Then it will be a nursing home, or you."

"And the nursing home?"

Alicia Sommers pulled her glasses off and rubbed her eyes, and returned the glasses to their perch on the bridge of her nose. "I don't want to take anything away from nursing homes. They do a marvelous job with patients that require long-term care. Nursing homes aren't designed to give terminally ill patients the kind of individualized care that allows the patient to be in control of their lives. Generally, they under-medicate patients who are in pain, and spend too little time in caring for their emotional needs. The medical profession has been slow to embrace Palliative Care, and nursing homes have been slower still. It is a matter of cost. Nursing homes, if they're to survive with what Medicare and Medicaid pay them have to control costs. Payroll is the single largest cost. They stretch the number of patients assigned to duty staff to control those cost.

"I can't tell you what you should do. But her best chance to be able to meet death with dignity is first to spend time with our Palliative staff and let us get her started on a program of medication that will make her final days as comfortable as possible. In the best case, she should be with family and find a hospice organization to help you with her care." Dr. Sommers stood. "I can supply you with the names of three hospice units that I feel are serious about their mission to help the dying.

"Well, you and your aunt have much to discuss. I will assign her to the Palliative Care Unit later today. If I can help with questions, let me know."

"Thank you, Doctor." I stood, and shook her outstretched hand.

She held my hand with one hand and patted it with the other. "Ruby is a vibrant, exciting woman. You have the opportunity to make the next couple of weeks one of the most meaningful in her life. To allow her to live the remainder of her time with dignity and comfort may be the greatest gift of her life. Talk to her openly and honestly. Find out what's important to her. Then see if you can make a contribution." She squeezed my hand, bid me goodbye, turned and left the cafeteria.

I fell into my chair in a state of panic. When I began to help Ruby, caring for a terminally ill patient was the last thing I had considered. It scared me thinking about the intensive care that an elderly dying woman would need.

My first thought was to get my book done and to meet my publisher's February fifteen deadline. I had little more than six weeks left. The doctor would not release her from the hospital for a couple of days. I sat and thought about options. These were choices Ruby needed to make. We had much to talk about.

Ruby and I had never talked seriously about anything. The weather, her health, her art, my books, her family and my progress with Emil were our main topics. The topics we discussed were wide but never deep. She tried to pry into the details of Em's and my relationship, but I had successfully cut her off from her intrusions. So our discourse rarely became that personal.

When I left the cafeteria for her room, I felt trapped and suddenly very responsible. When I moved her to an assisted living facility, I just did not think about caring for a dying person. In the elevator, I thought about going home, and to make some excuse to Ruby why I suddenly had to leave. I did not want to discuss her plans for dying, and I certainly did not feel I could commit to her staying with me in the process. For all her qualities, Ruby was a talker, and not a particularly quiet one. Her constant need for care and desire to bend my ear would destroy my peace and privacy - to a writer the twin Ps for success.

Aside from Glory-Jean, who was herself nearing the age when she would need care, I was Ruby's only kin able to help. When I intervened to help her sell her house and got involved in her care, I never anticipated what a burden it would become. The fact that I failed to envision such personal and intimate care was not Ruby's fault. There was no way to extricate myself at this point. I was in for the duration.

In the hall leading to her room, I suddenly remembered my mother and her protracted decline toward death. Ruby's and her situation were similar. Mother died of cancer in her fifties. She lived for twelve months after doctors discovered her cancer, a process much longer than Ruby's. I recognized the help that she would need, father put his career on hold for a year, and devoted full-time to her care. When it was determined that treatment would not alter her condition, my parents had the same conversation that Dr. Sommers recommended I have with Ruby.

Mother wanted to be at home, near her family. She had had a life-long love affair with the ocean, and asked my father to rent a place on the shore where she could listen to the waves. On the coast, a short distance from Orlando, my father found a home with sliding glass doors that faced the ocean. The living room became a hospital room. In the beginning, she could take short walks on the beach with assistance. As her health declined, my father installed a ramp for a wheel chair to carry her to the water's edge. In the final stages, he moved her bed close to the open doors where the salt air and the roaring surf contributed to her comfort.

What had not occurred to me until now were the tremendous financial and personal sacrifices my father had made for my mother. Mother was fortunate my father cared enough and had the resources to permit her to face death the way she wished. She died with dignity. Although she suffered, my father made sure that she died as free from pain as he could reasonably manage. For most of their married lives, my father led and mother followed. In these final days, she led and he became her servant.

Dr. Sommers' conversation resonated. I could either look upon Ruby's final days as either a burden, or an opportunity.

Ruby looked better than she had earlier, a more cheerful version. Her face brightened when I came through the door. She had brushed her hair and they had straightened her bed. I scrambled to think of a way to begin, what would be, a very intimate conversation.

"You know, don't you?" Her eyes looked through me as though someone had written something on the wall behind me and she focused to read it.

"Yes, I had coffee with your doctor. You're lucky to have her."

"She's so precious. I feel like she could be my daughter. She takes such sweet care of me."

"I like her. She cares an awful lot for you."

"What did she tell you?" Her question put me on the spot. I was not sure how deep their conversation had gone.

"Why don't you begin with what she told you."

"How are you and Emily?"

I pulled a chair up to the side of her bed, sat and then put her hand in mine. Her blue eyes looked dull, and her face drawn. "We can talk about Em in a minute. We need to talk about your health. I know it's hard. It's hard for me, too."

"She said I had only a couple weeks to live; the cancer I have is very aggressive." She looked at me and tried to gauge my reaction.

"How do you feel about it?"

"It's not unexpected. Jackie, I'm eighty-five years old. I can't live forever. Sugar, I don't think

44

anyone is truly prepared for this day. The older you get the more you think about this day coming.

"You know what's odd about it? When I turned forty, I didn't feel forty. When I turned sixty, my body told me I had aged, but I didn't feel sixty. As I lay here, I still have a child within me who's curious, fun loving and adventurous that never has really grown up or grown old. Even though my organs are failing faster than corn pops in hot oil, this child still wants to play, to explore, to taste life, to love and be loved."

"I've always said that about men. They never really advance in age beyond their sixteenth birthday."

"Well you know what I mean, then. I look old, but I don't feel old inside. I keep beating this old hulk into submission to do the things the child wants to do, and I've just run out of time and my body is giving up. There are so many older people I hear say that they've done everything they wanted to do. For me there's always more to do. One more thing I haven't done. One more painting I'd like to try."

"You don't sound disappointed."

"This may be hard to explain. Lord knows I barely understand it myself. Who I really am is in that child. It is the essence of who I am. When I die, the child continues to live on, exploring new things, in a new world, a better place without the limitations of this old body. The child isn't afraid of death."

I had never thought of life in such simple terms.

"I have a very simple faith, Jackie. The child and God have been close, in fact one, for my whole life. My time has come. The child is excited about it; ready to experience it. But there's a part of me that's scared."

"Afraid of the unknown?"

"I'm not afraid of that at all. Heaven awaits and I'm thrilled at the prospect. It's the process of dying that I'm afraid of."

"You mean the pain?"

"That's part of it, sure. I'll admit it. That worries me some. I've cared for most of my kin as they've approached death. I've stood by helplessly as they've suffered so. It's awful. I wouldn't wish that experience on anyone."

"Dr. Sommers said that it doesn't have to be that way. She said they've made advances in handling people who are . . . you know."

"I'm dying, Jackie. I don't have leprosy."

"She said that they have this program that adjusts medication to your level of pain to make sure you're comfortable."

"Well I suwanee, Jackie. I did understand what she told me. They want me to go to some Pal-something place this afternoon for a couple of days. It's kind of a school to learn to manage pain. Dr. Sommers said it wouldn't be too bad at first, but soon the medications would make things easier." She grabbed my hand. "You know what I'm really worried about, though. I don't want to be a burden to you." Tears fell. "You've been so precious to me."

"You won't be." I wanted to say come stay with me, but I stopped short. In the first place, this may not be what she wanted to do. In the second place, every second of my time for the next six weeks was committed to writing if I wanted to save my financial butt. I wanted to think more about all the options. To say I wanted her to come without thinking about all that entailed seemed foolish. What was clear to me was that I wanted her to do what she wanted to do. I wanted her to be in control of how she wanted to die as much as she had been in control of how she lived. "Ruby, when my mother was dying, my father asked her how she wanted to spend the time. I want to ask you that question. How would you like to spend the time you have?"

Her eyes narrowed. "I want you to write my story. I want to see Glory Jean, bless her heart – I know she doesn't have the money to come. I know that she may not be able to come for health reasons. I want to spend as much time as I can with you and Emily. I feel like we're still getting to know one another." She paused, looked around the room as though the words she needed were written on the walls. "I don't want to be alone when I die, Jackie. I don't want to be in some hospital ward or a nursing home."

As she shared the depths of her fear of loneliness, I related immediately. I had the same fear. When I reached that point in my life, I want loved ones to surround me.

As I considered her plea she said, "I've thought about this story for a long time. I want to see it on paper."

"Why is this story so important to you?"

"Jackie. I've wanted to write my entire life. It's something I want to do before I die. Artists cre-

48

ate objects that are valued over time. I want to leave something. Is that so difficult to understand? I want you to write my story. God gave me this story. Will you do it?"

"Yes, of course."

Juanita returned to the room to prepare Ruby for a move to another wing of the hospital. I bade Ruby goodbye, gave her a kiss on her cheek and explained the deadlines I faced, which she graciously understood. I promised to return with my voice recorder and begin her story.

Insatiable curiosity. That is why I write. It seems every story I write begins with the question, "What if?" I am a sucker for a mystery. As I drove back to Mount Dora, I was fixated on Ruby's promise of a story. What story could be so compelling that an eighty-five year old woman would place it on her priority list before dying? This is a story that "God gave her" no less. I wondered if my agent would buy into such a lofty endorsement.

5

I arrived back at my studio just as the sun set. I poured a glass of wine, plopped down in the chair behind my desk and gazed at the water through the picture window. The lake mirrored reds, pinks and purples broken only by bass breeching the surface of the water. The lights from Mount Dora glimmered like stars hung low in the sky. My office smelled of soiled laundry and dirty dishes in the sink.

When I opened my laptop to begin to lay out my next novel, I glimpsed an all-to-familiar red Mazda Miata, its top down and a white scarf unfurled in the wind. Not only was a visitor the last thing I needed right now it was the last thing I wanted. I scrambled around the studio and tried to straighten the mess of the last six weeks but finally gave up as the door opened and Em flew into the office her perfume colliding with the musty, stale smells of the studio.

At thirty-seven, dressed in yellow slacks and a baby-blue pullover sweater and a white scarf on her head, Em was still more beautiful than Jacqueline Smith. Light brown wavy hair to her shoulders, olive tanned skin, a thin face with high cheekbones, and light brown eyes contributed to her warm, friendly face.

In the awkwardness of the moment, I held an armful of dirty laundry I had picked up from the guest chair in front of my desk.

"Em," I said, confused about how to greet her, whether to hug her or shake her hand. She walked up kissed my cheek and solved the problem. The smell of citrus filled the air around her. As always, Emily dressed to perfection. No small detail forgotten.

She reached across the desk and scratched Hemingway on the top of his head with her manicured and painted fingernails. "Hard at it, I see."

"I have another novel to write in exactly fifty-one days, and the stopwatch is running."

"I know. That's why I'm here. First I want to know about Ruby." She untied the white scarf, slid it off her hair and laid it across the back of a guest chair. She picked Hemingway up off the desk, and held him. She pulled up a chair, sat, placed the cat in her lap then crossed her legs. I offered her some wine but she declined.

"What's wrong with Ruby?"

"I should've called you, I'm sorry. They discovered she has colon cancer. They operated the day before yesterday and found the cancer had spread to her liver and pancreas."

"That doesn't sound very good."

"I met with her doctor. She only gives Ruby a couple of weeks if that. The doctor told her yesterday."

"Poor thing. That's awful. How is she handling it?" Hemingway purred in her lap. She stroked his body and came away with a patch of hair. She balled it up and laid it on top of the desk. She set the cat on the floor, brushed her slacks with the palm of her hand and gave me that 'eeeeww' look.

"Better than I would. I asked her how she wished to spend the time she had left. She said she wanted me to write a story for her. She aspired to paint, of course. And what seemed most important to her was to spend time with me and you."

"She on the story jag again?"

"You should have heard her, Em. She said God gave her this story. A legacy, she said. She nearly pled with me. She made me promise to write it for her."

"What happens to her next? Will she just stay there in the hospital?" She looked at the glass of wine that sat on the desk in front of me and said, "I think I'll have a glass of wine. Not much . . . a small glass."

I got up, retrieved a glass from the cabinet and poured from the bottle on the desk, then returned to my chair. "Her doctor wants her to go to a ward at the hospital for a couple of days to put together a pain management plan. This is where they decide the medications they'll use to make her feel more comfortable as the cancer progresses. As the end nears, she'll require more and more help until she'll need fulltime medical attention."

"Where will she go for that? She can't afford anything like that."

"The doctor suggested that a hospice might be the answer."

"What do you think about that?" Her lips curled at the question.

"I don't know. I don't know anything about it. I thought I would check into one and investigate. Seems like a pretty lonely way to die, with strangers caring for you."

"It seems like a heavy load for you to carry especially with all the things on your plate. I'm surely not helping either with the divorce."

She looked around the room then at me. Her voice was steady and even. If there was emotion behind her words, it did not show in her face. I looked at her and could not believe I handled this so calmly. Every atom in my body ached to beg her for another chance.

"I was somewhat reluctant to come today for that reason. I don't want to talk things over. We've had many opportunities to do that and didn't. If I work for you, you have to understand that that part of our relationship is over. I think I can handle it. But can you?" Emily could compartmentalize life's issues. I admired the way she separated the unpleasant from the pleasant. She could be upset about something, but put it out of her mind if need be. I had no doubt that she could handle the strain of a divorce and still work with me. I, on the other hand, knew that I could not. We had had this discussion this morning. Why would Em make the trip when we had already gone through it, earlier?

"Lisa called you, didn't she? Is that why you came?"

"No, not exactly. I mean, yes, Lisa called, but that was not my sole reason for coming. Ruby may not be blood to me, but she's just as much my aunt as yours. I want to help in any way I can. You do need my help. I may want to divorce you, but I don't hate you."

"I don't know, Em. I appreciate what you're doing. It is just so soon. I love you, this is so difficult."

"Well, I understand, but you're in a jam and you need all the help you can get." She stood, brushed the cat hair from her lap. "Let's get this done. Give me a copy of the manuscript so I can look it over. Then you make up your mind whether you want my help or not."

Em lifted the scarf to her head and cinched it at her chin. I dropped a blank CD in the disk drive of my laptop, burned a copy of *Death in the Desert* and handed it to her.

"Call me as soon as you can and let me know what you want to do." She looked me directly in the eyes, smiled, gathered her purse and the disk, stepped around Hemingway and left.

6

My cellphone chirped as Emily pulled her Miata onto Lakeshore Drive. As she turned toward Mt. Dora, her headlights swept the oak trees hung with Spanish moss as she made the turn and disappeared into the darkness. All that remained of the sunset was the soft hue of purple in the sky coaxed aside by stars in the crisp clear heavens.

Billie St. John's name appeared on the display of my cellphone. Billie was my half-sister and lived in Key West.

"Merry Christmas, Billie. I was worried about you."

"Jackie, I'm sorry. I wanted to call yesterday, but I knew you were writing and I was afraid I would disturb you." Her voice was husky but feminine. Her accent was dusted with the remnants of her childhood in Charleston, South Carolina.

Before I could assure her she could call me anytime, she plowed ahead.

"Jackie, I have a real problem. I need your help. It's about the restaurant." She was nearly breathless and sounded on the verge of tears.

"What's up, Billie?"

"Our landlord has decided not to sell to us."

Billie owned a restaurant on Duval Street in Key West. When she started the business ten years ago the building she leased for five years was a disheveled, termite infested, two-story clapboard structure with a fallen-in roof. During the first five years, she reinvested money from the business to make leasehold improvements to the building. She landscaped the yard that faced Duval to create a courtyard restaurant. Five years ago, when the lease came up for renewal, the property owner doubled the rent, claiming that the improvements Billie had made increased the value of the property. With every cent she had tied up in the property and business, she could not afford to move the business elsewhere and she renewed the lease for an additional five years at the higher rate.

In the last five years, "The Mangrove," the name of her restaurant, was "discovered" by a food critic from the Miami Herald, then by Zagat's and business boomed. To answer the opportunity, Billie invested in the construction of a wing on the house that created an outdoor bar that ran left alongside the courtyard between the house and Duval Street. While I was there, her lease was due to renew and her landlord announced that he would not renew her lease and that he would put the property up for sale. Front footage along Duval Street had become increasingly desirable as national retail chains, attracted by the cruise ships that deposited bored, cash-flush travelers at the base of Duval at Pier B, gobbled up any available real estate from Front Street all the way to US1.

Like before, Billie had invested everything she had into the business and while she had been successful, she did not have the resources to make a twenty to thirty-percent down payment on the $1.2 million required to secure the loan. If she did not do something, she would lose not only her business, but also hundreds of thousands that she had already spent to improve the property. She was in an understandable state of panic.

On Billie's behalf, I called a banker friend, Bob Decker, in Mt. Dora and I agreed to put up the collateral she needed to buy the restaurant. When I returned to Mt. Dora, I did not have the time or opportunity to follow the proceedings, but according to Decker, everything had moved smoothly and the sale was to close on December 29.

"Billie, why don't you back up and tell me what has happened. I haven't talked to Decker in several weeks." Hemingway jumped up on my desk, walked toward me, stepped into my lap, circled then plopped down.

"After you left, we contacted a local attorney to help us work through all the issues in buying the property. She felt that if the owner knew that I was the purchaser that I would lose leverage to negotiate a price. The owner knows how much I have tied up in improvements and how important it is that I retain the property and the attorney felt that this put me at a tremendous disadvantage.

"She recommended that we form a separate corporation that would be unrecognizable to the landlord, and that she would negotiate with the real estate broker and the landowner. Jackie, this is just awful."

"Billie, I'm sure all will be fine. Just calm down and tell me the problem."

"Well, I don't know how he found out that I was involved in the sale, but he did. Now he refuses to close. He says that we tricked him." She blew her nose and did her best to compose herself.

"When I spoke to Decker, he said he didn't see any obstacles to the sale." I scratched Hemingway behind the ear and I was certain Billie could hear Hemingway purr.

"Jackie, we had a contract. All the inspections were done; all the contingencies had been lifted. The contract is solid. He told me there was 'no way in hell' he'd sell that property to me. If that wasn't enough, many of the servers from Sloppy Joe's come here to eat. We give the wait-staff a courtesy discount. One of Sloppy Joe's bartenders said our landlord mouthed off to several of the servers that there was no way he would sell his place to 'no damn lezo.'"

I did not respond right away. She cried softly while I thought about how to advise her. My heart broke for her. She had everything invested in that restaurant, emotionally and financially. She would be destroyed if she lost that property. Finally, I said, "Billie, sounds like you have a valid contract that would be awfully hard to break."

"That's what the attorney said. She also said that we would have to sue to force him to comply with the contract. Jackie, this jerk has more money than Donald Trump. The legal fees could be more than the property is worth."

"Did you tell your attorney about the remarks your landlord made at Sloppy Joe's?"

"No, I just found out about that. Why is that important?"

"I know squat about the law, but it sounds like he has discriminated against because of your sexual orientation. I'm pretty sure if you sue him and win you could force him to sell, pay all your legal fees and collect civil damages for his discrimination." My mind spun around the abusiveness of the situation. "In the meantime, your attorney should file for an injunction of some type that ties the restaurant up until all this is settled."

"It's overwhelming, Jackie."

"Billie, it may be, but you need to act right now on this. Forget the cost. Just press ahead. Fight. What've you got to lose?"

"If I can't keep this business . . . I'll lose everything."

"And if you file a suit and lose?"

"I'll lose everything."

"And if you do nothing?"

"I'll lose everything."

"Then the only way out of this is to beat this creep. Don't let him get away with this." It was hard to contain my anger. "I want to come down, Billie."

"My attorney is off until tomorrow. You don't need to come. I can handle it. I'll call her first thing and tell her about the Sloppy Joe's rant. I'm worried about Bob Decker. Once he finds out what a mess this deal has become he'll probably drop my loan."

"Don't worry about, Bob. I'll take care of him. You just get your attorney moving. As soon as I get some business squared away, I'll catch a flight down."

"Thanks, Jackie," she said as though a weight had been lifted. "I've been so concerned about my own situation I've neglected you. How is your book coming?" she asked, her tears nearly stopped.

"Finished the novel I started there at your house. The wolves are fed for the moment."

"That's wonderful. You left here with such hope and enthusiasm. "

"Yes, but I have to finish another one by the middle of February. The good news is I have the story put together in my head, and now I need to get it on paper. How is Alex with all this?"

"It's good she was in San Diego on a layover, or she would have hunted our landlord down and killed him."

Alex is an airline pilot and spends long stretches away from home.

"And what about, Emily?" she asked.

"Still intent on the divorce. That woman has a will of iron. I've about given up." Billie and Em had never met.

"Jody asks for you every time I see her here at the restaurant."

Jody was the first girl I ever kissed. Billie lived with my mother and father for part of the summer of 1961 and I met Jody during Billie's stay. In fact, Billie was a bit of a matchmaker. Jodie and I were fourteen then and Billie neared her eighteenth birthday. After Billie left our home in 1961, I had only seen her once since I reconnected with her six weeks ago. Jody had migrated to Key West when her husband passed away and Jody and Billie's paths crossed before I found Billie in Key West.

"Billie, I would love to see her."

Billie and I chatted for a few minutes, said our goodbyes and I pondered the breadth of our conversation and the events that unfolded at our re-union.

I met Jody at a municipal pool on Holly-wood Beach while Billie lived with us. I was so socially awkward Billie knew that I would screw the meeting up with Jody if left to my own bumbling, so she interloped into our budding romance until we were inseparable. Jody was my first love, but not for long.

I remember my mother told me once how southerners defined courtship; they called it sparking. She ignited a fire in me that took years to simmer. She was the inspiration for my very first novel, and I hoped that one day I would find her, or she would find me. It would be thirty-plus years later before I connected with her again. She was free, but I was not.

Because of the demands of my publisher, I had a very limited time with Billie and Jody, but both of them contributed significantly to my ability to write again. Jody and I did spend a magical evening together. She invited me to carry our relationship to the next step but I demurred. I explained that while Emily had left me, I was still in love with her. I explained to her that I needed to see it through with Emily before I could make any commitments to her. Jody said, "You know where I am if you change your mind."

The chemistry, the spark, when we first met on the beach over thirty years ago was still there. There were rough edges, too. We both wore deep emotional scars. I barely held my own battered life together without added complications. As I considered Emily, the next novel I needed to write, Billie and her issues with her landlord and Ruby, I could feel the panic grow in me. I wanted to help all of them, but I could not do anything for anyone if I did not survive. I held on, but barely.

7

Sometimes in life, we face frighteningly bad choices. In these desperate situations, life backs us into extremely dark corners and it forces us to walk down paths we would never traverse in the full light of day. This was my mother's situation.

My mother had been married when she was sixteen to a much older man, a man she did not love, to get away from an abusive step-father. Her first husband was even more abusive. It was not long after she gave birth to Billie that my mother left her abuser and divorced him.

In the process of my mother's divorce from her first husband, she met my father whom she truly loved. He was Roman Catholic and his family was devout. He was discharged out of the Navy in 1945 and wanted to return home and wanted Mother to return with him. They married in front of a Justice of the Peace and my father convinced my mother to leave Billie with a sitter while they returned to his home to find work. To avoid a conflict with his parents, they hid Mother's former marriage and child from them, moved into their home temporarily, and hoped to find work quickly. They planned to send for the child as soon as they settled. Returning WWII veterans found it difficult to find work. As my father searched for employment, weeks stretched into months and my father made it difficult if not impossible for my mother to return to Charleston for her daughter.

In the end, Billie's father filed for custody because my mother had abandoned her child. The abuse heaped upon Billie had only begun. Billie's father and new wife had a business that required them to be in Europe frequently and left Billie with a governess for months at a time: abandoned again. Billie's governess was a lesbian and Billie's need for acceptance and love created a hole the governess filled with both emotional and physical love. Billie's parents came home from a trip unexpectedly and found the two asleep in the same bed and they threw both of them out into the street.

The governess and Billie lived together until the money ran out, and the governess skipped out. With no place to turn, Billie called our mother and asked if she could come and stay with her until she could find work. After a couple of months when my father learned of her homosexuality, he removed her from our home and bought her a bus ticket. He abandoned her with her meager possessions in a

Greyhound bus station in Hollywood, Florida. Her young life had been filled with people who rejected her.

Billie finally met someone who truly loved her, sought counseling and put the pieces of her shattered life together. Now, Billie's landlord threatened Alex and Billie's storybook ending. I could not let her be abused like that again.

I had to force myself to push Billie's dilemma out of my thinking and focus on writing. When I was emotionally healthy, I had the ability to focus on my work and block everything else out of my mind. Em used to say to others that I could write in the middle of Grand Central Station, which I could. My mind swam with the complexities of life and it was difficult to dig down and find the voice to write. Once my fingers hit the keyboard, as it had happened in Key West at Billie's more than a month ago, the juice began to flow. My next book was another Dana O'Brian action-adventure novel. The family of a pilot missing-in-action in WWII contacted her. His plane went missing in the Himalayas between India and China in 1942. The Chinese, then an ally of the U.S. against Japan, were cut off and isolated — surrounded by the Japanese army. The Chinese's only source of supply was from U.S. bases in India. The only route to China by air was through the Himalayan Mountains. Its peaks were too high to fly over and its mountain passes and unpredictable weather were treacherous. In 1942, the aircraft the U.S. used to ferry supplies to China were not equipped to fly these routes safely. The planes had no oxygen to fly at high altitudes or adequate navigational equipment to circumnavigate the mountains with any degree of safety. The pilots (both civilian and military) were ill trained to fly in this challenging environment. Consequently, nearly half the flights in the early days of the airlift met with disaster.

The Himalayan terrain was inhospitable even under the best conditions. Snow at higher altitudes and dense forest and jungle at lower altitudes made visual searches by air, even in good weather, nearly impossible. When by chance they spotted wreckage, the terrain was nearly impossible to reach. Search and rescue efforts in the 1940s were a total failure with only a dismal fraction of the pilots or equipment rescued and recovered.

Word of Dana O'Brien's success in locating her grandfather's B24 in the Libyan Desert, although classified, spread through the ranks of military brass in Washington like an urban-legend. John Abercrombie, a 21-year-old Army Air Corps MIA pilot, grandson of a Major General Army intelligence officer, was the missing pilot they hoped Dana O'Brien would be able to find.

December 26

I was able to write for several hours then fell asleep in my chair. The chirp of my cellphone awakened me.

"Jack, you sound awful. You must have written all night."

"Em," I said, as I tried to clear the fog of sleep from my mind. "What time is it?"

"Eight-thirty. Can you meet me for breakfast?"

I looked at my wristwatch to verify the time, ran my hand across my face as though the act might drain the slumber out of me and said, "What's this about?"

"We need to talk about our divorce and I don't want to do it over the phone." She gave me the name of a diner out on 441 and asked me to meet her in twenty minutes.

Em was already in a booth, had ordered coffee and had mixed in cream and sugar the way I like it. She had pulled her hair back into a ponytail and had worn a black and yellow jogging suit and had a patina of sweat on her face and arms. Em religiously jogged every morning.

Emily pulled on a two-carat acorn that hung from a delicate gold chain around her neck. "Jack, I need to talk to you about mediation."

"Shoot."

"Jack Spears, my attorney, wants us to seek mediation rather than divide assets in court. He thinks that a court fight is in no one's interest, yours or mine. Reporters have called already wanting me to confirm rumors of our split. The publicity will hurt you more than me."

"Why can't you and I decide how to handle this and have Spears draw up the papers."

"He doesn't think it can be done that simply. He recommends an attorney named David Huff. He wants us to go see him day after tomorrow. Just an initial meeting. If we don't like him, we can find someone we do like. Jack will represent me. You should probably get an attorney to represent you."

"What do you want?"

"I don't think it would be wise for us to have this conversation now, Jack."

"We have to talk about it sometime, Em."

"Listen. I care about you. I may not want to be married to you anymore, but that doesn't mean I don't care, and that I don't want us to have a good relationship. Divorce settlements can destroy relationships. That's why Spears suggests we go to a neutral party to reach an amicable settlement. The mediator will work with you, me and our attorneys and try to find agreement."

"All right. Is this with our attorneys present?"

"No. Not the first meeting. We're just there to determine if we want to hire him. You know what I'm saying?"

"Can't we postpone this for a few weeks? This couldn't come at a worst time."

"No. There'll never be a good time for this."

"With the book due and Ruby . . ."

"Jack. Look at me."

I looked directly at her for the first time since I walked in the door. She was more desirable than ever.

"We aren't getting back together. You could delay this for ten years and it wouldn't change my mind. Am I clear on this?"

"All right, Em."

8

The drive to St. Vincent's Medical Center to visit Ruby was the longest hour and forty-five minutes in recent memory. I was angry at Em for her inflexibility. I was afraid to move from a relationship that had been the most significant of my life. I was hurt to the core. The most devastating piece of it was the loss of intimacy with her, the oneness of body and spirit. My life had become so intertwined with hers I could not imagine life without her. The chemistry between Em and I was immediate and life sustaining.

The emotional pit I had fallen into had nothing to do with her. Nothing. Had she not been with me I would have stepped over the edge and fallen into the abyss of insanity. She was a lifeline, a link to reality. In the end, she needed to protect herself. The rational part of me was okay with that. I was broken deep in the emotional part of me.

There is oneness in my marriage that I did not know I had until Em took it away from me.

At Saint Vincent's Hospital a middle-aged man now occupied room 301. The thin slight nurse at the station said they had moved Ruby to another room on the floor below. I inquired about her progress. She said she was well, progressing beyond their expectations. She gave me her room number and directions to the stairs.

On the floor directly below, in room 201, I found Ruby, or I should say I heard her booming voice down the hall and followed the sound. Parked outside her room was a large cart with food trays scattered on top.

"Whew, this is way too much food for a girl with such a trim figure. Honey, you best take some of this back with you." I could hear all this before I came through the threshold.

Ruby sat up in bed and a petite black woman with an ear-to-ear smile arranged the food tray on the tabletop and ignored Ruby's instructions. "Ms. Ruby, doctor's orders. When I come back to pick up that tray I want to see clean plates."

I watched Ruby pick at her food until the aide left the room then she dropped her fork on the plate. "The food tastes like cardboard and the water like metal. Hey, Darlin'. Come here you precious thing and give your Aunt Ruby some love." She surrounded my neck with her twisted hands and kissed me on the cheek.

The aide stuck her head back in the doorway and said to Ruby, "I mean to find a clean plate when I get back, hear me?"

Ruby nodded her head affirmatively.

"Good," the aide said and then scurried out into the hall and moved to the next room.

"They're all so sweet here. They treat me like a queen. Well, you look sharp today. Did you get your book done? Meet your deadline? Heard from Emily?" She said this in one breath.

"Have enough coffee this morning?" I sat in the hard recliner next to her bed.

"Don't be hateful to a dying woman, Jackie." She wrinkled her face into a mock scowl.

"Here it starts, bleeding your nephew for sympathy. Well, you'll get all you want from me." I smiled, and patted her arm.

"Well tell me, Darlin'."

"I sent the first draft . . ."

"Not the book, tell me about Emily."

"It won't work. We went to breakfast to talk and she was adamant that we won't get back together."

"You told her you were sorry for everything you put her through?" She sounded like Mother after I had a fight with one of my friends in school."

"Of course."

"Did you ask her to forgive you?"

"I don't think my sorrow or asking for forgiveness has anything to do with it. I went through some serious depression, and I started to drag her in that dark hole with me. The depression frightened her. I don't think she wants to risk being there again." I thought about Emily, and the pain I had caused. "I don't want to be there again either."

"I suwanee, I wish I had words for you, Jackie. All I know is seeing the two of you together was always a treat. The way the two of you related, it was like watching a couple in a waltz. You two were made for each other. It's a shame to see it end. I wish I wasn't in this hospital. I'd go talk some sense into that girl."

"It's not her fault. I'm to blame." After the words were out, I analyzed where the blame really belonged. I didn't feel right shifting the blame for my depressed state onto my parents, but that's where it belonged. I had been wearing a suit of clothes that someone had given me to wear. Once I realized it, I could elect not to wear them anymore. If I knew it, and kept wearing them, then I was to blame. "Tell me about your new room."

I could see that Ruby still wanted to talk about Emily. She scanned my face and pressed ahead.

"Are you sure there isn't anything else you can do? Have you tried writing her a letter? You're the writer — write something. Explain how you feel. Tell her you love her."

"Next we see a mediation attorney. She's insistent. I've done everything I know to do. It's done." The words have more emotion in them than I anticipated. "I have to accept it. It'll just tear me apart if I don't."

"I'm sorry, Darlin, I didn't mean to pry." She patted my hand and surveyed the small private room. "This is the pain unit. They call it something else, but I like my name better. I can pronounce mine." She smiles.

"The doctor will be in here directly to explain what they do here. The nurses have already told me. Women do all the work and men take all the credit. Isn't that the way it always is, sugar." She winks at me. "Once all the medication from the surgery has worn off, they want to evaluate my level of pain and teach me how to judge the pain in the future, so that they can make me as comfortable as possible. They say I can go home in a day or so."

"How do you feel about all of this?"

"I feel fortunate. They seem serious about helping me with the pain. I told one of the nurses that suffering is one of my worst fears. She told me this was the reason the pain unit was started."

"I brought my voice recorder. I'm ready to start your story." I lifted the bag to show her the seriousness of my words.

She edged closer to me, lowered her voice and almost whispered, "You'll love this story. I can't wait to start." Her look told me to get my stuff out and get ready.

I moved the lunch tray aside, placed the recorder in the middle of the table, and moved the table closer to Ruby. She readjusted herself in the middle of the bed to get more comfortable. Just as we were about to begin a man in a white smock glided through the door, the smell of cologne filled the room. The tall thin doctor had dark features and thick black hair combed straight back. He filed through pages on a clipboard.

"Ruby?" He looked at her and she confirms with a nod. "I'm Doctor Stevens. But I prefer Stuart." He extends a hand to Ruby.

Ruby shakes his hand by his fingertips.

And how do we feel this morning?"

"We feel good. And how are you today?" She emphasizes the word you.

With Ruby's hand still attached to his, he placed the clipboard on the bed, and patted her hand. "I'm well. Very well, in fact. Thank you for asking. I'll be looking after you while you're here with us. To me he said, "And you are?" He extended a hand in my direction.

"Jack, Jack McNamara. I'm Ruby's nephew."

Ruby said, "He's also looks after me."

I shook his hand. He picked up the clipboard and flipped through the papers. "Ah, yes. You're her health care surrogate. Good. Then it is good that you're here. I want to orient you both to the Palliative Care Unit, explain what we do here, and how we will assist you." Dr. Stevens was animated and expressive.

To Ruby he said, "Has your doctor gone into detail about your prognosis?"

"You mean about dying soon? Yes, Dr. Sommers talked to me about it. She said that you would help with the pain."

"Doctor Sommers. She's the best. I wish I could convince her to work with me. She has such compassion. A wonderful woman. Anyway, let me welcome you to the PCU. We work exclusively with terminally ill patients. Our sole purpose is to make you feel comfortable to make the time that God has given you as meaningful and enjoyable as we can."

He perched himself on the edge of the bed. "A couple of years ago, I became concerned we weren't meeting the needs of many of our terminal patients. Our doctors and nursing staff felt uncomfortable with the dying, and nothing in their training had prepared them to deal with dying patients. They only knew how to make them well. They were slow to admit that a patient was dying. As a result, we robbed the terminally ill of the ability to embrace and enjoy a very natural part of the life cycle."

I was impressed with the passion this gentle man had for his work. Unlike other doctors who always seemed to race against the clock, Dr. Stevens acted as if he had all the time in the world.

He looked directly at me. "We have several goals we try to achieve. First, we want to educate the patient about their condition and what they can expect as it progresses. We want them to know exactly what they're up against so that they can begin to prepare for it mentally. This is very important.

"We also provide counseling to our patients and their families. We have trained psychologists who treat the terminally ill. Each patient will face dying in a different way. Some will have religious faith to support them, others long held philosophies. Many are afraid, afraid of the unknown, of what life after death will be like. They're afraid of the pain and the potential suffering they must endure. And, they're afraid for the people they'll leave behind. Before a patient can begin to enjoy this most important phase of their life, they must move past fear in all its forms.

"Very often it is the spouse or other family members who fail to embrace death as a natural phase of the life cycle. I've seen it happen so often. A patient is ready to face death. There's something in their soul that allows them to face it. They know when their time has come and they're ready for it.

But family members won't let them go. They demand that doctors continue to try to heal, when there's nothing they can do. It is the patient's family who often refuses to accept the inevitable. As a result, the family robs the dying patient of the peace that can come through the dying process. Counseling the whole family, along with the patient, is critical to the needs of the patient."

I looked at Ruby who was intent on the doctor's every word.

"We try to teach the family that most patients want to go through the dying process with dignity. They want to be in control of the process in the same way that they controlled their own lives. And as much as family members want to wrist the reigns of control away from them, they should resist, and let the patient make decisions for themselves as long as possible.

"We also want to understand the patient's desires, goals and needs. We want to understand what they want to do with their remaining time and try to design the pain management program around those desires. We had a man once who had an inoperable brain tumor. He wanted to go on an African safari he had dreamed about his entire life. Since we caught the tumor in its early stages, we were able to design a program around his need to fulfill this life goal."

I was most impressed. I had never really thought much about dying until faced with Ruby's. My heart sang with agreement on each of the points that he covered. I had never really thought about that fact that there was no training available for the person on the street on how to face death. There was not a course in college, or any that I had come across in print on the subject of dying. Certainly, I had never heard of a hospital that treated death as a treatable condition.

He slipped off the bed, let go of Ruby's hand, stretched his back and read the expressions on our face to make sure we were with him. "And finally, we want to learn how we can communicate with each other regarding pain, not just now, but also in the final stages, when you may not be able to speak for yourself. If you don't have a living will, we suggest one. If you do have one, we want to understand exactly how you feel about prolonging your life and intervention to keep you alive when you can't speak for yourself. We want to make absolutely certain we understand what you want." He moved toward Ruby again, and touched her arm. "Any questions?"

"I'm not afraid to die. I'm afraid of the process. I don't want to suffer. My sister died from cancer and in the final stages she suffered so with the pain."

"This is a common fear. For years, doctors have always been afraid to administer drugs in sufficient quantities to make the patient comfortable. First, there has been a bias against over medication for fear of a lawsuit. Under medicating was safer, the logic went, than to risk legal action by the family. There has also been a bias against drugs because of the potential for addiction. I know this doesn't make sense with dying patients but there are still many doctors who have a reluctance to use painkillers for this reason. Sometimes, again, the family can be the problem. Let's assume that a patient is in pain to the point that they can no longer handle it. It would be better for the patient to put them to sleep with medication until the death occurs. The family members, unwilling to let go, can tie the hands of the doctors from medicating the patient to this level.

"When we put together a treatment plan, you'll give us instructions on how you want to handle the medications when you reach a point that you can no longer handle the pain. There's no reason why you should suffer. There's just no need, unless it is your desire for some reason to do so. Some patients would rather suffer than sleep. We want to honor your desires.

"This afternoon, I want you to visit with one of our counselors." To me he asked, "Are you going to look after Ruby when she leaves the hospital?"

"Well, that's something that we haven't talked about yet."

"Good. Good. In the meantime, Ms. Johnson, we have data to review and a few tests of our own to conduct while you're with us. Anything else you want to ask?"

I asked, "How many hospitals have programs like this, Doctor?"

"Well, Jack, the number is growing. Palliative Care is a relatively new field. I'm very fortunate this hospital has given us wide discretion, and, as a result, we're breaking new ground in care of the terminally ill.

"Some hospitals, while they've developed new and more humane policies in administering medications to terminally ill patients, they still only see the treatment as a pain issue. Here we've made an effort to treat the dying holistically, not here in the hospital, but also after they leave. Once we have a patient assigned to us, we try to stay with them for the duration."

I wondered about the cost of such specialized care. Ruby must have read my mind.

"How can I afford all this? I only have Medicare," Ruby asked.

"Most patients have more resources than they think. Our counselors will work with you and your family, and we have some charitable resources available to us if need be. Let's not worry about this now. Let my people worry about it. Well, that's a quick overview of the PCU." He picked up his clipboard, offered his hand to Ruby, then me. "The counselor will give you a list of phone numbers for you to call if needed. I have a superb staff who'll take excellent care of you. If something happens and you need me, my phone number is on the list. Call me any time."

I said, "Thank you so much, Doctor."

He shook Ruby's and my hand and left from the room.

"What a precious man," Ruby said.

"Ruby, the last thing I want you to worry about is money. I'll work things out with the hospital. Besides, this story will be worth a fortune. What I'll make from it will more than handle any expenses you have." Before she could argue with me, I asked her, "So what's this story about?"

I reached for the recorder on the table, checked to make sure it was set properly then pressed the record button. The question still rolled around in my mind, what story could be so compelling that she had to tell before she died?

Ruby sat up in bed and talked too loudly into the microphone.

9

Fulton, 1938

John Barnes nosed his truck into the driveway of Lydia Banes' home, a colored seamstress and single mother. The home had a fallen down veranda, unpainted clapboard siding and a rusted, galvanized steel roof covered in debris from the massive hundred-year oaks that towered over and shaded the ramshackle house. A mixed breed Beagle and what appeared to be a purebred Cocker Spaniel fought in the yard and when they took notice of John Barnes, they charged his tow truck, yelping and jumping up on running boards and scratching the driver's door with unclipped nails. A middle-aged black woman bolted through the torn, poorly constructed screen door yelling to the dogs and calling their names; the dogs quieted and moved away from the truck. She walked down the single step into the leaf-strewn yard, stopped and crossed her arms across her chest to insure that the dogs would not go near the truck.

"They won't bother you, John," she yelled then swished a bug away from her face with the open palm of her hand.

Barnes got out of his truck, and met Lydia in the yard.

"Lydia." Barnes said and put his forefinger and a thumb to the bill of his fedora. Her son Awesome had filled the yard with vehicles most with hoods open, or on blocks in various stages of repair. There were as many vehicles in this yard as there were parked in front of Taggart's garage awaiting his attention. The vehicles were all aimed at a solitary shed. The front half of the structure was new and roughly constructed — little of it plumb or square. The rear half was a much older shed with windows boarded over. A two-by-four pole nailed to the side of Awesome's "garage" supported two bare wires that ran to another twisted two-by-four attached upright to the house and then disappeared into a fuse panel on the side of the home. Barnes had heard that Awesome Banes had some crude machine shop tools and undoubtedly, this was the source of electricity to run them.

"What brings you to my door, John? I think I already know, though. It's the cars isn't it?" Lydia's voice was without accent a rarity this deep in the south even rarer for a Negress.

90

"I'm that obvious?" Barnes was over six-feet tall, heavily built and wore bib overalls. He stood nearly a foot taller that Lydia. He surveyed the woman in front of him. She wore a thin shirt-dress with a light sweater. Her hair was jet-black pulled straight back into a simple bun. Her cheekbones were high, nose long and thin, ears small and close to her head and her lips were uncharacteristically thin. Her most striking feature was her pale green eyes. The skin around her eyes was two to three shades darker than her face, which made her eyes appear brighter.

Lydia chuckled; her eyes squinted and created crow's feet at the corners. She said incredulously, "What do you want to do, offer him a job?"

Barnes looked down at Lydia's shoes, embarrassed that she had discerned his motives so easily. "Yes, that's exactly what I want to do."

Lydia and most of the other Negroes around the St. Johns River brought their second and third-hand cars to his garage until Awesome started doing repair work here at their home.

Awesome was a prodigy. At twelve, he had done small repairs on Lydia's car, at fourteen major repairs and at eighteen; his reputation had grown so that most of the Negroes brought their cars to Awesome Banes for repair. That was not a serious issue for Barnes. Most of the Negroes were poor and had difficulty paying for the repairs or he had to extend credit and couldn't collect payment. Awesome would barter with the Negroes and accept farm crops and other services in exchange for his work, a practice John Barnes long ago discontinued.

Awesome Banes began to attract the notice of John's white customers; that is when it got his attention. Awesome's impact on his business mushroomed in an unexpected way. Henry Ford introduced the 65 H.P., flathead-V-8 in the 1932 Ford Sedan and Coupe. It was the first mass-production automobile with a simple, easily modified motor. It wasn't long after the introduction of the vehicle in late 1931 that racing, in particular with young, white males from families with money, gained popularity. By 1938, the business of racing parts for the Ford Flathead was in early bloom.

Awesome had purchased a wrecked '32 Ford Coupe from Barnes when Awesome was sixteen. He stripped the engine and drive train from the mangled car and installed them in a rundown 1928 Model T. When he brought his roadster into the garage for gas, he was tight-lipped about the modifications he had made to the motor. Other young men who came into the station reported that Awesome had taken on all comers and had not lost a single race on Jacksonville Beach. That is when the rich young men from Jacksonville found their way to the simple Negro young man in Fulton, Florida. Even that was not a significant problem. What was a problem was the reputation he gained as a mechanical genius in southern Duval County, and the young men brought their parents to the prodigy for their work as well. That is when Awesome Banes got his attention.

He looked toward the shed, then to Lydia.

"He's not here, John. He should be back soon. He had to run to Jacksonville for some parts."

"Would you ask him to stop by the garage? I'd wait for him, but I really need to get back. I just thought I would try to catch him."

"Can I tell him why you want to talk to him?" She smiled. "I'm sure he'll be excited." Her eyes radiated.

"Of course. I'd like to hire him. He won't get rich, but it will be steady work."

"I'll tell him."

Barnes again pinched the brim of his hat. "Lydia." He got into his tow truck, backed out on to the gravel road as he watched her standing alone under the tall oaks.

Awesome Banes pulled up to John Barnes' garage in his modified Model T, the altered exhaust pipes burbled at idle. He shut the motor off, set the brake, got out of the car and slammed the flimsy door. A sign, hung above the two garage doors in the gable of the roof, read, "Taggart's Livery." The sign was a throwback to its days as a blacksmith and buggy shop, which opened in 1909. He did not know why Mr. Barnes had not changed the name of the business, but everyone in the area knew it simply as Taggart's or Taggart's Garage.

What had always impressed Awesome about Taggart's was its cleanliness. John had lined the cars waiting for work neatly in a row, with the fronts of vehicles aimed at the street as if they were for sale. Barnes' shop was equally as tidy; tools always put away, floors swept and clean and Mr. Barnes seldom had a spot of grease on him. If the car repair business were like baseball this would be the big leagues.

Barnes used a star-wrench to tighten the lug nuts on a '31 Chevrolet on which he had just installed new brakes. He heard and recognized the rumble of Awesome Banes' car, tightened the last lug nut and pulled black cotton gloves off his hands and met Awesome as he came through the garage door.

"Awesome," he extended his clean hand to the mulatto.

Awesome returned the greeting. "Mr. Barnes."

They shook hands while Barnes took the measure of the handsome young man who stood in front of him. He had his mother's green eyes, nose and thin lips. However, his skin was nearly white, his dirty blonde hair tightly woven and he stood a couple of inches short of six feet. What had always struck Barnes about Awesome was his confident easy manner. He stood board straight, shoulders back, chin high and he looked you directly in the eyes. There were many whites in Fulton that took exception to Awesome's confident air as "uppity" at best and "not understanding his place" at worst.

Barnes said to him, "Did your mother tell you why I wanted to see you?"

He smiled, "Yeah, but I want to hear it from you." Awesome's language was absent accent like his mother's.

He knew that Lydia Banes had pulled Awesome from public school very early in his education because of the abuse hurled at her not-Negro-not-white son by other children. She educated him at home a fact that both benefited him and hurt him. Awesome was intelligent and well educated which had the unintended consequence of further isolation from both his white and Negro peers. While he was Negro, he did not fit with those of his race. He did fit with the whites, but they did not accept him, in fact, in many cases, they despised him. None of this seemed to burden Awesome Banes. His enthusiasm and cheerfulness seemed undaunted as though he were oblivious to the insults launched at him.

"Well, because I see a real benefit from us working together." Barnes extended his hand toward the small office. "Let's go sit and talk."

Once inside the office, Barnes pulled an oak chair from behind a small wooden desk, which he placed opposite a grey canvas-covered bench seat that came from an old truck. He offered the chair to Awesome Banes, and he took the longer and lower seat.

"I can't tell you how impressed I am with you. You and your momma have come here since you were a baby. I'm amazed at what you've accomplished with your skills as a mechanic. You're an intelligent young man, Awesome and I'd like you to work here."

Awesome began to shake his head. "Mr. Barnes, I appreciate your kind words, but I really don't want to work for anyone. I'm good, really." Lines appeared on his forehead as though he found the discussion awkward or stressful.

"I don't know any other way to be except honest. The majority of your customers can't pay you and you don't charge enough for your work to the ones who can. If you make money, it isn't a lot."

"How do YOU know?" He sounded insulted.

"All of your Negro customers used to come to me. I still have an envelope full of unpaid bills and IOUs. And the white customers still buy their gas from me and brag about how little you charge for your work." Barnes held up his hands. "I'm not critical. I just feel you could make a lot more money working here."

"How? By working for Negro wages? I doubt it."

"No."

"That's what my momma said. You wanted to talk to me about a job, and that I wouldn't get rich."

"Fulton isn't that big. There are only so many customers to go around, and you'll hurt both of us if we continue to divide those customers. The racing stuff . . .," - Barnes nodded his head and made a clicking sound with his mouth - ". . . now, that's business worth pursuing."

"It's just a hobby; something to have fun with."

"You made my point. Yes, it is fun. But, the racing business is a gold-mine under your nose."

"I make enough money to pay for parts for my own car. Every time I work on someone else's automobile, I learn more. They pay me to learn." Awesome leaned back in his chair and rubbed his hands together.

"Awesome, the things that you're doing with racing are so new, so advanced, it goes way beyond anything I do here. And you accomplish it with worn out tools under the shade of a tree. It's incredible! I've been to school, and taken Ford sponsored factory training and the modifications you're making to these engines are beyond the ability and experience of even a well-trained mechanic.

"I'd like you to work here, not by the hour but on a percentage of the profit on each job you do. After we pay for parts, I'll give you 35% of the money from labor and 50% of the profit from parts."

Awesome said with a level voice, "Why only 35%, I get 100% now?"

"For starters, I have tools and a well-equipped shop. In the back, I have a complete machine shop for engine work. I've been in business here for over twenty years. I know how to make money in this business. You have an opportunity to make good money right now. You're right. I told your Momma that you wouldn't get rich, and that's true. Perhaps a few years from now that will be different. You can make a very good living right now; I can show you how."

"Why are you doing this?" His pale green eyes narrowed.

"I could tell you that you're talented and I want to give you a chance. I could tell you that I've seen the work that you do and it is impressive: very professional. Both of these facts are true. In the end, though, I want to make money. I know that if I show you how to make money in this business, I'll make money and benefit. That's what motivates me. That's what should motivate you. I can show you how to make a good career with your skill."

Awesome stood up and looked around like a cornered cat. "I need to think about this Mr. Barnes." He rubbed his palms on the front of his dungarees.

"You should think about it. It is a big step. But I can assure you, young man, if you decide to do this you won't regret it." John Barnes stood, extended his hand looked directly into the eyes of his would be protégé.

Awesome Banes reached out, shook Barnes' hand and held his gaze. "Can I get back to you tomorrow?"

"Take as long as you need. I'm in no hurry."

Awkwardly, Awesome Banes nodded to Barnes, backed away toward the office door, turned and left.

As he watched Awesome walk through the shop and heard the souped-up car roar to a start, he was even more convinced that his decision to pursue the young man was a good one. He had considered the potential opposition that would come from some of his bigoted white customers. He had already made a mental inventory of whom they were and decided that they were customers he really did not want. His only real concern was for his daughter's reactions.

Ruby's voice began to fade, and her energy waned.

"We should stop, Ruby." I reached up and turned off the recorder. "We can pick this up next time."

She adjusted herself in the bed, pulled the covers up to her chest, reached for my hand and patted it. "You don't know how much this means to me, Jackie."

"It's nothing. Why don't you try to get some rest and I'll be back tomorrow."

I gave her a hug, kissed her on the cheek and left.

10

On my way home from St. Vincent's, the sky to the west of I-95 was ominous with a bank of boiling clouds as dark as charcoal. The air smelled of rain and salt, lightning veined the sky. Thunder cracked so loudly that it sounded like an explosion; raindrops so large they sounded like hail hitting the windshield. Traffic crawled and all I could see in front of me was a torrent of rain and the faint blinking glow of emergency flashers.

Even the biblical rains could not distract me from replaying Dr. Stevens' conversation about end-of-life experiences. He conveyed the information in such straightforward terms and made it sound like she should deal with death as one might make plans to go to a movie. My thoughts, as the skies fell open around me, were selfish. I had never given death much thought. Even when my mother passed away, I was too young to grasp my own mortality. Then, I was in a state of denial. I had coupled my reaction to her death with my longstanding anger with her for what she did to Billie.

Now the subject felt very personal. I probably had fewer years to live in front of me than I had lived so far. I tried to put myself in Ruby's shoes. How would I want my life to go if a doctor had told me I only had weeks to live? Immediately, my thoughts went to Em. I would not want to face it without her. I would want to surround myself with the people I loved and by the few who loved me. Then I had a feeling of loss; the circumstances of our imminent divorce coupled with the bleakness of Ruby facing death.

Prior to Dr. Stevens broaching the subject of death and dying, Ruby's issues were merely problems someone needed to solve. The net sum of Stevens' Dying 101 class brought Ruby's plans into the reality of my life.

On my first visit to St. Vincent's, Dr. Sommers had given me a list of hospice organizations that served Lake County in general and Mount Dora specifically. As traffic came to a standstill in the blinding deluge, I pulled the information from the sun-visor and called Agape House in Eustis. It was Saturday and a long shot that someone in authority would be there. I reached the managing director Jeff Morrison who said he would be happy to go over the services they provide and give me a tour of their facility.

The building from the outside looked like a residence, a large, 1900s, Victorian, two-story home that you would find on Main Street in any rural community. An enormous porch wrapped around the front and the sides of the house. Unoccupied white wicker chairs and oak rockers lined the porch by the entrance.

The desk completely consumed the foyer. A robust woman in her sixties juggled a phone on her shoulder, shuffled papers on the desk and looked for something. She put her caller on hold.

"Can I help you?"

"Jack McNamara . . ."

The receptionist, still sorting through papers said, "Mr. Morrison is expecting you." She motioned to the living room. "If you'll have a seat he'll be with you shortly."

The living room resembled the lobby of a small hotel. Chairs lined the walls and a small television set, tuned to The Weather Channel, reported current weather conditions to an empty room.

"Would you be, Mr. McNamara?"

"Yes. I spoke with you on the phone."

Morrison was a portly man with short legs and arms and large fleshy hands. His nappy hair was nearly gray, his eyes danced with energy and his smile was warm and genuine.

"Of course."

He extended a hand. "I'm Jeff Morrison. I'm the hospice administrator. If you'll follow me we'll go to my office where we'll have more privacy."

I followed him out of the living room, past the receptionist, then up a flight of stairs to the second story. From the second story landing at the front of the house, we followed a central hallway to the back of the building. The sound of voices from several offices we passed filled the hallway. Although I could not see anyone, the din communicated an organization trying to keep up.

Morrison's office was small, smaller than the offices we had passed in the hall but he had it neatly organized.

"Won't you sit?" He waved me towards a single side chair next to the desk.

"Mr. Morrison, my aunt has just been diagnosed with terminal cancer. It has spread to her liver and pancreas. They say the cancer is inoperable."

"I'm so sorry." His concern was genuine.

"The hospital is planning treatment. An option the hospital has suggested is hospice."

Morrison sat down in the small secretarial chair behind his desk.

I continued, "I've never been in a hospice and I have a limited understanding of what you do. I hoped to get a tour and determine whether I should bring my aunt by also."

Morrison gathered up a packet of material and handed it to me. "These are some pamphlets that describe Agape House and what we do. We treat the terminally ill, obviously. We distinguish ourselves with the level of care that we provide to the dying. Sometimes we're more successful in meeting the needs of our charges than family members are."

"How so?"

"At times, family members can't accept that a loved one is dying. They look at death through their eyes instead of the eyes of the dying. As a result, they push the terminally ill to undergo treatments that diminish quality of life without substantially prolonging it. They take precious time the dying have and often increase the suffering they must endure."

I could see how this could have happened with Ruby. Doing everything I could do to prolong her life seemed noble and right from a very selfish point of view. What was best for her? I tried to put myself in Ruby's position. I would want to be in control of how my life ended. I would not want to be in some hospital probed, prodded, tested and hovered over by doctors and nurses. I would want to enjoy the little time I had left with people that I loved and cared about. I would want to be active doing the things I enjoyed for as long as I could.

"So how is a hospice different from a hospital?"

"We see dying as a process very much like the process of living." Morrison pushed back in his chair and crossed his arms across his barrel chest. "Family, friends, work, hobbies and interests are all active ingredients in a happy life. Just because a person is dying doesn't mean that these things aren't important." Morrison sat forward and rested his elbows on the desk. "Mr. McNamara, Agape House isn't a place where you drop someone off to die. That's not how we operate. In concert with our charge's doctors, our own physician, our counselors and your family, we become a small team involved in patient care. We try to look at the individual,

their needs and the way that person's family inter-
acts with them to determine the best way we can
walk along side our charges."

"Walk along side?"

"I'm sorry we tend to speak in a language all
our own. Some people need some support, information, medication and little else. Others need
counseling, intervention with family members who
have a difficult time letting go, and a lot of emotional support. We all face death differently. The
last thing we try to do is take control. We walk
along side our charges, sometimes behind, but never
ahead. We try to minister to our charges in a sup-
portive way."

"How do you feel about a person dying at
home?"

"We encourage it, whenever possible.
Whether our charges are here or in the home, our
services are still the same. In fact, when you see our
facilities, it will be obvious that we try to duplicate
the home environment, thus the reason for the
house. For some, staying at home isn't possible.
Having enough space, the absence of family members, fear family members have with death, are
some of the reasons why our charges choose to
come here. When they do, we encourage family to
come and treat the place like their home. We permit

charges to decorate their rooms with their own things to duplicate the comforts of home. Our first choice is always their home, or the home of a family member.

"While we're equipped to handle most medical situations here, there are occasions, either because of the charge's medical situation or complications that arise from that condition, that a charge has to be hospitalized in the closing hours. We do everything we can to avoid that. Hospitals focus on cures that save and prolong life, as they should. They see death as a defeat instead of an important part of living. Our focus is to help our charges make the most of the final moments of their life and to make them as comfortable as possible. "So, when hospitalization is required, we work closely with the family and the hospital to ensure that our goals continue to remain in the forefront."

"You talk about death . . . so . . ."

"Matter-of-factly."

"Yes."

"One of the dangers of work in this ministry is to become callous to death. We deal with it day after day, and of course you become accustomed to it, even minimize it. That isn't good. Death happens to everyone. People don't want to deal with it until they have to. We've found that the best service we can be to our charges is to provide information, support and medical attention without sensationalism or diminishment."

"Ministry?"

"Agape House is a Christian organization made up of paid-workers and volunteers. Although we charge nominal fees for our services of which Medicare pays a majority, we rely on donations from individuals and support from area churches to keep the doors open."

"Does your participation mean that you'll attempt to proselytize her?"

"We have charges of all faiths at Agape House, Mr. McNamara. We find that many we minister to have never given God serious thought, and their illness forces them to face what they believe about life after death. Some have no interest in God, and have no interest in learning more. Others are hungry to learn. Again, our goal is to walk along side. When our ministry is wanted and needed, we provide it. When it isn't, we don't. It's just that simple."

Silence fell between us as I tried to think of unasked questions. It appealed to me to have someone experienced with the dying support me in helping Ruby. Based on what Morrison said, I felt Ruby would like him. He certainly espoused convictions about patient care that fit with Ruby's concerns.

"One final question. My aunt is horrified of dying in pain. This is her greatest fear. How will you make her feel comfortable?"

"What hospital referred you?"

"St. Vincent's."

"Palliative Care Unit?"

"Yes."

"Your aunt is there now?"

"Yes, developing a pain management plan."

"Great. This is a good program. Our services overlap somewhat, but we're accustomed to working with them. If you agree to work under their out-patient care unit, they'll develop a pain-management plan that'll follow your aunt until she dies. Field nurses will work with her directly in her home providing medication to cope with pain. Although we have a staff-physician who does the same thing, we welcome the field-nurses into our facility to monitor their patient's progress in dealing with pain. Either way, whether through St. Vincent's or through our doctor, I can assure you that your aunt won't suffer unduly. If we feel that the hospital isn't aggressive enough in dealing with pain, we will intervene on our charge's behalf to increase or change medications."

He stood up. "I would be happy to give you a tour. We only have one charge with us right now. It will give you an opportunity to meet one of our caseworkers. Since most of our staff is made up of volunteers, we assign each charge with a caseworker and have volunteers who can help with patient care."

The tour of the hospice was impressive. Excluding medical equipment, monitors and bathrooms that had been upgraded to an institutional level, the hospice could have been easily confused for someone's home.

As I drove to Mt. Dora, I decided that as nice as the hospice facility was l would not want to be anywhere but home in the waning weeks and hours of my life. If I were terminally ill, I would not want to be in a hospital with teams of people trying to extend my life. I wanted Ruby to come stay with me. The crushing deadline I was under gave me pause.

11

December 27

I called my banker, Bob Decker, who had arranged Billie's loan to buy the building that housed her restaurant. Decker and I grew up together, went to college together and he had been one of the foundational blocks in all my financial decisions.

"Jack, I've already heard about the contract debacle." Decker had a voice like the veteran sportscaster for the L. A. Dodgers, Vin Scully. His deep, commanding and melodious voice exuded confidence and put you at ease immediately. "I wish there were more I could do to help but this has become a legal matter that has to play out before we can proceed."

"What about the contract? Doesn't it mean anything?" Contracts have teeth. I couldn't believe that more couldn't be done.

"Jack, you can't make the guy sign the papers unless a court orders him to."

"What's the next step?"

"Billie has a competent attorney in Key West. She suggested filing for an injunction to freeze any action the landlord might take until the issue of the contract could be resolved. I think this should be done immediately before the landlord can do anything to harm Billie."

"There's no other way?"

"No, Jack. I think Billie could use your support right now. She sounded lost over the phone. I think she's at the edge of what she can handle."

What about me? I said to myself. "Alright, I'll head down there."

"Call me if you need me, Jack."

"Thanks Bob."

I picked up the phone, called Billie and asked her to set up a meeting with the attorney for tomorrow morning, packed some clothes and my laptop and headed for Orlando International Airport. I picked up a standby ticket on the 8:10 p.m.

puddle-jumper that got me to Key West in a little over an hour.

While I stood by the curb of Key West International Airport and waited for Billie to pick me up all I could think about was Em.

Billie pulled to the curb in a disheveled Volvo station wagon eaten with rust, reached across the passenger seat and opened the door for me. I opened the back door, tossed my bag and computer on the seat then jumped in and closed the door. Before I could buckle my seatbelt Billie closed the distance between us, hugged me, and began to cry.

She pushed away, brushed the tears from her cheeks, hooked her short red hair over her ears and said, "I'm so sorry to involve you in all my problems. I know you have your own truck full. I feel really bad, Jackie." She reached out and grabbed my hand, patted it and began to cry again.

"Billie, we'll figure it out." I gave her hand a squeeze. "You have a valid contract, and your landlord has singled you out for being gay. This won't stand up in court, Billie, not for five seconds." I pulled a handkerchief out of my coat pocket and handed it to her.

Tears spilled down her cheeks onto her white sleeveless blouse and yellow knee-length shorts. She dabbed her eyes, took a deep breath, checked over her shoulder for traffic, put the Volvo into drive and aimed it toward downtown.

Billie parked on the street near her restaurant and we walked a block to "The Mangrove." The restaurant was a blend of old and new construction. She converted the house into a kitchen and dining rooms. The large front yard had two enormous Banyan trees around which Billie had designed a courtyard. The trees provided shade over the entire yard. The Banyans were covered in stringed white lights, which created a romantic atmosphere in the evening. Red brick-pavers covered the grounds and tables with green umbrellas filled the courtyard. Along the left side of the patio an outdoor covered bar ran from near the street all the way back to the house. Billie had the courtyard enclosed with a four-foot-high, white vinyl fence with a host station at the entrance gate.

The host led us to a two-top cocktail table near the bar. Without asking, Billie went to the bar gave the bartender an order and returned with two fluted glasses of cold Pinot Grigio. The bartender followed Billie back to the table with an ice bucket and remainder of the bottle of wine.

Billie ran a hand through her hair as if the act might remove the stress of the past few days. "Did you get your book finished?" She lifted her glass clicked it against mine, "Happier days," she said and tossed back nearly half the glass in one swallow.

"I finished it day before yesterday. If it hadn't been for you and Jody, I would have never had the first sentence written. That's the good news. The bad is that I have to have another novel done in six weeks."

Jody's mother, Helen, suffered from postpartum psychosis, lost all hope and murdered her entire family. She shot her husband and her five children in birth order then tried to turn the gun on herself. Jody received only a grazing blow that rendered her unconscious for a few moments. She regained consciousness and found her mother sitting in the middle of the kitchen floor, shaking uncontrollably, trying to reload the gun. Jody wrestled the gun from her and called the police.

Jody's mother got my writing career started. Before trying to do away with her family, she used her contacts as a freelance magazine writer to get a short story I had written into one of her the magazines. The connections I made through that short story led to an invitation to write a longer piece. I chose my loss of Jody's love as the basis for one of my novels.

Jody's aunt gained custody of her, and even before the funeral for her family, she moved Jody to Atlanta to shield her from the publicity and the trauma of such a horrific event. I had been as devastated by Jody's removal from my life as I was about losing Em. When I was here a month and a half ago, I learned from Billie that Jody was a widow and was living in Key West and had come into The Mangrove and recognized Billie immediately.

The gruesome events of Jody's departure were one of three equally horrendous events in 1961 that collectively lit an emotional fuse that would not detonate and bring my life to the very edge of sanity until thirty-six years later. It was Jody, just a month and a half ago, who ushered me back to a time in my life where I loved to write, and she reminded me of the power of love – love for her – that propelled my writing so long ago. Being with her and experiencing that distant time anew in her company, rekindled my need to write – a need that had been missing for over two years. There's no way I could be in Key West, regardless of the circumstances, without seeing her and thanking her for her intervention on my behalf.

Billie said, "Jody asks me every time she comes to the restaurant about your book and Em. If you get a chance you should at least call her, or if you're okay with it, I could call her and invite her to dinner tonight here at the restaurant."

"Alright, let's get together with her for dinner. But it will need to be short; I need to get a chapter written tonight or at least a good start on one."

Billie stood, made a quick call to Jody and set up the dinner. She returned to the table and sank into the chair. "She's excited that you're here, Jackie. I've never met Emily so I can't make a comparison to Jody. Jody is a real find: beautiful, charming, desirable and financially set. Emily has to be an amazing woman to compete with her."

I let the comment pass without acknowledgement, and she did not pursue it either. "I'll make sure you get out of here early so you can write tonight. My problems aren't helping you get your book done, are they?"

"If I can write some tonight and early in the morning I can stay on track. I don't want you worrying about me. Where's Alex?" Alex was an airline captain and Billie's partner.

"In San Diego. She has a few more segments to fly before she'll be off for two weeks. I talked to her on the phone last night and she was relieved that you've decided to come. We've both been in a panic over the restaurant. I'm so glad you're here."

"I'm glad to be here too, Billie." I looked around the courtyard and bar area and there was not a vacant seat. At the host station, a line had formed and backed up down the sidewalk on Duval Street. "Looks like business is good."

"Jackie, all of our hard work is starting to pay off. This year we doubled the business we did last year, and with Alex's help, this will be an extremely profitable year. This makes this issue with the landlord so heartbreaking. I'll lose everything if I can't buy this property."

She continued to tell me about the business and the work she had done to bring the restaurant to this level of success. She sat forward in her seat, her voice passionate and her pale, expressive, green eyes appeared sultry. She looked like Amelia Earhart, with her short flyaway hair, and freckled face. Her elbows rested on the edge of her table, her hands moved in exaggerated gestures. I acknowledged that I loved my sister. Despite all the hardship and rejection, she had dealt with in her life she fought hard and won. She was an inspiration.

As she shared with me all the details of the real estate transaction and the unconscionable behavior of her property owner - all facts I already knew – I listened intently and allowed her much needed time to vent. She shared my need to work my problems out verbally and when she had exhausted the topic she said that she felt better and two hours passed as though they were a few moments. It was an 'excuse me' from Jody that brought Billie and I out of our deep conversation.

Jody looked more beautiful than I had remembered from my last visit. She was tall and slender; her dirty blonde hair pulled straight back to a ponytail. She wore a long, orange, sleeveless, form-fitting sundress that accentuated her deeply tanned face and arms. I was at once glad I had made the trip and anxious to be in her company again.

12

The limbs of the banyan trees veined out in every direction creating a canopy that covered the bar and all the tables in the courtyard. Thousands of tiny, white lights hung in the trees seemed like stars someone had hung in the heavens. The soft glow of light gave the courtyard an enchanted appearance and, coupled with the effects of the wine, drained the stress from my spirit.

As Billie found another chair and got Jody situated, I wrestled with the feelings that seeing her and being with her produced. Although she was tall, Jody was graceful and fluid in her movements. By any measure, she was stunning. I was comfortable around her. Just as I experienced as a young boy, her persona exuded warmth and openness without speaking a word.

I stood and gave Jody a hug. She carried a light jacket over her left arm and she wrapped her right arm around my neck and hugged me tightly. She smelled of scented soap.

"Jody, you look marvelous," I said, adjusting my chair to accommodate the one Billie had gotten for her. Jody draped her jacket and purse over the back of the chair, pulled her chair close to the table.

"You look pretty good yourself." She bent over and kissed me on the cheek. "How is everything going?" Emphasis placed on "Everything."

I filled her in on the completion of the novel I started in Key West when I saw her last and my publishers demand that I have the last novel in the series completed by February 15.

"And Em?"

This was really the "everything" she was interested in. "We're still on course to split our assets. Despite my entreaties, she's firm on moving forward with the divorce. What've you been up to?"

I realized, other than her husband passing away, I knew little about her current circumstances. When we last met, all we really discussed were my woes and childhood events that involved us both.

Billie spoke before Jody could open her mouth. "Jack, you won't believe what this woman has accomplished in just a few short weeks. She found this little hole-in-the-wall down on Duval

Street and opened a gallery that features local artists. That little place jumps." Billie reached over and touched Jody's arm.

Jody patted Billie's hand. "You two wouldn't believe the talent that lives on this little island. The galleries that were here featured well-known artists and their prices were outrageous. I wanted to highlight lesser-known talent, consign their work and give them the exposure they deserved. When word spread about the opening, my gallery filled in a week and the demand for local works has been more than I ever dreamed, especially from tourists off the cruise ships. Surprisingly, I sell the most to locals. It is interesting that many of the buyers are artists themselves."

I asked Jody, "Do you handle just painted works?"

"Gosh no. We'll take just about any form of artistic expression. Sculpture, pottery, photography, woodcarving and blown glass. We even have a gorgeous quilt hanging in the window, and a video artist has set up a sixty-inch projection screen to feature his work." Jody fiddled with a lone pearl hanging on a gold chain.

Billie again, "In just a short time, her shop is the most coveted place for an artist to show. Jody is very selective about what she'll consign. She has an incredible eye and an uncanny ability to know what'll sell." Billie looked at her watch. "Jack, I'll give you two a chance to catch up. When I get to the house, I'll take your things up to your room and set your laptop up on the desk. See you in a bit." Billie stood, leaned over and kissed Jody on the cheek and said, "You're the best, sweetie."

Jody and I watched her walk out on to Duval.

"She and I have gotten to be good friends, Jack. She's a very special person. She's had it rough and doesn't deserve to suffer at the hands of this bigot," she said referring to Billie's landlord. Her eyes narrowed and she drew her hands into fists. "These are the nineties for crying out loud. Key West is the last place for a homophobe to live. I'll bet that eight to ten percent of the people who live in Key West are gay."

As I listened to Jody, I had to keep my own feelings of revulsion in check. I continually reminded myself that Billie was my sister, deserving of all the unconditional love I could offer her. "I agree Billie needs a break. She has worked so hard and been so successful. It seems terribly unfair that all of that would be taken away from her because of the hatred of one man."

I looked at her and she had locked her eyes unwaveringly on mine. I was not uncomfortable, nor did I wish to ruin the moment. Even in the pale light, you could see the tiny flecks of brown in her light brown eyes.

Jody spoke first. "Jack you and I are connected. We've been connected since the very first time we kissed when we were kids. I believe you feel the same thing. Am I wrong?" She reached across the small table and took my hand in hers.

"You don't mess around do you?"

"I lost you once and if I can help it, I don't want to lose you again."

"Jody. I'm not in a position to explore those feelings with you. Regardless of how I may or may not feel, until my marriage runs its course with Emily I'm not free. Discussion about us just makes things more complicated; more difficult."

"Please Jack, throw me some crumbs. I'm not asking for any more than some honesty. Do you share my feelings?"

I could not believe my conflicting feelings. I loved Em deeply, but she obviously did not want to be with me anymore. Jody was right. I did feel connected to her; more than connected.

126

"Since you press me, yes, I share the same feelings. I can't - I'm not in a position to act on those feelings. I'm in love with Emily and I made a commitment to her. Do you understand?"

She withdrew her hand from mine. "Yes, I understand. I don't like it, but I understand. But I want you to understand this." She shifted slightly in her chair facing me more squarely, "I don't give up easily. I don't have a single doubt about how I feel about you. Reluctantly, I'll give you space to work things out with Em. But let's not let what we have slip through our fingers again."

We spent the remainder of the evening talking about her, her business, her family and her migration to "the string of pearls," the Keys. I promised to keep in touch and she promised to keep her eye on Billie.

13

December 28th

I made it to Billie's a little past ten and she had already gone to bed. I pushed my conversation with Jody out of my mind, wrote until almost four this morning and finished two chapters. I collapsed exhausted.

As I awoke, my mind could no longer ignore my conversation with Jody the previous evening. As much as I grieved for the loss of my relationship with Em, I could not understand how I could have feelings for Jody, too.

I climbed the stairs to the widow's walk that stretched across the roofline of Billie's two-story home, a block from Mallory Square and a stone's throw from Pier B where the cruise ships moored. The morning air was cool, crisp and dry as I surveyed a city about to come to life. The rising sun had not cleared the trees and the serenity of the scene, broken only by the occasional jogger, seemed counter to the turmoil that had become my recent existence.

As I rested my arms on the rail and took in the brilliant aquamarine sea out beyond the Hilton Resort, I turned my attention toward the meeting with Billie's attorney later in the morning. Jody was right that Billie did not deserve the treatment she received.

I came down the back stairs to the kitchen and found Billie dressed and putting bagels in the toaster.

"Good morning. Glad you're up and about. Our meeting is in a half an hour. Bagel?" She held out half of a buttered, rye bagel, which I took from her. She pointed to the drip coffee maker at the end of the counter. "Cups, cream and sugar are next to the coffee pot."

The two-wall-kitchen painted in pale yellow with white trim was long and narrow with ample multi-paned windows overlooking a spacious garden to the rear of the house. At the extreme end of the kitchen was a spacious turret that surrounded an eight-sided solid oak table with beige fabric-covered parson's chairs. Plants Billie had hung strategically gave a warm touch to the room and made the kitchen feel like the extension to the gardens. At the other end of the kitchen was a breakfast bar with four counter-height stools that matched the style of the parson's chairs. I filled my coffee cup, moved to the bar and waited for Billie to join me. She wore powder blue slacks and matching long-sleeved blouse and sandals.

Billie blew the steam off the surface of her coffee and said, "Big day today. Kind a scary."

I said, "Sometimes things that are worthwhile are challenging to acquire. It will make the owning of your restaurant that much sweeter, Billie. How are you doing?"

"I'm okay. I just wish this were all over." She sat on a stool, took a long sip of her coffee and continued. I met Cynthia Pike through the association of gay and lesbian business owners in Key West. Her specialty is real estate law and her legal practice is pretty general."

"What's her take on your situation?" I took a big bite of my bagel while I waited for her to respond.

"I haven't talked to her yet about the 'Lezo' remark Coats made at Sloppy Joe's. I just made the appointment. But folks in the association who've used her said she was sharp and tough as kryptonite."

"It sounds like you got the right person." I finished my last bite, and took another slug of coffee.

"I don't know if I do or not. That's why I'm glad you're coming with me. Normally, Alex would go with me, but with her gone and time being of the essence, you're it." She finished her bagel, grabbed our plates then marched to the sink and deposited them. "So we will both find out how good she's."

We accessed Pike's office through an inconspicuous single door between two dress shops on Duval Street, only a couple of blocks from Billie's house. We climbed the dark stairway to a brightly lit, second floor waiting area. The receptionist desk was empty, an office door opened and a small, thin, young women in her late thirties said, "I thought I heard someone on the stairs. You'll have to forgive me, my assistant is on maternity leave and the temp isn't due until after lunch. So, we're making do." To me she said, "I'm Cynthia, and you're Billie's brother?" she said, extending a hand.

I nodded and shook her hand. Her hand was small but her grip was firm.

Then she shook Billie's hand and said, "Good to see you, Billie, I just wish the circumstances were better. Have you been feeding your brother all that marvelous food at The Mango?"

Pike stepped into the threshold of her office and gestured us in."

"The Mangrove," Billie said.

"Ah, yes of course." She glided behind her desk. "Please, sit down."

While many offices and businesses decorated in island décor, her office was large but spare of furnishings and ultra-contemporary in style. Her desk was metal and glass, and everything was immaculate.

"Bring me up to date, Billie?"

Billie gave her a succinct history in a well-organized chronological sequence, which culminated with the landlord's refusal to close the deal on the sale of his building because she was a lesbian.

"Do you have witnesses? Pike took notes on a yellow legal pad in front of her.

"Yes, several people, all servers at Sloppy Joe's. I know most of them. They frequent my bar and restaurant."

"Jack, what's your interest in this?" Pike coiled her shoulder length light brown hair around her ear.

"I'm just here to support my sister. I want to help in any way I can, financially if necessary."

Pike narrowed her pale green eyes, "If we have witnesses who can attest to what you claim your landlord said, then it would be a pleasure, no make that an honor, to handle this case pro bono. What's your landlord's name?" Pike looked through a file on her desk, pulled out a copy of the real estate contract and moved forward in her seat. "

"Ah, yes, Jeff Coats."

"Do you know him?" Billie asked.

"Yes, I'm well acquainted with Mr. Coats." Pike dropped the pencil on top of the legal pad. She pushed back in her seat. "First, if everything is as you've reported it, we have a classic civil-rights case where, at a minimum, Coats discriminated against you because you're a woman. Certainly if all else fails, we will approach the case from that angle. However, my real interest is to pursue this case as discrimination because of sexual orientation.

"While the gay community has been active in the courts trying to persuade judges to recognize sexual orientation under the Equal Protection provisions of Civil Rights Act of 1964, case law isn't well established. There's a case working through the federal courts, Romer vs. Evans, that addresses that issue directly, but I don't think the Supreme Court will rule on it until next year." She folded her small hands together, leaned forward and rested her elbows on the desk.

"The first issue is to freeze the sale of the property until our suit can be heard."

Billie looked at me and then at Pike. "I wouldn't put it past this guy to sell the restaurant to someone else as quickly as he can."

"As soon as I can interview the witnesses, I'll file an injunction with the Monroe County Court to prevent the sale of the restaurant until we can file a suit. We should have an injunction in a day or so. I'm afraid Mr. Coats has no idea of the number of influential people in the gay community. He has picked the wrong place to display his bigotry."

Billie said, "Coats has a lot of money, Ms. Pike."

"Billie, you wouldn't believe the influence and power that the Business Guild has in Key West. If Coats persists in refusing to complete the sale of the property to you, a lawsuit aside, we can bring tremendous pressure to bear on him and make his life here miserable. I don't think we will have to do that. This case is so cut-and-dry all the money in the world can't buy enough whitewash to make this go away."

I asked, "So you're sure that Billie will be able to keep the building."

"Nothing is ever one-hundred percent, Mr. McNamara. However, I think we can deal from a position of strength. I'm certain we can tie up the building while this goes through the court." She focused her attention on Billie. "Billie, I'm lesbian as well. Therefore, this case has special import to me. I'm not just fighting for you I'm fighting for me and all the other folks who are subjected to this kind of hatred. If you'll let me handle this case, I'll fight like hell for you."

Pike sat back in her chair, relaxed a bit and said, "Can I handle your case for you?"

Billie looked at me, then to Pike and said, "Yes, of course."

Out on the street, Billie said, "That sounds too easy, Jack." She paced back and forth as if she couldn't decide where she wanted to go."

"She seems like a competent attorney. Don't worry."

We walked down Duval to the restaurant. A cruise-ship was in port so tourists blocked the sidewalks window-shopping with their indecision about where to go. It was impossible to walk together and talk, so I followed her as she wended her way through the throng.

As we approached the restaurant there was a Monroe County sheriff's deputy leaning up against the host station as he fanned himself with a manila envelope. We walked up the two steps to the courtyard.

"Ms. Saint John?"

"Yes," Billie looked at the officer and then at the envelope.

The officer opened the envelope, pulled a document out and handed it to Billie. "You have a good day," he said. Then he bounced down the steps, got into the passenger side of a police-cruiser at the street and they drove off.

Billie scanned the document then handed it to me. "It's an eviction notice. It says I have fifteen days to vacate the building."

"Here, let's sit down and go through this." I scanned the contents. "Are you behind in your rent?"

"Of course not!"

"This says that you're 45 days past due."

"Jack, I pay my bills, and I pay the rent a week before it's due just to make sure I don't have a problem with Coats." Tears welled up in her eyes.

"Billie, you need to stay focused. Gather up your lease and cancelled checks, the names of the people at Sloppy Joe's who heard Coats' rant along with this eviction notice and we'll take them back to Pike. I'm no lawyer, but it seems to me Coats can't evict unless he gives you an opportunity to bring your rent payments current."

"Pike will have to sort it out. I don't have time to mess with it." She put her hand on my arm. "You should go, Jack. You've already spent enough time on my problems and I love you for it. You have a book to write and you have to work through a divorce.

"It's not a problem, Billie. I'll stay as long as I'm needed."

"I know you can and you would if I asked. But I've got it. If something comes up that I can't handle, I'll call you. You're the best."

14

When I learned of Billie's homosexuality a month and a half ago it took me back, I confess. My Irish Catholic upbringing did not provide margin for deviations from sexual norms. I know the arguments advanced by some that homosexuals are born with this same sex attraction and others claim they come by it through environmental circumstances. I have no special insight on the topic. What I do know is that what Billie suffered at the hands of my mother and father no one, regardless of who they are, deserves that inhumane treatment. So many people had abandoned and rejected Billie. It is a miracle that she had made such a successful life for herself. I owe a lot of that to her relationship with Alexandra.

I am in no position nor do I have the desire to judge her. I cannot fathom the hurt Billie has experienced in her life. I know that Alex threw Billie a lifeline and the two of them have made a life together. So, my questions about morality have no place in my relationship with Billie, nor will they in the future. She is my sister and love is transcendent. If the abandonment, rejection and ridicule Billie has endured over the years were seen as a trash heap, Billie's landlord added to the height and width of the toxic mess. No creature, not even a dog, should have to endure the vile and hate-filled battering at the hands of her intolerant landlord. As I boarded the small propjet bound for Orlando, I could not get Billie out of my thinking. I tried to pull my laptop out to write but I could not concentrate. I hoped that Billie's attorney's aggressiveness was equal to the legal onslaught that Jeff Coats would no doubt level at Billie. Finally, I was able to push Billie's dilemma to the back of my mind by concluding that "I" (or a surrogate of my choosing) could buy the restaurant then transfer ownership to Billie if it came to that. With that hope hanging in my field of vision, I was able to turn my mind towards writing.

When I reached home, it was nearly midnight. A lone note, on pink paper, on my desk in the studio, in Em's handwriting read: "1. Ruby called and would like you to visit her tomorrow at St. Vincent's if you can. 2. Don't forget arbitration meeting day after tomorrow."

Concerning the arbitration meeting, I thought Em moved too fast. As a friend of mine once said, "The train was leaving the station without me," and I could not run hard enough to catch it. It was consistent with Em's philosophy to face unpleasant things head-on and get them behind her quickly. The curtness of her note was an emotional punch in the face and I wondered how many more of them I could handle before I gave up.

Ruby's desire to see me was unexpected. I had not planned to visit her until New Year's Eve and frankly, I planned every bit of the time in the interval to write. My new novel, like most of my other works, will be about eighty-thousand words. I do not plan it that way it just always seems to come out to eighty-thousand words plus or minus. I have forty-five days to complete the next novel, which requires I write approximately seventeen-hundred to eighteen-hundred words a day. With several chapters already written, I was a little ahead of schedule. I was tired when I got in last night, but I could not go to sleep so I started writing and finished another chapter by three o'clock in the morning and then slept fitfully. Sleep has always been problematic and when I am writing it is worse. When I am in the flow of a story, or to put it in Ernest Hemingway's words when there's "juice" flowing, sleep was a distraction and my mind buzzed with what came next in the story. Another major interruption was discouraging.

Room 201 was quiet and Ruby sat in a chair next to her hospital bed reading her bible. The smell in the room was a combination of disinfectant cleaners, hand-soap, body odor and ozone from the television running without sound.

"Ruby?" I knocked on the metal doorframe to her room. She was dressed in a hospital gown, her left arm connected to an IV attached to a chrome pole on rollers.

She looked up, "Jackie, come in here." She bookmarked her spot in the brown, worn, leather-bound book, laid it on the bed and took off her reading glasses. "Well, I suwanee, if you don't look the site. You look wrung out?"

I walked over to her, put my arms around her, the flesh on her shoulders felt slack and without substance. I kissed her on the cheek and said. "I just haven't slept a lot. When I'm in the middle of a project, sleep is hard to come by."

I pulled the second, green, metal-frame chair closer to hers so that I faced her. Although she looked rested, the hospital stay had taken a toll on her appearance. Her blue eyes were more deeply set and appeared to be glazed over from medication, her cheeks more drawn and the tremors in her body from Parkinson's were more pronounced.

"I'm so glad you came, Darlin'. Tell me how are things coming with Emily? I talked to her on the phone and when I asked how the two of you were, she said she didn't want to talk about it, and so we discussed other things. She's such a sweetie, Jackie. And so beautiful."

I really did not want to get into it with her either, for discussing this with Ruby would lead to unsolicited advice and intense prying for details. I just did not have the energy. I answered her question with, "We're not doing well." I reached over and picked up her mangled right hand. "So what was so important that you needed to see me right away?"

"I need to ask you something." She seemed pensive like a child who wanted to ask her mother a question and knew the answer would be "no."

I said, "What is it?"

She paused, looked directly at me on the verge of tears, "Can I come stay with you?" She gave my hand a squeeze.

"Yes, of course."

"I would like to come and stay with you, now." She paused to let the weight of it fall then said, "Jackie, they're talking about my life expectancy in terms of weeks. The cancer in my liver is worse than they let on. And I've had friends who've had similar cancers and their time was short." She searched my face for signs of my reaction. "So whatever time I have, I want to spend it with you. You and Glory Jean are the only family I have left and god-bless her, Glory Jean can barely manage herself, much less care for a dying woman."

My first reaction was selfish and petty. I thought about the inconvenience and the time it would take caring for her needs. Then as I studied her warm and tender face, my opposition melted quickly. "Certainly, you can stay with me."

Bolstered by my reaction she said, "I'm supposed to be moved to a nursing home. I really don't want to go there, Jackie." Tears welled in her eyes.

"You don't have to, Ruby. We'll work it out. I'll meet with your doctor and have him make the arrangements."

I pulled my tape recorder out of my jacket, "Besides we have some work to do." I tapped the record button on and placed the miniature recorder on top of her bible on the bed. "Where did we leave off?"

A twinkle returned to her eyes, she shifted on the chair and took me back to the 1930s and Taggart's Garage.

15

Fulton, Florida

1938

Adel Barnes had always been both repelled by and attracted to Awesome Banes. His half-breed status created a conundrum in that considering him as anything more than a racial anomaly put her against the grain with most of the people she knew, her father excluded. Her father was not a religious man. He was raised in Michigan. After World War I, when released from the Navy, he came to Jacksonville. While he kept his views about Negroes to himself, his actions bespoke tolerance, acceptance and at times defense of Negroes who were abused or mistreated. He did not wear his views on his sleeve. While a quiet man, when angered he was immense enough to be feared and there was nothing that would set him off more quickly than a Negro suffering at the hand of a bigoted white man. "The only difference between that man and me is the color of his skin," he would say and mean it.

Adel Barnes was less dogmatic and more flexible with regard to her opinion. She had grown up in Charleston as a child and moved here when she was twelve to escape an abusive father. Her adoptive mother, Madara, a native of Jacksonville, who died three-and-a-half years ago from breast cancer, had been less tolerant and openly demeaned Negroes.

She had continuously shared her less than positive views with Adel. While her father's views and feelings were fixed, she had to deal with the realities of the hatred that existed between the coloreds and whites in the world around her. She was not powerful enough, like her father, to argue. While repelled by the conflicts of his race, Awesome Banes was attractive to look at. Both Adel and Millicent, Adel's older sister, had to pump gas for their father at his garage. As a result, the girls knew everyone in Fulton. Lydia and Awesome Banes were regular customers and although Awesome was closer in age to Millicent, she and Awesome were friendly; which was also part of the conflict. She enjoyed his frequent visits, more so now since he had become a customer in his own right. However, her admiration of Awesome Banes was distant, and her socializing limited, no more so than the relationship she enjoyed with many people who came to the garage to trade regardless of their race. The town was small and there was no other place to buy gas unless you drove to Orange Park or Jacksonville, so everyone came here.

It was her father's announcement at dinner that he had extended an offer to Awesome Banes to work out of his garage that forced her to confront the conflicting feelings she had about him. Her initial reaction was concern about what people in Fulton would think about a Negro working for her father? The first person to come to mind was Buddy Hines, her sister Millicent's boyfriend. His hatred of Negroes was unbridled. She could predict the guff Millicent would receive for her father's indiscretion. She had seen Awesome and Buddy clash during the infrequent times they were at the garage at the same time to buy fuel.

Buddy was the only child of Derrick Hines, an automobile dealer in Jacksonville. While Mr. Hines worked in town, their home was on a large tract of land in Fulton directly on the St. Johns River. The fact that the Hines' home was on the river was not significant. Adel's father's garage and an adjoining home abutted the St. Johns. However, the Barnes home and Taggart's Garage could both fit inside the carriage house of the Hines Plantation. Buddy Hines' grandfather had been a real estate developer and made his fortune subdividing large tracts of land in Orange Park and selling the pieces to "Yankees," on credit as "winter homesteads." As Ford automobiles became evermore popular, Hines transferred his wealth from real estate to Ford dealerships across northern Florida. In 1928, when the elder Hines passed, he left his son Derrick a depression proof economic empire. When the stock and real estate markets imploded, following his father's example, Derrick reinvested in real estate buying large tracts of land on the courthouse steps for the taxes owed. Derrick Hines knew that America could not avoid involvement in the looming war in Europe and had bet heavily that the economy would improve significantly and with it, real estate values would rebound.

Buddy Hines would sit at the concrete picnic bench behind the garage and regale the Barnes sisters with stories about his father's financial exploits as though he were a key and trusted business advisor. Millicent would fawn over every detail with patronizing compliments, "Oh, how wonderful," or "Your father is brilliant." Buddy bored Adel. She found his constant, insatiable need to be the center of attention burdensome. Praise to Buddy was more important than lifeblood itself. While good looking, Buddy had a mercurial personality. It was the ugly, anger-riddled side of Buddy Hines she detested.

Many others would struggle if not revolt at Awesome's presence in her father's garage. There would be few with the courage to say their piece directly to John Barnes, however, they would say it to her, every last one of them.

Adel looked at her father as he sat at the head of the table as though the information he just shared about Awesome Banes was nothing more than insignificant news, like talking about the weather.

When Adel came to live with the Barnes family, John and Madara legally adopted Adel. No sooner was the ink dry on adoption papers, Maddie succumbed to breast cancer just shy of her fortieth birthday.

If John Barnes felt burdened by the addition of a teenaged girl to their home, Adel never saw it. She had never seen even the slightest thread of partiality. She felt loved, wanted, and as much a daughter to John as if she were his natural child. Moreover, she loved him almost from the first day she came to Fulton. He was a patient man, unshakeable in his convictions, predictable in his behavior and Solomon-wise.

Millicent was another matter. From the day Adel arrived, Millicent Barnes' actions screamed envy, resentment and at times unbridled hatred. When Adel first arrived, John placed her in the same bedroom with Millicent treating them both with unwavering equality. However, he soon fathomed the error of the move. The simmering conflict erupted into war when Maddie died as Millicent demanded female supremacy in the household.

With obvious reluctance, Barnes placed Millicent in the master bedroom John and Maddie had shared for years and permanently installed himself in the small guest room he had slept in since Maddie's death. Millicent's move to her own room and her perceived status as matriarch softened the open warfare between the girls to skirmishes that became less intense over time. That is until Awesome came to work at Taggart's Livery.

16

Fulton, Florida

1938

At eighteen, Millicent Barnes was everything that Adel was not. She was tall, athletic, small of waist and amply curved. Adel was just over five feet tall, boxy figured, small boned and frail. Millicent had brilliant blue eyes, long dark-brown hair while Adel's eyes were green and her short hair the color of rust. Millicent had high-cheek bones, full lips, squared off jaw and dimpled cheeks. Adel's face was unremarkable and her lips thin but expressive. As alluring as Millicent was, Adel was plain.

Millicent's mannerisms were exaggeratedly female, so demonstratively so that one might equate her physical movements as theatrical; body and arm actions a Shakespearean male actor might make to convince an audience he was female. As attention seeking as Millicent's mimes were, Adel conducted herself with efficiency and economy. As outgoing as Adel was, she did not seek unwarranted attention.

There were other differences, too. Adel was a warm and empathetic, which drew people to her. While men looked at Millicent, they were more comfortable talking to Adel. Millicent's stunning physical appearance was as much an attraction as it was an obstacle to both men and women. People tended not to take Millicent seriously, while placing confidence in Adel who they perceived fairly or unfairly as more grounded.

When Adel first came to live in the Barnes home, the competition between the girls was primarily one of status in the home. As John Barnes introduced Adel to the customers of Taggart's Livery and Millicent exposed her to her circle of friends and other teens Adel's age at school, the competition shifted to relationships.

Adel's gregarious personality and unassuming ways endeared her to Fulton's residents almost immediately. Adel made friends with no effort, and Millicent, despite her physical assets and assertiveness, was challenged to make enduring relationships. It was the attention of young men, however, which turned an otherwise tentative truce between the girls into heart destroying combat. Every boy in whom Adel took an interest Millicent would do anything - go to any lengths - to destroy that relationship. There was only one young man with whom there was no competition, Buddy Hines. Hines only loved one person, himself.

To Hines, Millicent was the most-beautiful girl in the county: a possession, a status symbol. She sought his company for similar reasons. He was good looking, came from a wealthy family, an anomaly in 1938. Millicent tolerated Buddy's arrogance and abrasiveness in exchange for the social status the daughter of a mechanic did not have. As deep as her need for social acceptance, her love of Buddy Hines was parchment thin.

Adel Barnes hugged herself and tried to stifle a shiver. Dressed in denim bib-overalls, a green flannel shirt and men's small work boots, Adel tightened the long sleeved shirt around her. A cold north wind white-capped the choppy waters on the St. Johns River and rattled the fronds on the cabbage palms that dotted the field between the back of Taggart's Livery and the river. John Barnes had constructed a thickly made picnic bench from rough-sawn cypress. The wood was concrete gray from weather and petrified from the sun.

As she faced the river, the wind blew her short hair into her face. She turned her head until her face squared with the wind. The sky was still gray and overcast as a cold front labored south.

Boats crabbed into the wind to remain inside the channel.

In spite of the piercing cold, the aggressive wind and gloomy skies, this was her favorite time of year and favorite place to be. Between chores, school and pumping gas for her father, she enjoyed the solitude of the bench and the river. She read there, studied schoolwork, prayed and worked out all of her problems there by the water's edge. It was not her exclusive place, however. Her father ate his lunch at the bench as well, and spent many an hour perched on the tabletop with his feet on the seats working out the grief of losing his wife. That is where she and her adopted father talked into the twilight hours, when the lights of Orange Park winked across the river.

It was Saturday, and lunchtime. Adel had made lunch for her father and Awesome and snuck down to the river in the hopes of catching a few moments of solitude. She sat on the bench, faced the water and adjusted to the cold air. She opened the wrapper to her sandwich. She asked God to bless her food and no sooner had she taken the first bite of her sandwich she heard a voice behind her.

"Am I interrupting anything?" Awesome said inching his way into Adel's periphery. "Mr. John said to come out to the bench that he would be here in a minute after he finished with a customer."

Saturday mornings were particularly busy with people coming to pick up repaired vehicles. Consequently, it was payday, too.

"Not at all; just starting to eat. Sit," she said, and gestured to the opposite side of the table so that Awesome would have his back to the water. "How is the first day going?"

Awesome unfolded his napkin and exposed a sandwich identical to Adel's. With the first bite in his mouth, he said, "Pretty slow, actually; at least for me. Every time your father begins to explain something to me he gets interrupted by a customer or the phone rings."

If the cold bothered him, he did not let on. He wore a short-sleeved khaki shirt. He sat forward in his seat, perched on the edge, hungrily attacking his food. He kept slapping the napkin down to thwart the efforts of the wind to launch it.

"Yeah, Saturdays are pretty crazy. This afternoon should be quiet though. Everyone will have picked up their cars, and he usually uses the time to clean up the shop and prepare for Monday morning," she said.

"Clean up? You could eat your lunch off the floor now. What does he clean up?" Awesome's brow furled and his blue eyes widened.

"You make that sound like a problem," she said, and took another bite from her sandwich.

"Not a problem for him. I worry about me. I try to keep myself organized, but Mr. Barnes . . . now that man . . ."

"Yeah, I know. It took getting used to when I first moved here. I'm a bit of a slob myself, but it didn't take long to take up his habits. He never scolded me or said anything about my mess. When you see how clean and neat he keeps everything, it gives you something to live up to, you know, like a goal. Now it is like second nature. You'll get used to it."

Adel had always looked upon Awesome as cocky and overconfident. She had to admit, though, that what she knew of him was limited to the few minutes they spent together when he came into the garage to refuel.

"So how do you feel about all this, Awesome? Big step, isn't it?"

Awesome, deposited the remainder of his sandwich on the napkin and looked straight at her. "You've no idea how much I respect your father. Ever since I was big enough to stand on the running board of a car, I've admired your father and the business that he built here. He has always treated me with respect when everyone else in Fulton treats me like a freak of nature." Tears welled in his eyes, then he caught himself and sucked the tears back in.

"He has a lot of respect for you, too, Awesome. He wouldn't have brought you in and offered his garage to you if he didn't. He has never done that with anyone." She looked past Awesome as a fishing boat headed south on the river porpoised past them in the rough water. A deck hand threw junk fish out of their nets off the stern of the boat and Pelicans dove into the water in their wake for a bit of lunch.

Adel surveyed the man in front of her. Even though his nose was not as broad or his lips not as full, there was no mistake about his Negro lineage. She had known Awesome since she came to live with the Barnes. His frequent visits to the garage to trade kept her in touch with him at least once or twice a week even if he only bought a cold drink they sold in the office.

"I have a lot of respect for him, too. I would love to have a place like Taggart's one of these days."

"You love to repair cars that much?"

"Repairs are the cake that the frosting sits on. It's the racing I like."

158

Awesome spoke metaphorically often. When he talked, he painted mental pictures that were easy to see.

Awesome continued, "And it isn't the racing so much as it is the challenge of getting the car to go faster. I love the mechanical piece of it, the things that make an engine tick."

Adel hoped he would not regale her with one of his long-winded technical discussions he engaged in with her father. He would get started talking about carbs, intakes, and manifolds and such as if he spoke a foreign language. When he was in this mode, Adel would say 'ah-huh,' 'right' and 'yes' to him until he wore himself out or she yawned. A yawn would stop him dead in his verbal tracks. He must have read something in her face, paused, looked back over at something he heard on the river, then turned back, and looked directly at her.

"The reason I took the job was very simple. Yeah, I can do the repair work and it will pay the bills, but your dad has one of the best machine shops around. My machining tools are worn out relics, antiques that other shops had thrown away. There's only so much I can do with junk. The fun is to improve on what others do only do it better; creating improvements, that no one else has tried. It is the technical part I love." His face was expressive, his eyes narrowed with intensity, he rubbed his hands together in front of him as though he were about to cut into a juicy steak.

"I would think the fun part would be racing, being behind the wheel; going fast." She coiled her hair behind her ears and leaned in so she could hear his deep voice against the strong wind.

"Anyone one can mash the gas pedal to the floor and keep a car going in a straight line. Few people really understand how to make the car go faster. Making the parts that create the power, that's where the fun is. Your father is right. That's where the money is, too!" He said it like "That . . . is . . . where . . . the . . . money . . . is," he bobbed his head up and down with each word.

"John seems a little old for that kind of stuff," she said, talking over the engine noise of a tug as it pushed a barge on the river. Adel called her adoptive father John, a term of familiarity that annoyed her 'sister' Millicent.

"Your father is quiet. He doesn't flaunt his knowledge or try to impress. He knows more about mechanics, more about engineering then I'll ever hope. His greatest gift is he knows how to make money. He's a very smart guy, making a decent living out in the middle of nowhere. He sees the opportunity in racing, the same as me. Not in the racing itself, but in the equipment and engine parts that can be sold to the people racing the cars." Awesome looked up over Adel's shoulder.

"What're you guys so engrossed in discussion about?" John Barnes said as Adel made room for him on the bench next to her. He unfolded his napkin with the sandwich in front of him.

Adel said, "Awesome was just talking about how great the opportunity was to make and sell auto racing parts."

John said, "Yep, he's right - absolutely right. But that business requires a lot of capital and the only way to get it is to fix a lot of cars." He winked all-knowingly at Adel.

Adel could see air seeping from Awesome's balloon of enthusiasm.

"John, Awesome knows that. He was just talking to me about the potential and why he was so excited about it."

"As well he should be. Fixing cars puts grits and biscuits on the table. The stuff he fiddles with, those contraptions he has taped and held together with baling wire hidden under the hood of his old wreck out front - that's where the future is." He looked at Awesome's down cast face. "Young man, you're truly a genius. You have talent and ability way beyond what you think. It is incredible the things you've been able to do with trash and junk. I've seen that jalopy of yours go down the beach wide-open sounding like hell had opened up and it is remarkable. And I can help some. Yeah, I've got a good machine shop, but you're trying to do things that require much more sophisticated equipment than I have. I know it takes money, more money than I have. So, unless you have a stash under a board in your house that I don't know about, we both need to hustle some business to pay for the racing. You understand that, right?"

Awesome nodded. The corners of his mouth moved from negative to neutral. He looked at Adel and smiled.

"Wondered where ya'll were," a feminine voice floated across the wind.

Adel knew it was Millicent before she came into view. She could see it in Awesome's eyes as they tracked with her movements. She came to rest at the end of the picnic bench, hip cocked to one side with a hand resting on it.

"Well, are you going to make room for me?" Millicent said to Awesome.

Caught wherever his mind had gone, Awesome jerked to attention. He slid to the side so that when Millicent sat on the bench she was directly across from her father.

Adel smelled the all too familiar light jasmine perfume that arrived before Millicent took her seat. Millicent feigned a southern accent that could disappear with a change in mood. She wore a shirt-dress, flats and a sweater buttoned at the waist. She had pulled her hair back to a clasp then her hair hung straight down to the middle of her back. She wore no discernible make-up and did not need it. Her blue eyes and dark features gave her face all the color it needed.

"Awesome Banes, I swear. What has Daddy gone and done?" Daddy came out 'Daiddy.' She folded one arm on top of the other and looked over at Awesome expecting an answer.

'Here we go' thought Adel, but her father interjected before Awesome could open his mouth to answer.

"What he has done, Millie, (Millie was spoken very firmly) is acquire the services of one of Duval County's brightest mechanical stars. We, including you, are very lucky to be a part of that decision."

Millicent cut her eyes back toward her father and said, "I hope for all our sakes that the people of

Fulton see it that way, too. Good Lord, people are talking already."

Adel was all too familiar with the gossip even as early as this morning. She finally caught Millicent's gaze and tried to warn her off this line of conversation with a slight movement of her head to the side.

Awesome started to speak and John cut him off, raising his forefinger into the air. John then looked at Millicent and pointed that same finger at her. "Millie, I don't care what people think or their idle gossip. And frankly, I don't want to hear it or know what it is." He turned to Awesome. "Young man in this house, in my home and in that garage (he pointed with this thumb over his shoulder) we're all the same. And as far as I'm concerned, if I have customers who see it differently, then I don't need or want their business." He turned and looked at each of them, Adel, Awesome and then a final look at Millicent. "Are we all clear on that?"

Adel and Awesome nodded agreement, but Millicent said, "Buddy is about to come apart at the seams. I just got off the phone with him and he yelled and screamed at me that no one in Duval County would ever do business at Taggart's again. His parents are beside themselves."

Millicent's comments hung in the air like swamp gas. Adel looked at Awesome who had dropped his gaze to his hands folded on the picnic table. The clouds on the horizon to the north were dark and swollen with rain.

Adel said, looking at Awesome, "I wouldn't pay any attention to a thing that boy thinks. He has a streak of hate running through him as wide as this river."

"I'm just saying . . ." Millicent began to elaborate until John cut her off.

"That's the problem, Millie, you've said enough. I don't want to hear any more of it." He tapped his forefinger on the tabletop. "No more."

Millicent shoved herself up from the table and stomped across the yard to the house.

"I'm sorry, Awesome. Forgive me."

"It's not your problem, Mr. John. I hear that stuff every day. It's unusual when I don't. Don't think a thing of it. My only worry is that what Buddy Hines predicts will come true: that my working here will hurt your business. I wouldn't want that."

"People will talk, Awesome. I have no control of that. I have faith in the people of this community. I know them. A few will cause a problem. I really don't want those customers. Do you understand?"

Before Awesome could respond, Adel put her arm through her father's and gave it a hug. "Awesome, let John worry about the community. You should just focus on the work, and your dreams, and everything else will take care of itself."

Awesome looked at Adel and then John Barnes. "I just hope you know what you're getting into Mr. John. As for me, I'll be fine."

17

Ruby tired of the story. I turned the recorder off and I sat with her awhile until she fell asleep.

On the drive back to Mount Dora, I considered the mammoth writing task ahead. I was in over my head. I needed to edit the book I just completed and I just didn't have the time to do it. I really didn't want to use Emily, but I didn'tt have any choice until I found someone else.

I called Lisa on my cellphone and she bluntly informed me that she had zero success in finding an editor. "Jack, it's the holidays," she said as though I shared the mountain hideaway with the Grinch and that I was his co-conspirator in destroying Christmas. "You need Em, Jack; despite the rotten circumstances you need her."

So I caved in and called Em and asked her to read the draft I had given her the day before yesterday.

Emily and I worked as a team to complete a novel. With no revisions, my first draft of a story went straight from brain to paper without any effort to clean it up. I did not begin the edit process until I had read the first draft through in one sitting and let the completed story coagulate. Then I set it aside for a few days to let the theme simmer into clarity. With the goal of honing the theme to an edge, I would begin the revision process then present Emily with a clean copy. This was the normal process. On this novel, I threw the rules out the window.

It has always been difficult for me to write for an unseen audience. As a child, I had always written my short stories for my mother. I would live for the moment when she would finish one of my stories and compare them to one she had just read in this magazine or that. When Emily began editing my work, I soon wrote for her pleasure and praise. After she read something, I had written she always began with what she liked, then her criticism.

Like me, on her first pass through the story, she read for content. Then we would discuss the story. If there were revisions she felt I should make, I would rewrite those sections first while she did the final edit. She would verify facts that I had used, make sure that character descriptions were consistent throughout and catch grammatical errors that I missed.

However, it was the discussions Emily and I had following her first read that I enjoyed the most. Yes, we celebrated with wine and a toast on the dock, but it was the discussion after her first reading that I looked forward to. These were all about the craft of making a book into a novel: taking something mundane and making it magical.

Em had printed the manuscript from the CD and brought it to the studio. "Well, how soon can you get started reading the manuscript?" I asked.

"Nearly done. I started reading it the day you gave it to me. Just a couple of chapters left." She made herself comfortable, hugging her legs lost in the final chapters of *Death in the Desert*.

I watched her as she read the final chapter. It was as though the past two years of marital difficulty had vanished. It was the old days, when we were blissfully in love, and all that mattered to us was each other and the writing. As I scanned her face, I searched for clues about how she liked what I had written; it seemed inconceivable that divorce attorneys labored away at that very moment to rip apart the only meaningful and satisfying relationship of my life.

Emily slapped the final page down on the pile, drew her reading glasses away from her face, brushed the spray of hair that she had been twirling around her finger off her forehead, and announced, "I'm done."

It was well after lunch when she had finished. "Before you say anything, let's go get something to eat. You can tell me what you think then."

"Doesn't this have to be sent to Lisa today?"

Lisa Catera was my agent. "I over-nighted the manuscript to her day before yesterday. Reynolds and Ryan is pleased with the draft, and agreed to give us another week or so to clean it up. They've already given Lisa a deadline on the last book in the series. How about some lunch?"

"I'm game." She stood and reached to the ceiling in a stretch. "Where do you want to go?"

"I thought we would eat at the Lakeside." The Lakeside Inn was across the lake in Mount Dora. "I thought I would drive you in your Miata."

Em looked out the plate glass window toward the Lake and at the convertible parked in the driveway.

After a long pause she said, "Alright."

Em loved Lake Dora. When the weather was agreeable, she insisted we watch the sunset from the deck of the boat before it took on water and sank to the bottom. We frequently enjoyed the twenty-minute boat trip to town, to eat out or shop.

As we drove down Lake Shore Drive, Lake Dora stretched out in front of us like a mirror. Emily wore my jacket like a cape as she pulled her hair back into a short ponytail to keep her hair out of her face. The air was cool but not cold, refreshing compared to the stuffy warmth of the studio. Emily tilted her head back, closed her eyes and let the sun warm her face. The wind blew her light brown hair off her face. Even though she may have reluctantly agreed to the drive, she soaked in Lake Dora now and relished it.

"Beautiful day, isn't it?"

"Mmmmm." She slid down until her head rested on the back of the seat. With her eyes still closed, the short trip to town passed in silence.

We parked in the hotel parking lot and walked the short distance to the Lakeside Inn. The inn was built in 1883, as a winter resort for the wealthy of the north. However, it had a hard time competing with destinations like Miami or even

Winter Park, so its financial viability was challenged from the day it was built. Several entrepreneurs tried to transform the inn into something noteworthy and failed. So, the cycle of financial hard times, bankruptcy and renovation were part of its heritage. There were even plans at one time to demolish the grand structure. It survived the wrecking ball, survived financial hard times and through it all, remained an enchanted icon. Like the Hollywood Beach Hotel of my youth, the Lakeside Inn would forever remain an emotional anchor tying me to this captivating town. The Veranda restaurant was crowded with vacationers and locals alike, but the views of the sun on the lake and the romantic atmosphere made it a regular venue for Em and I.

After the waiter brought her a Pina Colada and me a draft beer, we ordered our food.

"Jack, I don't know how you did it, but it's one of your best novels so far. It's a great story. I liked it the first time you told me your idea. That plane sat there all those years in the desert without discovery. Sort of tickles at your curiosity, doesn't it?"

"I wish it had been totally my idea, Em. There was an American, WWII, B-24 that crashed in the Libyan Desert in 1944. It lay in the desert undisturbed until oil explorers discovered it in 1959. It was an idea I just couldn't pass up."

"A WWII bomber carrying a German doomsday nerve gas discovered fifty-five years later in Muammar al-Gaddafi's Sahara sounds far-fetched. When you told me what the story was about, I wondered if you could make it believable. You pulled it off, though. Your story sounds so plausible. The plot was so simple it read like something out of the newspaper. I loved it."

"Thanks, Em. So what didn't you like?"

"The title. *Death in the Desert*, is depressing. What was the name you gave the airplane? Lady something?"

The Tainted Lady.

"Yeah, that's a great name. Here we have this bomber with all this nerve gas sitting in the worst possible place on earth. What about *No Place for a Lady*?"

I said, "Already thought of that. There's the Rod Steiger movie by that name. There are also several novels with that title. Since you like the name *The Tainted Lady* so much, why don't we use that as the title?"

"Good, let's use it."

I asked her, "What else?"

"Mostly research items. First, you have the bombers flying out of Suluch, Libya in 1945. I'm not sure the Army Air Force still had bases in Libya then. Didn't most of them move to Italy by 1944? What about the B-24? Can it fly from Libya to southern Germany without refueling? We need to check the range of the airplane?"

"So what if we find that they didn't fly out of Suluch in 1945? What if the bomber can't fly that far? I'm out of time. I can't rewrite the story."

"We change the dates, and we install specially made fuel tanks to the B-24. Nothing that can't be fixed easily."

"Anything else?"

"Just a lot of clean up. You haven't edited yet, have you?"

"No time. We can both work on it. We have a week."

"Even with the editing and having to make some changes, it's your best. Two months ago, you were hopelessly blocked. What happened?"

The waiter brought our food just in time. I did not want to tell her about meeting Jody Holland. She was in Key West while I visited Billie.

174

"Getting away helped. I started with one sentence. I didn't ask anymore of myself than one sentence. The best sentence I could write."

"How did you do it so quickly? It usually takes you four or five months to write a novel."

"I learned something with this story. Even though I was terribly blocked, I'd written that entire story in my head several times. For months, I'd made refinements, pumped up characters, added twists and turns to the plot, and thought about the little nuances I'd add. When I was finally able to write, it just poured out. I was barely able to type fast enough. I'm always in such a hurry to write the next story. In the future, I want my stories to ferment more, to mentally ripen before I sit down to write them."

There was a long silence. She rubbed the tip of her finger around the rim of the festive Pina Colada glass. "Are you still depressed?"

"No, I feel pretty good."

"Alright. What happened to make you feel better?"

"LuAnn," LuAnn Calder was my therapist, "she suggested I try to find out what happened to Billie."

Emily had heard the story many times. Emily became impatient. "So?"

"Do you remember me telling you about the short-story my mother entered in a fiction contest?"

"You mean the newspaper contest; the one where your first story was published?"

"It was featured in the paper the same day that news of Ernest Hemingway's suicide was reported. A few days earlier Mother and Father got into this huge fight about my mother's encouragement to write. After he reamed her out, he took me for a walk and told me that writers were a bunch of wackos. He told me then that Hemingway was in the nut ward at the Mayo Clinic. I told him he was wrong.

"My father couldn't wait to bring the newspaper home with Hemingway's story on the front page. He told me that I would end up just like him if I pursued writing as a career. Then Helen Holland killed her entire family save Jody then tried to kill herself and she was a writer. And, my mother wanted to write and she suffered with depression.

"I guess I'd forgotten how profound a summer that was. I decided that my father had destroyed my mother's life, and had almost succeeded in destroying mine. When I was in Key West, I decided that I wasn't going to let it happen to me. And I learned that I've hated my mother all these years for something she didn't do."

Emily leaned forward with her elbows on the table. Her brown eyes were wide and intent and looked through me. "That was a lot to throw at a fourteen year old. Your father actually told you that about Hemingway?"

"I know how you feel about my father."

She withdrew from the table and sat back in the chair. I let the silence between us run its natural course. She always defended my father, so I spared her any further assault on him.

She leaned toward me again. "What a hateful thing to say to a young boy."

"Well it stuck. When I was in the Keys, I suddenly realized that I had lived out his prophesy and what had happened to Hemingway, Helen Holland and my mother and happened to me. It was like all the programming in my life led me to the point of total depression, a point I realized I didn't want to be."

"Why didn't you tell me about any of this?"

"I didn't remember any of it. It wasn't until I was there in Hollywood, surrounded by my old house and the Hollywood Beach Hotel that I remembered."

"And now?"

For the first time since Emily left me, her attitude toward me had softened. I could see it in her eyes. There was warmth, concern and empathy.

"I feel better than I've felt in a long time. I'm writing and that always makes me feel good."

The waiter cleared our table. Just before the waiter delivered the check, a procession of wait-staff came from the kitchen carrying a bouquet of roses, then a cake with candles. They gathered around the table, with smiling faces and sang 'Happy Anniversary to you.' The lead waiter laid the roses in front of Emily and it was then that I noticed her reddened face, the tightness of her jaw, and a glare which signaled her displeasure.

She waited until all the waiters clapped and reveled in the happiness they created before she teed me up.

"Before you say anything, I just wanted you to know how happy you've made me. It isn't our

178

18

December 30th

David Huff's office was on the seventeenth floor of the Florida Union Bank Building in Orlando. Em had written out the address and directions and had left them next to my keyboard in my studio. He was an attorney with a large six-name law firm, and although he had risen to partner, his name was not on the marquee.

The receptionist showed me to a seat in the sparse, cold but elegant lobby and announced my arrival to Mr. Huff. An older thin woman came into the lobby, called my name and escorted me to the conference room. Emily and Huff were already huddled at one end of the glass enclosed conference room. One wall was a solid glass window that overlooked downtown and Church Street Station, a local downtown tourist attraction.

"Mr. McNamara, David Huff." The short thin man, ten years my junior, circled the mahogany table with an outstretched hand. "I'm a big fan of yours. Read all your books. We were just talking about your next project. Emily tells me you're just about ready to release another book."

I shook his hand. Emily raised an eyebrow behind Huff's back. "Yes, we're just now finishing it. It'll be a year or more before it hits the bookstores. Wheels of progress . . ."

". . . move slowly. Around here, too. Sit down." Huff ushered me like a maître d to a chair on the other side of Emily. He sat at the end of the table between us. Emily was elegant in a navy blue blazer and white blouse. Her light brown hair curved down to her shoulders and framed a soft and friendly smile.

Huff surveyed each of our faces, an attempt to read the mood before beginning. "Jack Spears called me a week or so ago and explained your situation. Divorce is never easy. While the assets that you will divide are substantial, I want both of you to know I'll make every effort to find an amicable settlement that will work for both of you.

Huff flipped over a manila folder with a few sheets of yellow legal sized paper clamped to one flap. "Jack before you came in I asked Ms. McNamara to give me an idea of her expectations from the divorce settlement. Nothing specific, just what she hoped to achieve. Ms. McNamara, please repeat to Mr. McNamara what you told me."

Em clasped her hands together on the table, looked at me, and looked out at the skyline. "What's most important to me is that Jack and I remain friends. I already have all the furnishings out of the house that I want, and I have all of my possessions. I'd like to keep my car, and I want a fair financial settlement. I want something that's fair for both of us."

"And you Mr. McNamara?"

"Jack. You can call me Jack."

"Okay, Jack. What're your expectations?"

What I wanted was Emily back and to totally avoid this meeting. "I want the same thing. We don't have any children. We don't have that much property, just the house in Mount Dora that I don't think Emily wants and a house on New Smyrna Beach, which I'm certain, she will. The rest is in the stock market, retirement accounts and savings."

"Well just to make you feel comfortable, this isn't a negotiation session. I'd prefer we conduct such a session with both of your attorneys present. Fortunately, Florida law is specific in terms of the division of property. Each of you is entitled to one-half of all the assets that you've accumulated during your marriage. Generally, you can keep assets that you had prior to the marriage, unless there has been some pre-nuptial agreement that gave away those rights. Can I assume that there's no pre-nuptial agreement?"

Huff looked at me and I shook my head.

"Good. Good. Are there any known disputes of the division of personal property?" He looked at me.

"None as far as I'm concerned. I think Emily has what she wants."

He looked at Emily.

"I'm fine."

"Good. There are no children. That simplifies things dramatically."

"The only issues that you'll need to discuss with your attorneys are any claims of alimony, if any, and whether there will be any dispute over the division of financial assets."

"You sound a little pessimistic," I say.

"The situation may get a little sticky because of the future earnings from your work, Jack. Since you're paid in advances against royalties, you receive revenue for your books well into the future. The book is an asset that the two of you acquired during your marriage, but the revenue from that asset will continue to accrue after the marriage is dissolved. Future revenue from present assets will be something that you both will want to discuss with your attorneys and we will have to work through in mediation. I also understand from Jack Spears that movie deals, and foreign publication of a book can come years after you publish the book. Another situation where an asset you both acquired when you were married continues to produce revenue long after the marriage is dissolved."

Emily searched my face for a reaction to Huff's explanation. Even though I had made a decent living from writing prior to meeting Emily, it was not until we were married that my career started to produce significant income. While I still received royalty checks from some of the novels I had written prior to meeting Emily, the revenue was inconsequential. Splitting present and future revenues with Emily for all the books I had written while I was married to her, seemed fair to me. Since this was a sizeable amount of money, I did not think that Emily would need alimony.

I looked at Emily. "Do you expect alimony?"

"No. Are we still going to be working together?"

"I'm still thinking about it, Em"

"Well we will need to work out how you'll pay me. But no, I don't want alimony."

I turned to Huff and said, "I'm okay with dividing revenue from all my existing works with her evenly, even the ones before we were married, including future revenue. Anything I write from here on is mine."

"Jack, you should be advised by an attorney on this. We aren't here to negotiate. I explained that at the outset."

"Look, David. I don't have the time right now for a protracted negotiating process when we don't need one. Why can't you draw up an agreement that divides all of our current assets?"

"It isn't that simple." Huff flipped through his notes. "What about a residence for Ms. McNamara. You have a home that you both acquired together. What about the equity?"

"She can have the house at the beach. We'll have both the house and beach-house appraised, and if the beach-house is valued less than the Mt. Dora house, I'll pay her the difference in cash."

"But Jack, you love the beach. Are you sure about this?"

"You can always rent it to me if I want to use it," I said, although I didn't foresee that happening.

"That's fine with me." Emily looked at me and nodded. "I agree with Jack, David. This isn't that complicated. Can't you draw up an agreement that we can both look at?"

Huff was nearly in a panic. "How about loans on the cars?"

"They're paid for. He has his car, and I have mine." Emily was as impatient as I was.

Huff read a checklist as though trying to find a reason to avoid the simplicity. "I know Jack Spears will be concerned about doing this so hastily."

To Huff, Emily said, "Jack Spears will be fine." To me she asked, "Okay if he begins to put together an agreement? He can always call us if he has a question."

"Fine with me."

We both looked at Huff who yielded to our need for efficiency, no doubt disappointed that the many billable hours he anticipated mediating a long and complex divorce were disappearing.

"Very well. Although, it is unwise for both of you to proceed without the benefit of counsel, I'll draw up an agreement as you've asked. But I want to make it clear that I do so with strong objection." To me Huff said, "Mr. McNamara, I'll need the name of your accountant, and your permission to obtain copies of all your investments and retirement accounts. I'll also need copies of all literary contracts that you have for all the properties you've sold where you continue to receive compensation. I'll also need the name of the appraiser you'll use to establish the value of your home and the beach property."

"Em handles all of that. She'll make sure you get all this information. Okay, Em?"

She nods.

"And who'll handle our fees?"

"It was my understanding from Spears that we split those. Is that right?"

"If that's agreeable to you all?"

"Fine with me," I said to Huff.

Huff got names, addresses and phone numbers, dotted his i's and crossed his t's, escorted us both to the lobby with assurances that he would be in touch to get copies of the agreement to us and to set up a final meeting.

Emily and I rode down the elevator in silence. In the lobby, she turned to me and said, "Thanks, Jack. You made that very easy."

"So did you. I hoped that if we had to go through this, we could do it without hurting each other. I hate to see it come to this." Then I caught myself. "I know, I know. I said I'd let it go."

"I feel badly too, Jack. I must admit."

I wanted to scream, "Then why are we doing this?"

She touched my arm. "I'm done editing the first ten chapters. I'll have to come by the house and get into the filing cabinets to get the papers Huff wants. I'm going to work at my apartment to finish the rest of the novel. It shouldn't take more than a couple of days. That's plenty of time to meet Reynolds and Ryan's deadline."

"Lisa is pressuring me for a synopsis of my next story"

"I guess we could spend some time on the synopsis when I come by tomorrow. I gotta run." She patted me on the shoulder and left me in the lobby. I thought about this meeting all morning. I was determined not to let it bring me low.

19

I called Ruby's doctor and conveyed her wish to come home with me. I explained, with Ruby's okay, I wanted to bring in hospice immediately upon our arrival. I set a time to pick her up after lunch the next day.

New Year's Eve

There is a point at which you must accept the fate of things and fall into line with reality or they break you. With every fiber in me, as much as I loved Ruby, I did not want the intrusion of her into my life at such a complex time. Yet, at the same time I understood why she would choose being with family over a hospice facility. I just would not want to live out my remaining weeks imprisoned like that. My hope was that, that fate would not befall me.

I pulled my black SUV to the curb of St. Vincent's. Ruby was in a wheel chair parked at the curb as a young nurse's aide hovered over her. She gave me a weak wave as I pulled the truck even with her. I got out, walked to the passenger side, gave her a hug and kissed her on the cheek. She was bundled up with a heavy overcoat and a hospital blanket on top of it.

"Hey, Darlin'. It is so nice to see your sweet face," she said, giving me a fierce hug.

With a sweep of my hand I said, "Your chariot to freedom awaits, dear lady."

It was then that I regretted bringing the SUV. Ruby looked up at the height of the passenger seat as though it were Mount Everest.

Ruby was not a large woman but it took great effort for the aide, with Ruby exerting all her strength, to stand up from the wheel chair. Even with the side steps and the handholds in the doorframe, it took both the aide and me to lift and push Ruby into the passenger seat.

"Whew," she said, trying to catch her breath. She patted the hand of the aide and said to her, "Sweetheart, thank you for caring for this old decrepit woman. God bless you."

"My thanks as well," I said, and patted her on the shoulder.

With a struggle, Ruby buckled her seat belt moving away from the door as I closed it. As I walked around to the driver's side, it suddenly occurred to me that I had an hour and a half drive and no clue what Ruby and I would talk about. In the past, my talks with her were awkward with uncomfortable periods of silence as we both fished around for common ground to share. On most of these occasions, Em was with me and the two of them talked unabashedly about the most inconsequential things. Now I regretted not bringing my recorder, she could have continued with her story. Ruby already had the topic of our conversation set.

"What's the latest with Emily, Darlin'?" She tried to turn in her seat to make eye contact but gave up with deep breaths of exertion.

"Still hell-bent on a divorce." I did not want to get into this with her. I pulled onto the onramp of I-95 merging into a line of tractor-trailers. "Ruby, I really don't want to talk about it. Nothing I've done so far has swayed her in any way. And when Em makes up her mind about something it would take a miracle of biblical proportions to get her to change it." As soon as the words were out of my mouth, I knew I had chosen them poorly.

"That's what I want to talk about, Sugar. God can't let this happen. Have you prayed about it? Have you turned this over to God to handle?"

"Here we go," I said to myself. To Ruby I said, "Em has made it plain that she's leaving me. There's nothing for God to do here, assuming that he's so inclined. We met with attorneys yesterday to split up our property. It's just a matter of drawing up the papers and it is all over."

Ruby was undeterred. "Lord, Jesus . . ." she began.

I looked over at her. She had her hands clasped in her lap, her eyes closed, and her head bowed.

This had only happened a few times in my relationship with Ruby where she insisted on praying aloud, in my presence. Awkward does not begin to describe the feeling I had, entrapped, where I was forced to participate whether I want to or not.

Ruby resumed her prayer. ". . . I'm praying for Emily and Jack that you would restore their marriage and heal all the damage that has been done. That you would change Emily's heart and you would draw forgiveness from her. Father, these two people belong together. You meant for them to be together and I don't believe that it is your will for them to be apart. Lord, I know that things don't look good for them now, but I pray that you would work a miracle. I pray that you would show Jack, in a very personal way, that you're in control of the situation and that he can rely on you. It is in your name that I ask it. Amen."

The silence that followed was uncomfortable. Ruby raised her head and looked straight ahead at the bright sunshine and passing pine forests along the highway. I wanted to believe in the possibility of an answer to Ruby's prayer but I struggled. First, my view of God was not as a genie in a bottle that, once rubbed, wishes come true. I just did not think God worked that way. While I believed that God existed, I did not see God as a personal God. In my mind, God was in control of the larger circumstances of life, all the things over which I had no control. For my part, He gave me talents and abilities for me to manage my life with and He expected me to do it. When I succeeded, I used those gifts properly and when I failed, as I had with Em, I had misused those talents. What I got from Em, I deserved. It was as simple as that.

Ruby finally broke the silence. "You should be on your knees every day about this, Jack, and have faith that God can change Emily's heart."

I wanted to change the subject. I did not want to get into a religious discussion with her. "I went to see Billie in Key West. She's in some serious trouble right now. If Em has told you about all this tell me."

"What kind a trouble is she in? That poor girl just can't get a decent break."

With the SUV in cruise control, I paid more attention to Ruby than I should have and ran up behind a car too quickly and braked hard. Ruby pushed her foot to the floor to brace for a crash - frightened by my driving.

"I'm sorry, Ruby; I'll pay more attention to what I'm doing."

She nodded agreement without speaking.

I continued. "Billie went to renew her lease and her landlord wouldn't renew it. Then he decided to sell the building. Billie thought if she tried to buy it under her name that the landlord would try to gouge her so she formed another corporation to buy the building and the landlord agreed to sell it. After they signed the contract, the property owner found out that Billie was behind it and refused to honor it. Then he served her with an eviction notice."

"That's horrible, Jack. Why is this guy being so difficult?"

"Because she's gay."

"What's she doing?" she said, keeping a wary eye on the truck traffic around us.

196

"Billie got an attorney and she's fighting it. I flew down and went to her first meeting and she got a female attorney, who's also gay, to take her case without charge. She believes this a classic discrimination suit."

Ruby said, "I remember when your momma was pregnant with Billie and when she left her with a sitter to go with your daddy. I tried to do the best I could to care for that young'un but your momma put me in an awful spot when she didn't come back for Billie. Your momma's ex-husband hounded me to give Billie up, but I stuck my ground. Then he went to court for custody and I had no choice but to turn Billie over to that animal. He didn't care a lick about that child. He just wanted to get even with your momma for divorcing him. As soon as he got custody, he could have cared less about her welfare.

"Over the years I was the only connection between Billie and your momma, until your momma got so sick and was on her deathbed. Billie had a difficult life, Jack. I won't judge her for the choices she made, but the path she took back in the days when a lesbian was considered deviant was a harsh road to travel and she suffered for it."

The cab of the truck got quiet as we both thought about the challenges Billie faced.

"I pray for that girl every day, Jack. God has placed her on my heart and seldom does a day go by that I don't think about her and ask God's mercy on her life."

I expected her to break out in prayer again but she fell silent instead. Our conversation turned to the mundane. The pressure of the deadline to finish my next novel distracted me. I was also concerned about how things would go with Ruby living in my home and the conflict that would exist between sequestering myself to write and caring for her needs. As we made the turn off I-95 onto I-4 I began to doubt whether I could finish my book on schedule.

20

Just outside of Sanford as we made our turn toward Mt. Dora on State Road 46 my cellphone rang. There was no number displayed on caller ID and that could only mean a call from Reynolds and Ryan, my publisher. I dreaded this call. A whack on the head from Lisa was bad enough but dealing with the big guns was never a pleasant experience.

"Nathan," I said, trying to be as positive as possible. This was Nathan Barksdale with Reynolds and Ryan.

"Hello, Jack. It's been a while. How are you feeling?" his gravelly voice oozed with condescension.

"Good and you?"

"Very well. I got the draft of *The Tainted Lady*. It needs editing obviously, but it's a great story, maybe one of your best, Jack."

"Thanks, I'd usually send you a finished product, but I guess I needed to prove to you that I'd finished it." As the words came out of my mouth they sounded pissy and I meant it.

He ignored my barb and continued, "Jack, we've been friends for a long time and I hate it that our relationship has deteriorated of late. But, you put me in a helluva spot with the board of directors. The advance we gave you was one of the biggest we've ever given for a work of fiction. I was the one who championed that deal when a lot of my subordinates and board members were lobbying against it."

"Nathan, I was sick. I assure you it was not intentional."

"I gave you the benefit of the doubt. But when you wouldn't accept my phone calls and you ignored me and left me hanging in the wind . . . well . . . that's when my patience ran out." His delivery, in his customary style, was smooth and even. He never raised his voice.

"I'm sorry, Nathan. But until I started writing again, I couldn't promise that I could write a single word or a sentence."

"That's fine and all, but the reality is that you're a year past your deadline, and as good as *The*

Tainted Lady is, I still have one very pissed off board. The hit to our profits this past year was horrendous. The board is threatening to bypass me and cut the lawyer's loose."

I never knew with Nathan what was theater and what was true. "I appreciate your patience but I feel that the board has a very short memory. My last nine novels have been blockbuster hits. You've made millions off my work. I understand the position that I put you in, but my contributions to the success of Reynolds and Ryan should be worth something."

"I may understand that, Jack, but my board doesn't. It's the old what-have-you-done-for-me-lately mentality. When you were only three months overdue, you had a little slack. When it went over a year, especially when we heard squat from you, that created a bridge too far, Jack."

"So what're you saying? Let's cut to it."

"Alright, you must have a completed draft of your next novel by midnight February 15. Our lawyers are preparing legal written notification to that effect today. You miss that deadline and not only will we come after you for reimbursement of the advance we gave you, we will sue for punitive damages equal to our losses this past year due to your failure to perform."

"Is that it," I said with as much irritation as I could muster.

"No, that isn't all, Jack. At our board meeting last night, the board passed a resolution, which bars me from handling any more of your work. The board is done. The only good thing to come out of that meeting was an agreement that the board won't seek legal action if you meet the deadline. At that point, our affiliation is over." He delivered every word as matter-of-factly as did someone talking about the weather.

I was stunned. "What?"

"I'm sorry, Jack. It is because of our long relationship that I didn't want you to hear about this in a letter."

I wanted to say, "You Bastard. How dare you do this after all the money you've made off my books." However, I held my tongue. Every book I had written under the R&R banner had been on the New York Times bestseller list for months at a time. All of them sold at least 2 million copies worldwide, two topped 4 million and three had been made into movies. At one point, my books represented sixty-percent of R&R's profits.

"Jack?"

"There are plenty of publishers who would love to handle me," I said unconvinced of my bargaining power.

"I hope so, but your bouts of depression are well known."

I did not want to argue. In fact, I wanted to be done with the call. So I bade Nathan goodbye totally forgetting that Ruby sat there listening to the whole conversation. Ruby started to speak and I cut her off. "Ruby, this isn't a good time." Then we rode the remaining distance in silence. I dreaded the call from Lisa.

Em's Miata was in the drive. When we pulled in Em came out the front door, went immediately to Ruby's side of the SUV, opened the door and threw her arms around her and they rocked back and forth in an embrace.

Em said, "Ruby I'm so glad you've come to live with us, I mean Jack. You look terrific."

To me Em, said, "You, on the other hand don't look so good. Everything okay?

"No," I said as she broke her embrace with Ruby. I got out of the truck, walked around to the passenger side and Em helped Ruby slide out of the seat to the ground. "Barksdale called me and said they loved the draft of *The Tainted Lady* so much they fired me."

Em's mouth fell open. She looked at Ruby as though for confirmation and then looked at me. "You're kidding, right?"

I shook my head, "I guess they had their fill of my sparkling personality."

She still looked at me in disbelief to the point of awkwardness.

"Let's get Ruby inside and then we can talk about it."

Without any discussion, Em assisted Ruby up the walkway to the front door and I pulled her belongings out of the back and packed them inside to a bedroom Em had prepared for her. Just as I set her bags on the bed, my cellphone rang again only this time it was Billie.

Billie said, "Jack, I hate to bother you but I have a huge problem." Before I could ask her what it was she blurted out, "The bastard cut the power to the restaurant. Do you believe it? This is New Year's Eve, one of the busiest nights of the year."

"When did this happen?"

"An hour ago."

"How do you know it was Coats? Could it be just trouble with the lines?"

"I called the power company and they told me that they had a letter from Coats' attorney that the power was to be cut off in connection with an eviction." Billie was out of breath and on the verge of sobbing over the phone.

"Did you call your attorney?"

"She's not in the office." Then she began to cry uncontrollably. Amid the sobs she said, "My walk-in frig is full and the restaurant is filled to capacity. I can get through lunch, but if I can't get the power back on, I'll have to close for dinner. Then there's the holiday. And if it isn't turned back on today I'm ruined." More crying.

I did not know how to respond. I scraped the walls of my brain and tried to conjure a solution. "I'm so sorry, Billie," which was all that I could manage.

There is silence - save Billie's crying.

I remember when I bought the boat that sits on the bottom of Lake Dora, I asked the guy who sold it to me repeatedly if there were any issues with the boat. He assured me there was none. I brought the boat home and launched it into Lake Dora and it leaked, and not just a small leak either. I called the guy back, told him about the problem and told him I wanted to return the boat and get my money back. I said to him, "You knew that boat had a leak issue didn't you?

He said to me, "You had every opportunity to test the boat before you bought it. No – I'm not returning your money."

I said, "You deceived me, doesn't that bother you?"

"Look, pal. It's just business."

The revulsion I felt then was a tenth of what I felt as I listened to Billie. "I don't know what to tell you Billie except to get your attorney on the phone. If you haven't heard from her by the end of the day let me know and I'll fly down in the morning."

"What can you do, Jack?"

"I don't know Billie, but I can be there for you. We will figure something out. Listen, I know things seem pretty dark right now, but I know that it will work out."

With that, Billie pulled strength up from within, pulled herself together. "Alright. I'll continue to try to reach her. I'll let you know what happens."

We said our goodbyes and I wondered what shoe would drop next. The darkness of depression crept in like an invading marine layer over the coastline. I fought it, struggled to see the positives in the situation but I did not have a lot to work with.

21

Em had gotten Ruby settled in her room and down for a nap. She sat at the kitchen table editing *The Tainted Lady* manuscript and I walked through the courtyard to my studio. No sooner had I put my hands over the keyboard the phone rang.

"Lisa."

"Hi Jack. Barksdale called me after he got off the phone with you and gave me the good news. What're we to do?"

"What do you mean, we? I have a book to write by February fifteenth to save both of our butts from financial ruin. You, Lisa, need to work your magic and find us another publisher."

"How are you handling this?"

"Are you asking me if I still able to write? Isn't that what you really want to know?" I snapped.

Lisa said, "I know you're angry, Jack. You don't have to take it out on me. I'm worried about you, not the writing."

"I'm sorry, Lisa. That was uncalled for. It's just that two of the most important relationships in my life have ended at a time when I'd just crawled out of a hole. It's a little much."

Hemingway crawled up onto the desk, swished his tail in my face, curled up in a ball and nudged me to show him some affection. "Well at least the cat loves me," I said to myself. To Lisa I asked, "So what're the prospects?"

"I don't know, Jack. I'll be very honest we may be in for a rough ride."

"Why? I'm selling more books than ever and I think *The Tainted Lady* will do well."

"Jack, the industry is in transition. The struggling mega bookstores see a shift coming toward electronic books. The major publishing houses have their own stable of successful writers. Finding another publisher may take some time."

"You're just a bundle of positive energy, aren't you Lisa?

She retorted, "Maybe this isn't such a good time to have this conversation.

"No, I'll behave."

"You've had a charmed life, Jack. I've handled all the ugly details of your career. This is a tough business and grows tougher every year. The majors stick to established writers with proven records of accomplishment. They take few risks anymore. If you're a new writer and you have a Pulitzer class novel, forget it. The chances are slim it will ever see the printed page unless you publish it yourself. And," she hesitated, "your bouts with depression have been New York's worst kept secret."

"Yes, and I'm writing again," I felt like I needed to defend myself.

"I know that and you know that, but to a publisher there's always a risk you'll relapse and they could be left holding the bag like RR. I don't like it any more than you but that's the reality."

"There we go with another slug of optimism."

"I'm just trying to control expectations," she said. "I may be worrying for nothing. You pay me to accurately assess the markets and figure out a way to capitalize on them. This won't be a piece-of-cake."

"There isn't a thing I can do about it. All I know is that I must finish this next novel. After that we can figure out our next move."

"I'm not waiting that long," she said. "After the holiday I'll make contact with the big three and try to gauge their level of interest. Em said that your aunt has come to stay with you."

"Yeah, and it couldn't have come at a worse time. I really don't have a choice in the matter, though. She's family."

"You're carrying a pretty heavy load, Jack. If it gets to be too much you ought to talk to Luann or call me."

"I will, Lisa. Thanks for checking up on me."

No sooner had I gotten off the phone with Lisa, Em swept into the studio.

"I had a thought last night I want to go over with you. It's about the beach-house."

"You don't want it?"

"No, it's not about the settlement. I thought of Ruby. I know she likes the beach and I thought the ocean air and walks on the beach would lift her spirits. I know if I had to deal with what she faces I'd want to be there." Her eyes were expressive and gleamed with excitement. She smiled showing sculptured teeth.

I asked, "What about hospice?"

Em said, "I'll find a hospice near New Smyrna. I'll call today."

"And what about my studio, I need a quiet place to write."

"You let me worry about that, you can work here until I get things set up and then you can use one of the bedrooms at the beach-house as a studio."

It had been nearly three years since I had stepped foot into that house. It was a simple home, right on the ocean. Nothing extravagant. I said, "We should probably get Ruby's thoughts on it."

"You know she'll love it, Jack."

I knew she was right. "When do you want to do this?"

"As soon as I can work things out. I know the beach-house will need a good cleaning. I haven't been there in a long time. I thought I'd go over to New Smyrna and check it out. I just wanted to make sure you were okay with it before we made the move."

"I think it is a marvelous idea. I don't know why I didn't think of it right from the start."

Later, when I took a break and looked in on Ruby, she said, "Em told me about the beach. That's marvelous, Darlin'. That's not an imposition on you is it?"

"Not at all. Em will take care of everything."

Em and Ruby sat on the couch. Then Em said, "I have the name of a hospital in Volusia County that operates a non-profit, faith-based hospice. I'll try to call them in a bit."

"Oh, I so love the beach," Ruby said. "What a surprise."

I left Em to make the arrangements and wrote the remainder of the afternoon.

After dinner, we all sat in the living room: Ruby in her pajamas. Em said that she had contacted hospice. "As soon as we were settled in New Smyrna I'll call them and they'll come to the house and enroll Ruby." She looked exhausted.

"You ought to turn in early, Em. This has been a long day for you."

"Nonsense this is New Year's Eve. I think I'll make some popcorn, mix some margaritas and see if Dick Clark is on TV yet."

"We will join you in a while. Ruby and I have a story to write."

Ruby asked, "You aren't too tired are you Darlin'?"

"Not a bit. Let me go get my recorder." I went into the studio and got the recorder. When I returned, I smelled the popped popcorn and heard ice grinding in the blender. I sat the recorder on Ruby's lap, hit start, and she returned me to Fulton Florida

22

Fulton

1938

Adel followed John Barnes out to the parking area in front of Taggart's Livery to the front of Awesome's 1928 Model T roadster. John walked around the rusted and stripped down vehicle, shook his head and peered inside the engine compartment. With a casual look, the many modifications impressed him.

Adel noticed that Awesome had removed all the fenders, the convertible top and the most of the parts of the hood surrounding the engine compartment. Awesome had wired the headlight buckets to the supports and the windshield was cracked in several places.

Awesome walked out of the shop and wiped his hands on a rag. "Ain't it a thing of beauty?" he said closing the distance to where Adel stood amused at her father's curiosity.

John and Awesome had spent the afternoon cleaning up, preparing for Monday's business and John had given him a cook's tour of the garage and the machine shop in the rear of the building.

"So show me what you've done to this hunk-a-metal, Awesome. You've been so closed lipped about what's under the hood."

Awesome walked to the front of the car and lifted what was left of the hood.

"Start at the top and work down," John stepped closer to the engine compartment and then sat on the front tire so that his knees nearly touched the motor.

Adel walked around to the front, rested her forearms on the radiator shell and peered into the engine compartment.

"Okay, the twin carbs are Stromberg 97s."

John stopped him already. "You have two of them, how did you find the intake manifold to do that."

"I read in popular mechanics about a guy named Edelbrock in Southern California who had built a cast-aluminum, twin-carb intake called the "Slingshot." More fuel, more power. I wrote the man and told him what I wanted to do and he sent me one. Then I found the carbs on a couple of wrecked '36 Fords. I swapped some work out to get those. Then I took the jets in the carbs and drilled them out for more fuel flow.

"The exhaust manifolds I made myself. Less resistance in the exhaust system, more power."

Adel saw the pipes curving out of the engine. They were collected and welded together into a box and then, out of the box, twin pipes ran under the car to the mufflers.

"They aren't very pretty, but they do the job. When I'm racing I open the back end of the boxes," he pointed to one of the boxes on the driver's side where John sat.

"Those are the things you can see on the outside. The radiator that Adel is leaning on is a pressurized unit out of a wrecked '38. I found someone who modified it and doubled its size to handle the extra heat the engine generates, but it is the inside of the motor, the things you can't see, that make the real difference."

John nodded his head repeatedly as if to say, "I'm following you."

Awesome continued, "The '32 engine that I bought from you, John, didn't have a lot of compression and more compression produces more power. When I wrote to Edelbrock, he directed me to several other racers who modified the cylinder heads, filled the chambers with metal and milled the heads down. They also helped me find pistons with high domes. As a result, I boosted compression from 6:1 to about 10:1."

John whistled, "Is that why you have two batteries?"

Adel stood on tipped toes to see over the front bench seat and found the two batteries clamped down to the floor.

"Yeah, when the engine gets hot, it takes both batteries to start it. Then I discovered that if I polished and widened the intake and exhaust ports I gained some power there as well." Awesome moved a couple of steps back and admired the fruits of his work. "It doesn't look like much, but it will fly, Mr. John."

Adel listened with interest but once Awesome started talking about the Stromberg thing, she was lost. All she knew is when Awesome opened the exhaust boxes up and revved that engine you could hear his car on the other side of Fulton.

"What about the drive-line Awesome, have you done anything there?"

"Yes. The stock gears were too low. Some racers in California use modified camshafts to increase the lift of the intake valves and keep them open longer, which increases fuel in the cylinders. The newer flatheads have a slightly hotter cam that increases horsepower, but not enough to make a big difference in speed."

Adel yawned and tried to feign interest.

John Barnes stood and walked around the car again. "Why did you strip the car down so much, weight?"

"That's part of it, but mostly to make it smaller in the wind. I usually take the windshield off when I'm racing and tuck my head down as low as I can, that adds about five miles-per-hour more to my top speed." Awesome turned and backed his butt up against the driver door then crossed his arms over his chest.

John asked, "How do you know that? I thought you were barrel racing?"

Adel asked, "What's a barrel race?"

Awesome said, "Two barrels are placed on the beach a mile apart. The first barrel is the start line. The cars race to the other barrel, turn around it and race back. The first barrel is also the finish line. I do that, but that's not my favorite type of racing. I want to break the top speed record for a production car, at least on the east coast, maybe a world record one day."

John Barnes asked, "What's the record?

"Last I heard it was 357 miles-per-hour at Bonneville Salt Flats in Utah, but it changes frequently. The California racers are leading the way, but they have the dry-lake-beds in the desert that are a lot harder and flatter than the sands on Jacksonville Beach. In addition, we have the ocean breezes to contend with. Usually at sunup we have the best conditions."

"So how fast are you going?"

"When I first started, I was able to go a little over 85. Then I started making changes to the motor and gradually increased my speed. I clocked my last run at 134, but I had a little tail wind. The car starts to get very unstable at 130 especially with the undulations in the sand on the beach. Heck it's unstable after 100, but very hard to control after 130. The beaches at Crescent Beach and Daytona are wider and harder, but I just can't afford to go there. Maybe if the sand were harder, I could do better."

A car Adele didn't recognize pulled up to the gas pump. She left her father and Awesome to compare notes. They talked about how to make the car more stable when she left them engrossed in conversation.

The pumps blocked the view of the driver, but the car, what she could see of it looked brand new and a beige color she had not seen before. As she walked closer to the pump, she recognized the curly blonde hair of Buddy Hines. Adel walked around the pump to the driver's side as Buddy stood between the pump and the car and craned his neck toward the house.

"Where's, Mil?" He said, not looking at her.

"Well, hello to you, Buddy. Yes, it is a beautiful day and I'm well thank you."

"Just put the gas in the car, Adel," his voice trailed off as he took off toward the house. The car was indeed new, albeit last year's model since the 1939s hit the showroom floor in early October. It was a club-coupe convertible with stitched leather seats. Fender skirts, painted the same color as the car, covered the rear wheels and a spare-tire was mounted to the rear bumper. The engine ticked as the exhaust and engine began to cool.

Adel pulled the nozzle off the holder, cranked the handle on the pump, pulled the stainless steel cap off the tank and began to pump the gas into the car. She could hear Millicent and Hines talk as they approached the car.

To Adel Buddy said, "Why is he here?" Hines pointed to Awesome and John still engaged in discussion.

"He works here now, but you knew that right?" Adel said then held her breath and anticipated a stormy reaction. Adel looked first at Hines then to Millicent.

Millicent said, "I told father what you said, Buddy. I told him that no respectable person would trade here with a Nigger on the payroll. He wouldn't listen. I tried. He said he didn't care what people thought." Millicent tied a scarf over her head, pulled open the passenger door and slid to the middle of the bench seat. "Mmmmm, this one's yummy. So much nicer than that other car your daddy gave you." Millicent slid her white-gloved hand over the leather seat as one might smooth out the cover of a bed.

Adel eased up on the nozzle as the fuel bubbled in the neck of the tank.

Buddy opened the driver's door, told Adel to
put it on his tab and then just as he got ready to
close his door he must have thought better of it,
stepped out of the car, slammed the door shut and
said, "I can't let this go."

Hines was just over six-feet-tall and solidly
built. He wore brown corduroy pants, a long sleeved
white shirt and a light brown sleeveless sweater
vest. His polished brown shoes were dusty from the
sandy-shell paving.

Adel scurried after him and left Millicent to
admire Hines' new car.

"Mr. John, may I have a word, please?" He
came to a stop, spread his feet wide apart, hands at
his side opening and closing them into fists.

John Barnes had his back to Buddy, but Adel could tell from the look on her father's face when
he spun around that he knew what this "word"
would be.

"Sure, Buddy, what's on your mind?" John
still sat on the front tire and now faced Buddy.

"Could we talk privately, please?"

Adel took a position between the two men. Awesome was still leaning up against the car door arms folded across his chest. The chill in the air from lunch lingered.

"If I'm right about what you want to talk about, I think you should say it in front of all of us." John Barnes looked down at his knee and brushed away imaginary matter with a couple of sweeps of his hand.

Buddy fumed. His face was red, his cheeks filled with air – he looked like a balloon about to burst. Buddy looked at Adel for support but didn't receive any.

"Alright, I won't say anything that half-breed Nigger hasn't already heard . . ."

John Barnes bolted up and stood nose to nose with Buddy. "That will be all of that, Mr. Hines. Not another word."

Buddy started to open his mouth to speak and Barnes stepped even closer forcing Buddy to back up another step. "Buddy, so help me, you say another word and you'll never set foot in my home or business again. Do you understand me?"

Buddy's hands were now in fists as though he were about to swing at John's face. Red-faced, breathing heavily, spit forming at the corners of his mouth, he suddenly jerked one-hundred-eighty degrees and stomped off to his car. Millicent now stood behind the car, her hand to her mouth ready to burst into tears.

To Millicent, Buddy yelled, "Get in the car . . . now!"

Millicent looked first at her father, then back to Buddy who did not bother to open the door but climbed over it to get into the driver seat. He started the car and ground it into first gear.

"Mil, get in the car now or so help me."

Millicent narrowed her eyes at her father, began to cry and bolted for the passenger door. Buddy revved the engine, popped the clutch sending dust and shell in Adel's direction with Millicent half in the car. She managed to wrangle the door closed, but hugged it as Buddy sped off in the direction of Orange Park.

Adel turned to Awesome, "I'm so sorry, Awesome. That was awful."

Before Awesome could speak John turned toward him, the cloud of dust from Buddy's exit still filled the air around them. "You okay, Awesome?"

"Yeah, it isn't like I haven't heard that crap from him and people just like him before. This all began a long time ago. We've grown up together. Somewhere along the way, his bullying and taunts turned to hate. My skin isn't dark enough for him."

"You can't help that," Adel said, and stepped closer to John and Awesome.

John combed his hair with his fingers then swished away the remnants of dust still boiling in the air. "Awesome, I can't control what Buddy or anyone else thinks. I can control what happens here in my business or home. I'll not stand for that kind of blind hatred. I don't care who it is."

Awesome moved dirt around with the end of his boot and looked at his shoes in silence. John was silent, too. Adel felt for both of them in the awkwardness of the moment.

Adel said, "Awesome, would you start the car with the exhaust boxes open? I love the sound of that car." Adel walked around John, put a hand on his back and rubbed his shoulder then motioned Awesome to the door of his car with a nod of her head.

Present

Ruby's voice faltered and her eyes drooped. "That's all I can do tonight, Jackie. Why don't you spend some time with Em? This is New Year's Eve for heaven's sake. You don't want to spend this time with an old dying woman. Just help me to the bedroom. You need a break."

I helped settle Ruby. Em had already made me a drink and set it next to the recliner in the den. The ageless Dick Clark counted down the closing seconds of 1995. Em and I toasted the New Year, acknowledged the profound events that had marked it and within minutes of the ball drop Em found the master bedroom and I found the couch in my office and collapsed in instant sleep.

23

New Year's Day

I was wide-awake at three a.m. and wrote until Em got up at eight and worked her way out to my studio. I had written two chapters and started the clean-up work on what I had written.

"You look like crap," she dropped down into the guest chair.

"And you look as beautiful as ever." And she did. Her face was flawless. Her hair was backlit by the sun through my window. She smelled of orange blossoms and wore just a hint of jewelry; she was a sight that I never got tired of admiring. While she wore jeans and a long sleeved flannel shirt tucked in at the waist, she made them look elegant.

"Jack? I thought we talked about this?"

"I'm not flirting with you. Just stating the truth."

She ignored me. "I checked on Ruby on the way through the house. She's still asleep. She's so sweet, Jack." She sat down in one of the guest chairs in front of my desk.

"Things are a little crazy right now." She carried the manuscript with pink sticky-notes jutting out from numerous pages. "I'm nearly done. We need to go over a few things in the manuscript before I send it to Lisa." Em stood, and left the manuscript on top of my desk. "I'm really sorry about RR, Jack. You're a good writer. Lisa will find another publisher soon. I know it." She backed away from the desk towards the door. "Don't worry, okay? I'm headed to the house to think through what we need to take to the beach."

I picked up the phone and called Billie.

"Hey, Happy New Year. I was just ready to call," she said. "I have power this morning. Pike got in late yesterday afternoon and reached a judge. The court ordered an injunction and the power company had to turn the power back on. The judge ordered Coats not to interfere with my business until Pike files the suit and the judge determines if the suit has merit."

"You have to be relieved, Billie"

"I am, Jack. I'm very relieved. Pike said if the judge allows the suit to go forward, I'd be able to continue to operate the restaurant without interference from Coats until the suit is settled. She also said that his actions so far have created pain and suffering issues that entitle me to punitive damages."

"I like the way that sounds. I can still come down if you need me."

"I'm good Jack. Alex will be home late tonight and she doesn't have another trip for nearly two weeks. So, I'm okay. Really."

"You were worried about your freezers being off. Any damage?"

"When I told Pike about the power cut, she rallied the troops at the business guild and within an hour I had a generator parked in back of the restaurant. We handled the dinner crowd last night and the walk-in frig was fine until the electric company restored service. I was so impressed. Last night, despite all the drama, patrons slammed the restaurant and bar. It was the best New Year's we've ever had."

"Billie, I can't tell you how pleased I am."

"Jack, I've gotta run. Take care."

I wrote for a couple of hours then drifted into the house to check on Ruby. Ruby and Em were in the living room. I stood next to Ruby. She said, "You have such a beautiful home, Jackie. Em has told me the history of the house. And your studio - I'm anxious to see where you write."

Em said, "Why don't you give Ruby a tour." Ruby placed both her hands in mine. I pulled her up off the couch to a standing position, found her cane and handed it to her. At barely five feet tall, her head came to my shoulders. We inched through the house and out to the studio.

As we walked through the threshold I said, "You'll have to forgive the mess, but I haven't had time to clean up in a while."

Ruby scanned the studio, "You sleep here, too?" She looked at the unmade couch/convertible bed.

"This past six weeks since Em left me, I lived out here. I hardly ever went into the house."

"This gorgeous home and you live in your office? I suwanee, Jackie, that's no way to live. Help me into that chair." She aimed herself at one of the guest chairs in front of my desk. "We need to talk." When she positioned her backside in front of the chair, she half sat and half fell back into the seat and leaned her cane up against my desk.

"Ruby, I don't want to get into a discussion about Em." I circled behind the desk and sat down and Hemingway had already jumped up on the desk to investigate the visitor who invaded his domain.

She adjusted herself in the chair and said, "This is much larger than Em, it's about your life and what you do with it."

"Ruby, this isn't a good time for this."

"It will never be a good time. It is always the right time to talk about God and how he can help you. I've never seen a person more in need of God's help than you."

"Can't you talk to Em about this? I've got to finish this novel." I wanted to say that I had had enough distractions already, but I stopped short - I knew that it would hurt her feelings.

"This has nothing to do with Emily. It has everything to do with you." She picked Hemingway up off the desk and within seconds, he purred and nestled into her lap.

I started to speak and she cut me off.

232

"We ARE going to have this conversation, do you understand?" She sounded like my mother when I was a kid and had done something wrong. "I want to understand your relationship with God."

"What're you talking about?"

"Do you believe in God?"

"You mean do I believe that God exists?"

"Alright, Darlin' let's begin there. Do you believe God exists?"

"My parents raised me in the Catholic Church. I was an altar boy when I was a kid. I went to Catholic schools until I graduated from high school."

"You're sharing with me things that you've done, not what you believe. It would be like me asking if you loved Emily and you answered by telling me all the things you do for her. Now let me ask again. Do you believe that God exists?"

"I guess," I felt uncomfortable as Ruby tried to pry me open like a can of tuna.

"Is that how you would respond if I asked if you believed in Emily?"

"Of course not. Where are you going with this?"

"Every religion in the world bases their beliefs on some form of behavioral system - on what you do. Christianity is the only religion based solely on a relationship between you and God. This relationship isn't built on what you do for God, but what He has already done for you."

Her statement brought to mind a survey that I had seen in a national newspaper where a high percentage of people believed that God existed but they saw Him as some distant figure, elusive and unapproachable.

She continued, "How do you know God exists?"

"I don't know, Ruby. I guess I see God in nature and I don't think nature came into being by random chance. But, I don't buy that the world was created in seven days, either. I think it was a nice story, but I just don't believe it."

"Alright, then you see God in nature," she said.

I never thought about it in the way Ruby asked, but I had no trouble answering in the affirmative. "I guess so."

234

"Do you see God in me?"

I knew what her next question would be. 'Did I see God in myself?' I guess I believed that God existed and He controlled all the things I did not. In the past, when life or death circumstances or things had confronted me were beyond my control, I prayed as a last resort. I did not think, however, that God was interested in the minutia of my life. "I know where you're going with this so let me antici-pate the question and answer it. I think God is out there or up there somewhere and he may have been involved in my life in some remote way, but no, I don't see God in me."

"Then this is where we will begin. If I told you that He's in you, what would it take for you to believe what I'm saying?"

I began to get irritated and felt a little badg-ered. "I don't know. What difference does all this make?"

"You're about to lose the most precious thing in your life - Emily. There's only one person who can save your marriage and that's God himself. You have that power within your grasp all you have to do is reach out and take possession of it. You just have to have faith. But you can only access that power through a relationship with Him." She laid the cat back on the desk and said, "Now help this old woman out of this chair."

I walked around the desk, retrieved her cane, grabbed her hands and pulled her to a standing position. She looked up into my eyes. "God wanted me to come here, to be with you. He wants you in His life. I won't rest until I see that happen."

With that, she turned away from me and said over her shoulder, "You should try to get some sleep, Jackie. I can make it back to the house myself." I would not have it, and helped her back to the living room where Em had just gotten off the phone.

Ruby collapsed into a chair, and I sat on the couch with Em.

"Well I talked to Florida Hospital Hospice and they'll call Ruby's doctor in Jacksonville for her records. They said Ruby would have to sign a consent form for treatment but that they could get her to sign it when they make their initial visit. I gave them the address of the beach-house and I'm to call them when we're ready to receive them."

"Are you okay about this?"

"Yes. The doctor at St. Vincent's explained hospice care, especially for someone who wanted to

236

remain at home. And I don't want to be in pain, and he assured me that they wouldn't let that happen."

It was Em who had the courage to ask the question "You okay with this, Ruby?"

"You mean about hospice, or about dying?"

"Dying. I don't want to pry if it is too personal of a question."

Em had the capacity to dig down into people's emotions and get them to open up. She is the only person I have ever known who I could talk to about anything without reservation.

"Nonsense. Darlin' you ask me anything you want. Dying?" She looked straight at me for some reason. "I'm ready! If that's what the Lord wants from me, I trust Him. He has blessed me with a wonderful life. I couldn't have asked for more. I have Him in me, but in Heaven I'll be able to see him."

"So you're not afraid?"

"I didn't say that. I said I'm ready to go. What scares me is the pain and how the end will go. Selfishly I don't want to suffer. But Jesus suffered when He died, but He was God. I'm just little old me. It just means I'll have to hold on to Him more tightly. He's my strength."

"The doctors say that they can keep you out of pain, right?"

"That's what they say, but I've lost a lot of my friends to cancer and it can be a mean and nasty enemy. I pray every morning that I'll be able to handle it and not be a disappointment to Him."

Without thinking about the statement, I said almost instinctively, "There are few things I know for sure, but one of them is that you could never disappoint Him. It is evident that you have a close relationship with God."

"Jackie, that's my hope and prayer. I pray hard that God would work a miracle." She looked directly at Em and then me. "That he would heal your marriage and put your two back together."

There was dead silence in the room.

After the awkwardness faded, I excused myself, went back to the studio and fell into bed. As I drifted off to sleep, I argued with myself over her assurance that God lived in me. I certainly could not claim any evidence whatsoever that would demonstrate that belief.

24

New Smyrna Beach

January 3rd

I have always loved New Smyrna Beach. It is a quaint little town and city leaders, over the years, have resisted commercialization to maintain its seaside charm.

New Smyrna Beach is a coastal town south of Daytona Beach. The Intracoastal Waterway, that parallels the ocean, dissects community. The mainland is west of the waterway and beachside is a long narrow strip of land between Ponce Inlet and Canaveral National Seashore east of the waterway. While Daytona Beach is heavily commercialized, New Smyrna is mostly residential. High-rise condominiums have marred Daytona's beach. By contrast, New Smyrna's city leaders limited condominiums to eight stories.

Two causeways link beachside with the mainland, the north causeway and - as luck would have it – there is a south causeway. The beach itself was divided in half. The north beach is open to vehicular traffic, and the south is not.

There are cycles of life in New Smyrna that are dependent on external forces. Many of the homes in New Smyrna, especially beachside, are owned by three distinctly different groups: locals who live here full-time, northerners who migrate here during the winter months to escape the cold and folks like Em and I from middle Central Florida who used the condos and homes as weekend get-a-ways. The population doubles or even triples from January through the end of April. Then the population swells again from June through August when Central Floridians flock to the coast and clog the island with cars. During the summer holidays, Memorial Day, Fourth of July and Labor Day, the island strains, many times unsuccessfully, to accommodate all the visitors. And while there is no place to escape the horrid traffic and crowds during these holidays, homes along the south beach, where vehicles are prohibited from driving on the sand, are protected from beach congestion. Winter crowds are mainly retirees and in the summer, the younger crowd takes possession. During the lulls, in late spring and early to mid-fall, when the weather is idyllic, the locals get a break.

The beach itself is one of the most beautiful in Florida, perhaps in the top five on the eastern U.S. coast.

Our home was on the south beach. While the house was a ramshackle, it was right on the ocean. A one-story, concrete-block structure built in the 1950s, it sat up above the dune that separated it from the beach. Except for the living room that faced the ocean, all the rooms were small. The only redeeming characteristic of the house was a wide, covered porch that extended all the way across the front of the house.

It was six-forty-five a.m. and just barely enough light to see. January can bring with it periods of extreme cold. It is common for these snaps of winter weather to bring morning temperatures to near freezing. North winds that swoop down across the ocean then across the porch can make you wonder if this is really Florida and not a beach community in New Jersey.

On this particular morning, the low was about 45 degrees: cold but not uncomfortable. I walked over the dune down to the beach and headed north. I liked to walk until the sun broke the surface, to watch the fiery display and then to turn around and walk back to the house.

In the summer months, when I made these pre-dawn treks, I found mammoth sea turtle tracks when the shelled-creatures came ashore. They dug a pit in the sand, laid their eggs, covered the nest then paddled back into the ocean - all in the same night. The turtle tracks are a combination of depressions in the sand made by four flippers as the turtle pulled its body along the sand and the center a smooth path where the turtle slid its belly across the surface. The tracks in and out formed a U from the ocean to the pit and return.

Before the sun emerged, predawn foot traffic on the beach was non-existent which was why I loved to walk at this time in the morning. I thought about what I would write that day and formulated changes I wanted to make to my pre-planned plot. Although it had only been three years since I was here, I had forgotten how much I enjoyed it.

That morning, I mulled the conversation I had had with Ruby in my studio in Mount Dora about God. I suspected the topic would continue to come up and I needed to prepare for her probing questions. 'Did I believe God exists and do I believe He's in me?' I had not considered questions like that since I was in high school. In addition, the other question she asked regarding whether I have a relationship with God. That one I could easily answer, no. I was smart enough to figure out that you cannot have a relationship with someone you do not know

and you have not even considered in years. Did I
believe He exists? At some level I did and then the
evening that Em left me and my failed attempt at
suicide flooded into my mind, when I had doubted
my own sanity, when I had lost all hope and when I
cried out to God to help me. I had to admit I believed in God. At the moment of my most broken
state, I reached out to something larger than myself
for an emotional foothold and in that instant, I decided that I wanted to live. Did I pray to God? No,
at least my prayer was not audible. It all happened
deep inside me. I was not crying out to the sky
above me, I desperately called out to something
deep in my soul. Something so deep I had never experienced before. It was only then, as I watched the
sun prepare to breach the horizon that I acknowledged to myself that it had happened.

There was an old expression that "there are
no atheists in a fox hole." Until then I had only seen
it as a clever quip. However, I knew it to be true.
Was it a product of my Catholic upbringing, the result of the nuns of my childhood indoctrinating me
in catechism? Had they so successfully brainwashed
me as a child, had they so indelibly written their
code on the memory cells of my brain that in my
moment of despair I defaulted to that code? As I
walked along the water's edge - waited for the sun
to break the surface of the water - I admitted to myself that that was not the case. I reached out to God
not from my mind but from something much deep-

er, a place where I had not been touched since I was a child. As I reached down to pick up a small Conch-shell rolling in the surf I had to admit that from that point of absolute despair when I reached out to God, it was a turning point, a move back toward life. It was at that point that, not only did I want to live, I received the "want to" to climb out of the pit. At that point, I would have done anything to make that happen.

I stopped on the sand inches from where the small surf lapped at my feet and I marveled at the sunrise. Deep purples at the horizon gave way to pink, they fought with the reds and yellows as the sun inched into view. The clouds between the horizon and me were on fire and the sun trickled out on the ocean to produce a brilliant yellow path.

Ruby and Em were up by the time I returned to the house. They both sat on the porch with coffee at the ready both still in their pajamas braving the cool temperatures. Em had parted her hair on the left side and it hung in waves to her shoulders. Her make-up was freshly applied and pastel greens of her long-sleeved flannel top made her richly tanned face even more attractive.

Ruby had on a white terry-cloth robe, pink slippers and hugged herself to stay warm. Her red hair looked unkempt, but she smiled at me as I approached.

Ruby said, "Jackie, this is such a beautiful place and what a beautiful sunrise. Thank you so much for allowing me to come here." Ruby drew out her words like my mother, a trademark of her southern upbringing. I was often amused by the subtleties of her speech, like the way she said 'time.' She pronounced it 'tom.' "This is one of my favorite places and has been since I was a child. God's presence is so apparent here at the beach."

"Are you warm enough, Ruby? I can go in and bring you a blanket. You look like you're shivering."

"I'm fine, Darlin. You don't need to worry about your Aunt Ruby. Get a chair and come sit with us."

I walked in the house, got a blanket, a cup of coffee, came back through the door and slid a chair from the other end of the porch to a spot opposite Em and Ruby. I handed the blanket to Em and sat down in front of them. I knew she was cold, but I also knew that she was too stubborn to admit it. She accepted the blanket, leaned forward and wrapped it around her shoulders; the warmness of the look I received from her was all the thanks I needed.

Em was nearly as tall as I was, with a slender but not thin figure. I always felt that Em could have been a model if she had chosen to do so; she was that beautiful. I had always wondered what she saw in me. Even as attractive as she was, she was warm, friendly and approachable – one of the most loving people I have ever known.

"So are you ready for the hospice people, Ruby? They'll be here at nine o'clock." Her voice was husky but smooth and sexy, at least to me.

"Yes that will be fine. Just need to shower and run a rake through this mess of hair and I'll be ready. Emily says that you guys haven't been here in a long time." She took a sip from her coffee then reached over across a small table and patted Em on the hand. Her blue eyes sparkled.

I was amazed at how she could handle a hot cup of coffee with her hands so knurled but she managed beautifully. "I haven't been here in over three years." To Em I asked, "You?

"I was here the last time you were."

To both of us Ruby asked still lightly rubbing Em's hand, "What happened to you ya'll? You were so much in love. I've never seen two people that were so compatible. What went wrong?" She looked at me. Then she made eye contact with Em.

246

Em pulled her hand away from Ruby and turned slightly away from her. She narrowed her eyes, looked directly at me sans her earlier smile.

I did not want to get into this, but I also knew that my aunt would not leave it be. Better to deal with it and get it behind us. "Ruby, I'm to blame. I did all this, not Em. I've put Em through hell these last two years. It was enough to extinguish anyone's love."

"And what about now, you're getting better right? Is that what you said?"

"Yes, but in Em's defense . . ."

Em turned back toward Ruby, moved forward so that she sat on the edge of the chair and clasped her hands in front of her. "I don't need you to defend me, Jack. I'm perfectly capable of speaking for myself." To Ruby she said, "Ruby you have no idea of the darkness we've lived in for the past two years. His depression was so bad most days, Jack never got out of bed. Even with medication, he was a zombie. And when he was in that state, he was mean, confrontational and drove me out of his life. I know he was fighting for his life, but so was I. He may have been sick, but he brought me to the brink of my own mental health. Things were so bad, Ruby, that I realized that he was making me sick

247

and if I continued to stay with him it would do me in.

"And the hurt he inflicted. He stomped the love out of me. He ground it into something so small it finally just blew away. I'll not live my life that way. I just won't do it." Then she reached over, placed her right hand on Ruby's shoulder and said, "I know you mean well, Ruby. I still care for, Jack. But, I'll not be put in that position again; it is too risky. It is just not going to happen!" Her eyes narrowed.

I added, "Ruby, I understand where Em is. Yes, I've made progress. Yes, I believe that I've turned a corner permanently. However, I can't assure her that my depression won't return. I love her. I want her back in my life again, but I don't want to hurt her again either."

Ruby just bowed her head and started to pray as she did in the car coming home from the hospital. Em looked at Ruby then me and shook her head.

"Father I've never wanted anything as much as I'd like to see you reunite Emily and Jackie. You have the power to restore their marriage if you will it. They're such wonderful people and I pray that you would find it in your heart to restore the love

Bill Cronin

that so tightly held them together. I ask it in Jesus' name, Amen."

She inched to the edge of her chair, reached out and grabbed my hand then Em's. "I know you both think that this is over. Em, right now you're still recovering from your wounds. But I know with everything within me that the two of you were meant to be together."

I was speechless. Em answered her unbridled optimism.

"Ruby, I appreciate what you're trying to do, but this will be the last time we talk about this. I want to be with you and share this time with you, but if this conversation continues, I'll not be able to stay here. Do you understand? I love you very much, but I won't discuss this again. Do I have your word that you will not bring this up?"

Ruby suddenly looked all of 85 years old, and sad beyond description. "Yes, you have my word. I won't bring it up again. But I'll continue to pray for the both of you. And pray hard. I'm sorry if I made you mad, Emily. I wouldn't hurt you for anything in the world." Then her face crunched up, she put her hands over her face and began to cry.

Em looked at me, rolled her eyes and said to Ruby, "Sweetheart, I'm not upset with you." She slipped out of the chair on to her knees and knee walked to Ruby, put her arms around her neck and consoled her. "It is just that this topic is very painful for me. I'm barely over it, barely holding it together. You must understand." She rubbed her shoulders and slowly her crying abated.

Ruby pulled some tissue out of the pocket of the robe and dabbed her eyes then said, "I just love you ya'll so much."

We gave her assurance of our love for her then we all migrated into the house where it was warmer. Ruby, still sniffling from her cry, wandered into the bedroom to prepare for her shower.

No sooner had Ruby vacated the room, Em lit into me, "You put her up to this didn't you," she fumed and paced back and forth.

"Em, I swear. She started on me when I picked her up from the hospital. I told her I did not want to discuss the matter with her but she was insistent. I didn't put her up to this."

Her shoulders eased out of their braced position, and she stopped pacing and looked at me nearly in tears. "I want to help, Jack. I don't want to leave you in a lurch when things are so stressful. I warn you, though, that we can't have another discussion like this again. Are we on the same page?"

"Yes, Em. I'm sorry this came up. I'll talk to Ruby and make sure she understands how sensitive this is."

Ruby's efforts were driving Em further away. I knew she meant well, but hope of ever getting Em back faded.

25

At promptly nine o'clock, the three people from hospice showed up with either bags or brief-cases.

Paula Smith, a portly woman in her mid-fifties, with short closely cut, black hair and black rimmed glasses introduced herself and in turn, introduced a very tall thin man, Jerry Drinkwater as the chaplain and Pamela Davis, an attractive woman in her mid-thirties as the registered nurse who would be in charge of Ruby's care.

Em, ever the host, showed everyone to seats in the living room with the hospice staff facing the ocean. Em and I flanked Ruby opposite them.

Paula Smith addressed Ruby. "Ms. Ruby, we received your files from your doctor in the Palliative Care Unit at St. Vincent's. Are you familiar with hospice services?

Ruby cleared her throat and replied, "Somewhat, but I'd like you to go over it with me."

"Certainly. May I call you, Ruby?

Ruby nodded. "Please, I'd prefer that."

"Good. First, before I start, I just want to ask you a couple of questions. Have you and your doctors agreed not to pursue a line of curative care?"

"Excuse, me. Curative care?

"Sorry, let me explain. The medical profession, at least the majority of them, focus on preventing disease and curing you once you contract it. That's curative care. There comes a point, like with some forms of cancer, when doctor's feel a person can't be cured, or the patient has decided, for quality of life reasons, not to pursue curative treatment. Hospice care isn't about curative treatment, in fact, we generally don't accept a patient into hospice care if they're pursuing curative treatment somewhere else. So, have you and your doctors elected to discontinue treatment for your cancer? I have a form here from the doctor to that effect; I just want to make sure that you're in agreement."

Ruby got right to it. "You mean do I know I'm dying? Yes, I know that. The doctor at St. Vincent's said that while they could begin me on a course of chemo, they felt like it would only marginally extend my life and accomplish no more than making me miserable."

"Alright, so you understand that our sole purpose is to make you as comfortable as we can."

"Yes, I understand that." Ruby reached out and clasped Em's and my hand.

"Good. The reason this is important is that we want to begin our relationship with you with honesty. Honesty about your medical condition. Honesty about the process that you'll go through. Honesty about the impact of the disease as we go through the next weeks." Paula leaned forward resting her elbows on her knees. "Do you have any questions about this before we explain our care plan for you?"

"As long as we're all honest here," Ruby squeezed my hand, "how long do I have to live? The doctor at St. Vincent's talked about couple weeks."

Paula coughed, "That's hard to say. I'm not really qualified to answer your question. Let me talk about each of our roles and then I'll ask Pam to address it.

254

"I'm your case worker. I have overall responsibility for your care, but generally, I coordinate with Medicare, Medicaid and any insurance companies that may be involved.

"We're a faith-based organization of the Seventh-Day Adventists as is the hospital system we're affiliated with. We've learned from your records and personal information that you're a nondenominational Christian and are very active in your church. We try to coordinate with the patient's local church to meet their spiritual needs, but since your church is so far away, we asked a local nondenominational church to supply a chaplain. This is why Jerry is here. He'll talk to you privately after we finish with orientation, and answer any final questions you may have."

Jerry had a deeply tanned face from his eyebrows down. His baldhead was as white as a snowbird. What caught my attention was the warmness that projected from his thin face, his light gray-blue eyes and sun-bleached, light brown, neatly trimmed eyebrows. He cleared his throat. "Ruby, I'm so pleased to be here and to be of any service I can. Sometimes people struggle with the dying process and need God to help them get through it. We will talk after a while but I just wanted you to know that I'm honored to be involved in your care."

"Pam is the nurse assigned to your case and before she explains what's next, I'll let her try to answer your question, Ruby."

Pam had thick, natural, light-blonde hair and iceberg blue eyes. She had piled her hair on top of her head into a twist. Pam said, "We get asked this a lot and it is a legitimate concern. Unfortunately, it is a very difficult question to answer. There's one thing I've learned in the twelve years I've been working with hospice: God is the only one who knows the answer to that question. The patient has a lot to do with that. I worked with a man several years ago who wanted to make it for his son's birthday. He lived longer than any of us projected. He passed away within hours of the birthday celebration. Others grow weary of the extended period of poor health and progress toward death quickly.

"So while I can't offer specifics, I can share with you some generalities. I've looked over your file. Given how much your cancer has spread, a couple of weeks sounds like a reasonable prognosis. But I want to be honest here." She leaned forward and shifted on the sofa. "Your cancer is extremely aggressive."

Although I did not look at Ruby, her voice sounded as though she were on the verge of tears. She said, "God spoke to me in the hospital and said that I didn't have long. He impressed upon me that

I'd not last more than a week or two. I'm ready for that if He wills it."

Jerry broke in, "Ruby, I can count on my hand the number of patients who have the kind of faith that you just expressed here. It is clear to me that God is in you - every ounce of you testifies to the truth of it."

To Jerry, Ruby said, "The bible says that when I'm weak, He is strong in me. I know He's here," she pointed to her heart, "and I know that He will lead me through this."

"Amen," Jerry said, his face beamed.

To Pam, Ruby said, "So are a couple of weeks a pessimistic view?"

Still leaned forward, still intently engaged, Pam said, "I just don't know, Ruby. I know that the desire to live is a powerful force. I can't speak to what God told you, but I'd not rule out what He said either. At times, I'm astounded at the miracles and supernatural events that leave me no doubt of God's involvement. Who am I to contradict what God has shared with you? Does that answer your question?"

"Yes, child. And I appreciate your candor more than you know."

Pam continued, "I'll call on you twice a week to check on your progress. If I need to come more often, I can. Are Tuesdays and Fridays good with everyone?"

Everyone including Rudy nodded affirmatively.

"Good. A nurse's aide will be by a couple of times a week to check on supplies, medications and to take care of any needs you might have. As time passes, you'll need her help with baths, help making your bed and other comfort needs.

"Our job," Pam continued, "is to make you as comfortable as possible."

"I'm afraid of two things," Ruby let go of my hand. "The unknown and the pain."

"On the pain, I can assure you we take that very seriously. There's a balance in medication for pain. The more we medicate the more out-of-it you'll be. As the cancer spreads, the level of medication may be such you may sleep most of the time. Some patients would rather be awake and try to handle some of the pain on their own. I assure you that we will take our lead from you. You seem to be a person who speaks their mind, so I know it won't be a problem. As for the unknown, I'll be honest I can't help with that. Generally, the progression goes like this. First, you're still able to get around, to ride in a car. Then you won't feel like riding, but you still can move around outside, then only inside, then only in your room, then only in your bed. Your world will progressively get smaller. I can't say when those stages will come or how you'll handle each one. We just take it a day, and at times a moment, at a time."

Ruby started to sing, "'One day at a time, sweet Jesus, one day at a time.' I just love that song. And, yes, of course that's true, just as in living, God only gives us a day at a time. We take things as they come." She paused, thought for a moment and said, "Young lady . . . Pam . . . you and I are going to do fine together."

Paula continued. "We also understand that caregivers need support and help, too. We have volunteers who can stay with Ruby while you run errands, or go on a date, or whatever. We know that caregiving can be a twenty-four hour seven day a week job. If needed, we can bring Ruby to the Hospital for a few days to give you both a break. That's, if it is needed. Are there any questions?" She looked at each of us. She looked at Pam and Jerry. "You guys have anything you want to ask Ruby?" Following a reasonable period of silence she said, "Well, I think I'm done here. Pam will stay and give you an initial exam, and Jerry would like to spend a few minutes with you."

Jerry raised a finger as though testing wind direction, "I think I can accomplish what I want by praying for all of us. Would you please bow your heads?" As Jerry prayed for Ruby's comfort and the closeness of God during what was ahead, my mind backtracked to my thoughts early this morning. "Do I really believe this stuff?"

Jerry finished his prayer, promised Ruby that he would come see her every week and that she would be continuously in his prayers. He and Paula bid everyone good-bye and Pam remained, escorted Ruby into her bedroom for a physical exam and to take her vital signs.

Em and I remained in the living room. She looked at me and said, "What've we gotten ourselves into, Jack?"

Em found a small table and chair and placed it by the window in the bedroom that looked out over the porch and dune to the ocean. I had to stand to see it but it was a view just the same. I started writing at ten-thirty a.m. after Pam left and emerged from sequestration just before Em called us all together for dinner. Em had placed dinner trays out on the porch in a triangle so that we all faced each other, and although the air was cool it was still comfortable by January standards. The roar of the surf and smell of the salt air were invigorating.

After we all sat down, I asked Ruby, "So what're your thoughts about the hospice people?" I dug into the steak that Em had grilled.

"I liked all of them, but I really liked Pam. She's as beautiful on the inside as she is out. She's so patient and gracious; an answer to my prayers. I've prayed that I'd feel comfortable with the people who cared for me. And, I really do. It is such a relief." She swirled her salad in the bowl with her fork while she talked."

Em asked her, "What makes you so sure that God told you that you only have a week or two to live?"

"He speaks to me all the time. I just know his voice. It's not like a voice from heaven or anything like that, but an internal voice. He plainly told me when I found out from the docs how much the cancer had spread, that I only had a couple of weeks left to live and that I shouldn't leave any unfinished business. He also told me . . . never mind, I promised you I wouldn't talk about that."

Em said, "Thank you, Ruby. I appreciate your respecting my wishes on the matter."

Ruby took a bite out of a sourdough roll.

I asked her, "Does Pam's presence diminish your concerns about how this will go?"

"Very much so, I get more and more comfortable all the time." She took a small bite of her steak and, still chewing, asked me, "Can we work on the story after dinner? Before anything happens to me, I want to finish telling it."

"It's that important to you?"

"More than you know. Yes, it is important."

Em and I cleared the dishes and put the TV trays away. I got Ruby a jacket and I put on one as well. We sat on the porch and faced each other. I placed the recorder on a small table between the two chairs, pushed the "rec" button, made sure the red record light flashed. I nodded for her to begin.

26

Jacksonville Beach

1938

The sky on the horizon was a deep purple, rays of yellow tipped with orange and pink fought for their space as the sun inched its way into view. Pelicans flew in formation, skimmed across the flat ocean, and yawed across the small swells that rolled to shore. The wind was still and cold and there was not a cloud in the sky. The only sound was swells lapping at the sand.

Adel had never been to the beach this early in the morning. Awesome had driven to a deserted part of the beach and parked facing the water.

"Okay, I'm going to put a stake in the sand here then run up the beach, he nodded to the north, put a marker down a mile from her. Then I'll go on a mile or so further, turn around and open it up. When I get to the marker, (he nodded north again)

I'll flip on my lights and you start the stopwatch then hit it again when I pass the stake here. Got it?" Awesome looked at Adel and smiled broadly.

John and Awesome, over the past two weeks, had labored every night in the shop working on the suspension of Awesome's car to make it more stable. She did not understand everything they did, but she knew enough to know that they were welding additional pieces to the frame and connecting them to the front and rear axle. She heard them discussing the pros and cons of the additional weight, but Awesome had ordered a special camshaft from one of his friends in California. It arrived yesterday. John and Awesome had worked until late to install it. When they started the engine last night, it sounded different. It did not idle as smoothly. Adel thought there was a problem, but the men looked at each other with grins ear to ear, so it must have been okay.

Awesome got out, opened the exhaust boxes, took off the windshield, laid it on the sand and got back inside the car. "Wish me luck."

Impulsively Adel kissed him on the cheek, pulled away, looked at him, patted him on the arm and said, "Good luck." She slid out of the front seat closed the door and Awesome pushed the starter button with his toe and the beast exploded to life.

Awesome backed up, turned the steering counter-clockwise, eased out the clutch and rumbled north up the beach.

Adel saw the brake lights come on, and could barely make out Awesome as he put a stake in the ground a mile down the beach. Then he drove further another mile to get the car up to full speed before he passed the stake. Before she could hear the roar, she could see the car. She hit the stopwatch when the headlights flashed on. The sound was deafening as Awesome raced toward her; dust, sand and smoke bellowed in the wake of the two headlights. The car sounded like it would explode as the headlights streaked past her. She only hoped that she had tripped the stopwatch at the right moment. As soon as Awesome passed her, he let off the gas. Fire shot from the exhaust as he gradually applied the brakes and came to a stop. Her turned around on the sand, eased back to her and cut the engine.

"Well?" He removed his goggles, looked wide-eyed at her and was still breathed heavily from the adrenaline rush.

"Twenty-four seconds." She stated firmly. She was not all together certain that she had done it properly. She read Awesome's headshake as problematic. "That's not good?"

"Adel, that's one-hundred-fifty miles-per-hour, that can't be right."

"Looked pretty fast to me."

He kept repeating 'can't be right,' with both disbelief and excitement. "We need to do this again."

"What about the modifications you made. Are they helping?"

"Some, with the unevenness of the sand, it still feels like driving down rail-road tracks. I can just barely keep it under control."

"Any way to fix it?"

"Lift the radiator cap, and put a whole new car underneath it," he smiled.

Adel playfully slapped him on his shoulder. Before she could wish him well, he had started the engine and headed north up the beach again. Adel determined to concentrate more fully on the stop-watch. She watched as Awesome turned off the lights and rumbled down the beach moving away from her. During the two months since Awesome came to work at the shop, she had grown fond of him. She looked forward to their lunches on the bench by the river. John infrequently ate with them, but Millicent had joined them on the bench nearly every day over the past three weeks. Adel was glad to see Millicent warm to Awesome and Millicent began to be a buffer between the explosive Buddy and Awesome.

Adel could barely make out the illuminated brake light. Precisely at the burning of the head-lights, she clicked the stopwatch, and mentally counted the seconds as the storm of dust and smoke shot in her direction. She clicked the stopwatch at just a shade less than twenty-four seconds.

Awesome shut the engine off, bounded out of the contraption and before he could ask, Adel yelled, "twenty-four seconds."

Awesome started to jump up and down, grabbed Adel by her waist and they both started jumping up and down; Awesome yelled with every cell in his lungs. Then he kissed her. It was not a peck on the cheek, but full on the lips. It was not just a casual graze; it was passionate. It was Adel's first and she felt it in every nerve all the way to her toes.

Without acknowledging the significance of the moment, Awesome broke from her and danced a jig, repeating, "I can't believe it. I can't believe it."

They sat on the sand, watched the ocean and hardly spoke a word. Awesome's breathing subsided, and Adel still clung to the fire inside her that the kiss had ignited. She wanted to talk about it, to hear him say something to her about what had just happened. He would occasionally look at her and smile broadly, but she could not tell whether it was the physical contact they just shared or the euphoria of the land-speed run.

Finally, when the exhaust had cooled enough to close the headers, Awesome stood up, offered her his hand and he pulled her to a standing position next to him. He hugged her, pulled away slightly and said. "Adel, this is one of the happiest days of my life."

"Mine, too," she said.

27

January 4th

I have a reputation with Em when she wakes me from a dead sleep. According to her, as she shakes me, I bolt straight up to a sitting position and yell something unintelligible. This must all happen at a subconscious level since I do not remember it.

"Jack, please wake up, there's an emergency call for you. Jack can you hear me. Jack!"

"Wa . . . What?" I tried to focus on her voice. "What is it, Em?"

"Here," she handed me my cellphone. "You have an emergency phone call."

"Yes . . . hello." I tried to position the phone on my ear so I could hear clearly.

The voice on the other end was professional and business-like. "Mr. McNamara, are you a relation of Paul McNamara of Orlando?"

"Yes. He's my father."

"This is the charge nurse in the intensive care unit at Orlando Regional Medical Center. Your father has had a stroke. The ambulance brought him to the ER about two hours ago. They stabilized him and admitted him to the ICU about a half-hour ago. Fortunately, he had his cellphone in his pocket and we found your number."

I was in shock and feeling guilty. We had had a blowout argument at his house over six weeks ago. I had gotten as angry at him as I had ever been with anyone; in a rage actually, all over the way he had treated Billie. First, he abandoned Billie when she was just a toddler and prevented my mother from sending for her. Second, when she was seventeen years old and came to stay with her mother, he threw her out of our home when he discovered that she had had a homosexual affair. The last words I spoke to my father I demanded that he go down to Key West and apologize to Billie for what he had done to her. I stormed out of his home and have not talked to him since then.

I asked, "Is he okay?"

"I wish the news were better. The stroke was severe. He's unconscious, and suffering from severe seizures. We've given him medication to control the events, but we don't know the extent of the damage until he's conscious. Are you his healthcare surrogate?"

"No"

"Do you have a legal document he signed that gives you the legal authority to make healthcare decisions for him if he's incapable of making them himself."

"No, definitely not."

"Well you're his next of kin and absent that document, you're the only one I can reach. Can you come to the hospital please?"

"Yes, of course. It will take me about an hour and a half to get there."

"Don't hurry unnecessarily. But come as soon as you can."

"What floor and room?"

She gave me the information, she said how sorry she was that she had to call so early in the morning and that she would be at the nurse's station when I got there. We said our good-byes.

Em sat on the bed next to me. "It's your father, isn't it?"

"Stroke. He's in critical condition in the ICU. They want me to come to the hospital as quickly as I can."

"I'll stay with Ruby. Jack, I'm so sorry. "

I heard someone say once "God never gives us more that we can handle." I don't believe it. In fact, I know that it isn't true.

I was still angry with my father for the deliberate pain that he inflicted on Billie. Very angry. I had pushed it out of my mind to be able to write and to function. However, even in the hour of his need, I was still livid, seething that he did not have the gumption to face her and set things straight. My anger extended to the possibility of a premature departure from this earth without giving Billie some emotional closure. She probably did not care what my father thought, but I did.

I got on I-4 at Deland and made eighty to ninety miles-per-hour all the way to Orlando. The hospital was just a couple of blocks off the Interstate. I parked my car, took the elevator to the ICU and met up with the in-charge nurse who called me. The name on her tag read, "Nancy Spellman – RN."

I introduced myself, "I'm Jack McNamara, you called me about my father. Can I see him?"

"Of course, but he's still unconscious. We have him on a respirator and at this stage; it is wait-and-see. He can't breathe on his own, but there is brain activity. The next twenty-four hours will tell us a lot. I want to stress how serious things are. We lost him for a few minutes, his heart stopped but we were able to revive him."

"What are his chances of survival?"

"I wish I could offer you some hope, Mr. McNamara. The doctors just can't say right now. It all depends on the level of damage done to the brain. If the damage to the brain isn't too severe, your father could move out of a coma, into a vegetative state and then to consciousness. If that happens in the next three days or so, that would be a good sign."

"And if he doesn't recover in the next couple of days?" My thoughts raced. My yelling at him in anger and him striking me marked our last time together. It would be awful if he left this world with our relationship in this state of estrangement. My relationship with my father had always been difficult. His bigotry and disapproval of my profession aside, I never got used to his abrasive personality, his inability to see the pain that he inflicted on others or the view that the whole world revolved around him. That everything in it was there for HIS personal benefit. Despite his shortcomings and narcissism, I still loved him. Inexplicably I respected his strength of character, however misguided it could be. I knew that the bravado on the outside was camouflage for a person who struggled with the nuances of life since Mother passed away. I knew he was lonely. I knew that he had few close friends. The severity of those things he kept well hidden. I had often wondered if his strong opinions, like a life-vest, kept him from sinking emotionally and he held on to them tightly. Even if you threw another larger life-vest to him, he wouldn't take it, afraid if he released the one that he held tightly to his chest he would drown.

Nancy Spellman's words brought me back to our discussion. "The longer he remains in this state the chances begin to build against his recovery. No two patients who suffer a stroke are the same. Let's give it time, okay?" She looked directly at me to gauge my reaction. "Before I take you to see him, I'd like to get some information from you. Why don't you come around the desk and sit here."

She pointed to an armless chair on wheels sitting next to her.

I sat and gave her all my personal information. She keyboarded the data into the computer. After we finished with her paperwork, she swiveled her chair toward me.

"Are there any other siblings of your father's?"

"No," I said. "They've all passed away."

"Since your father didn't name a health care surrogate, and there are no other close family members, until he's able to make decisions for himself, that responsibility falls on your shoulders. Your father is on life support and if his condition should deteriorate, you may be required to make a tough decision: whether to keep him on life-support or have us disconnect him. I pray that it doesn't come to that. However, conditions could change quickly. So you need to prepare yourself for that eventuality."

"So how will you know when that moment of decision has come?"

"People in a coma have some brain activity, and those in a vegetative state have more upper and lower brain function. When the brain activity ceases, for all practical purposes a person has deceased. The decision to remove a person from life support is straightforward. Coma and vegetative state patients are more of a challenge if the patient can only live with external intervention such as lung and heart machines. When doctors feel that there's little likelihood of recovery and no brain activity then next of kin, with assistance from medical staff, decide whether we should remove them from artificial support. That can be a very hard decision for next-of-kin to make. It is made even more difficult when the decision is thrust upon someone without having had the opportunity to think it over."

I thanked her for taking the time to explain everything. I knew my father would not want to remain in a coma or any other state where his life depended on a machine. I had no doubt about it.

Nurse Spellman tidied up around her computer terminal, stood and said, "I'll take you to his room."

Father's room looked like a laboratory. Machines of every description blinked and beeped with regularity. It struck me immediately the number of tubes, lines and paraphernalia attached to his body and arms. The most obvious was the large tube inserted into his mouth and throat. I assumed that was a respirator. I could only guess at the rest of the devices. His eyes were closed and there was no movement in them, like there would be with a person in REM sleep. His arms were at his side and they had covered him with an egg-white blanket up to his chest.

"I'm afraid there isn't much to see. As I said, we're in a waiting mode. I'm sorry I had to call you so early in the morning, but now that we've down the administrative part, there's nothing more you can do. You should probably go home and get some rest. If there's any progress, we will be in touch immediately." She placed a hand on my shoulder, "I'll be praying for your father, Mr. McNamara. I'm afraid that's all we can do." She left me with my thoughts and quietly departed the room.

My mind churned to the point that I was overwhelmed. I had to struggle to hold off thoughts of Billie, Ruby, Em and the pressure of my writing deadline, so that I could focus on my father. As I watched his chest rise and fall keeping beat with the pump that fed oxygen to his lungs, I knew that I was tap-dancing on the line of what I could cope with. I fought to hold back the dark edges of panic. Unlike the night Em left me weeks ago, there was something deep inside me to draw upon, strength that heretofore had been absent.

Em used to tell me before she gave up helping me, that when I was overwhelmed, to mentally write down the things that crushed me on imaginary three-by-five cards, spread them out in my minds-eye and prioritize them in order of their urgency. Pick up the most important thing, focus on that and ignore the rest.

I sorted through my mental cards. Father's situation was urgent, but until his condition changed there was not a thing I could do save be ready for decisions when needed. Em also was urgent, but again, I could not do anything about it – she neither wanted me, nor would permit my intervention; my doing something would make the situation worse. At the moment, despite the difficulty I had being around her, I needed her help getting *The Tainted Lady*, finished and delivered to R&R and her willingness to help with Ruby was a godsend.

Then there was Ruby. I was already doing everything I could for Ruby. It was a matter of just being there.

Finally, there was the enormous pressure of finishing my next novel by the deadline. I began to feel angry about RR's inflexibility. Those feelings faded quickly as I thought about the harm that I had caused them. I made a promise and a commitment to them. They may not want me as a client anymore, but I owed them my best effort. If I left this relationship with them, I wanted it to be on good terms as much for me as for them. I did not want to make it worse by bailing on them or incurring their wrath. They had been extraordinarily patient with me. I owed it to them to make things right. Therefore, although there were pressing matters, until something changed I needed to write.

I stood up next to Father's hospital bed and clasped his hand, "Dad, I know we didn't part on the best of terms. I was angry and I regret that very much. I hope you'll forgive me."

I looked around the room to confirm that he was okay, patted his hand and placed it back on top of the blanket, and resolved to come back later tonight or have Em do it, to get some sleep and grind away on my story.

28

It was five-thirty a.m. when I pulled into the drive behind the beach-house. The night air was cold, a waxing moon hung in the sky like a torch and the air was still. I could hear the surf pound on shore, even from behind the house.

As I came through the front door, Em sat at the kitchen table with a cup of coffee waiting on me. I had called her after I left the hospital and had given her a bare-bones synopsis.

She propped her head up with a hand made into a fist. "Are you okay?" Even in the midst of our current marital impasse, she projected warmth, empathy and graciousness. It was hard for me to comprehend her caring and concern without a willingness to put our relationship back together.

"I'm good, I guess. It was hard to see him like that – this pillar of strength and manliness reduced to breathing through a tube. He would be horrified if he were conscious."

"I truly love your father. He's a good man. He has a soft heart, covered by a rock-hard veneer. It has always been a disappointment that you two have struggled with each other so much."

"That's because he sees me as this weak, spineless, milk-toast of a man who writes drivel for the masses."

"He's proud of you, Jack."

"Ah, huh."

"This is pointless," she said as I poured a cup of coffee and sat down across the table from her. "I want to go see him. He shouldn't be by himself."

I was not sure if she was critical of me leaving him or she was thinking aloud for herself.

"Em, he's in a coma. He can't hear or see and isn't aware of anything. They are taking good care of him. They'll call as soon as his condition changes."

"But what if he wakes and there's no one there he recognizes?"

"He'll be fine, Em. I must write. I have to write and if I don't I'm in deep trouble. I can't be

281

with Ruby for long periods or my book will not be finished in time."

"She's alright, Jack. She doesn't need someone hovering over her. For now, she gets around okay and can look after herself with only minor effort on our part. Don't worry. I'll take a shower, get dressed and go to Orlando to be with him. You get some sleep and then write. I'll be back by dinner and then maybe you could go down to the hospital and stay with him a while."

Em showered, dressed, patted me on the shoulder and left for Orlando as I finished another cup of coffee and watched the sun come up. During the winter months, the sun rose far to the south in purples and pinks and bursts of yellow. The sun's slow-motion trek to clear the horizon made me drowsy so I stretched out on the couch and fell quickly to sleep.

I awoke to Ruby banging pots and pans together as she pulled them out of the bottom draw of the electric stove. I checked my wristwatch and it was nearly ten a.m.

"Good afternoon, Darlin'. Are you going to sleep all day or try to get some writing done?" She went to the refrigerator, pulled out eggs, bacon and butter. "You ready to eat? I've got coffee waiting for you."

I pulled myself off the couch. The living room and dining area were in the same room. The kitchen was a two-wall affair where the long end opened into the dining room. The walls were painted in shades of tan, but the paint was faded, peeling in spots, and soiled at all the wall switches. The kitchen was dingy and worn-looking, but you could see the ocean from anywhere in the room.

I went into the kitchen, gave Ruby a hug and said, "Are you sure you're up for this?"

"Darlin' I may be dying but I'm not dead yet. How you want your eggs cooked?"

I told her, poured myself a cup of coffee, and got out of the kitchen and let her perform her magic. It was not until she joined me at the table that I realized she had only cooked breakfast for me.

"Where's your plate, Ruby?"

"I'm just not hungry. Nothing has any taste."

"Why is this story so important to you?" I had been intrigued with her tale from the beginning. As good as the story was, though, I did not see anything in the tale that would motivate a woman to tell it as a dying wish.

"This story has been in my head since I was a kid. I've wanted to write it since I can remember, but I never did. Maybe I didn't have the confidence, or maybe life just crowded it out. I don't know. But, Darlin', it is very important to me. I want this story out of my head before I close my eyes for good. I hope you make a pile of money off it. You'll write it, Jack, won't you?"

I did not have the heart to tell her it was not the type of story I liked to write. It meant so much to her that I didn't have the heart to refuse. "Of course I will."

I explained what had happened to my father and the events of the morning.

"Sweetheart, that's awful. I never cared for your father and all the pain he caused your mother. Jesus loves him, so, I guess so can I. I'll pray for him."

I waited for her to bow her head and break out in prayer, but she didn't. "He needs prayer for sure. I hoped that he could make things right with Billie."

"Then that's what I'll pray for." She paused for a moment. "Have you thought about the question I asked you the other day?

"You mean do I think God lives in me?

"Ah huh," she said.

"To be honest I see no evidence of it. But it is a nice thought." Then I explained the attempted suicide and the call out to God for help.

"Yes, Emily told me about that, you poor dear. It answers one question, you believe in God. And it appears that he has answered your prayer, you appear to be well on the road to recovery."

I had not made that connection but what she said was not lost on me. I remember as a kid the nuns taught us that the priest changed wine and bread into the body and blood of Jesus, that when we took communion we took Jesus inside of us. I remembered that I had the thought, if I could take communion and have Jesus in me, why did I have to take communion again. Would not once be enough. I also struggled with the truth of it. Was Jesus real? Did He really die for me or was this just some nice story to make us feel better?

"How do you know all of this is true? And don't tell me that the bible says it is."

Ruby took a napkin, dabbed her lips, set it down and said, "Alright, I won't quote the bible. I'll give it to you from my own personal experience. I'm an old woman and lived many years. One of the things I've learned is that there's a hole in each one of us, a need so deep, that only God can fill it. As human beings, we try too hard to fill that need with money, or power, or possessions, addictions, or sex. Those things just don't satisfy a thirsty soul. Why? God made us to be in a relationship with Him through Jesus. When I stopped pursuing those things, when I began to look to God to meet my deepest need, only then did I understand what it meant to be happy, to be satisfied and at rest. I know it to be true because it works. Do I have physical proof of God's existence? The beauty of the sunset, the love that I see in you and Emily, these are enough for me. For a skeptic, they'll never find the proof they seek, it only comes by faith." She pushed her plate away, grabbed mine and set it atop hers. "So, I'll ask again. Do you believe you have God in you?"

"To be honest, I'd have to answer no."

"And where do you think the strength came from to fight your way out of the dark hole you were in?"

"I don't know, Ruby."

"I think you do, Darlin'.

We sat in silence. The whole concept of God in me disturbed me. If it was true, and I candidly did not believe it was, what would the implications be? What do you do with something like that? It almost seemed impossible to accept something so unbelievable.

She did not press me for an answer. "You need to get your behind in there and get that novel done."

"I'm sorry my writing takes so much time away from you. I should be helping you."

"That will happen soon enough. You need to get that R&R monkey off your back and focus on other things in your life that deserve your attention."

"Ruby, why is this God thing so important to you?"

"You're dealing with some pretty tough stuff. I can see God's handiwork in all of it. I came to a point in my life where I recognized I couldn't live without Him. I didn't possess the power to deal with life; that I needed Him. When I consider all that you're dealing with, you may come to a point when you recognize that you're at the end of your rope and recognize you need Him. I want you to remember there's no problem in life that the nearness of God can't resolve. Now go, get some work done. Don't worry about me. Maybe we could walk down to the beach and I can continue to tell my story."

I wrote until nearly dinner and made substantial progress. Em came home, we all ate together and I returned to the hospital to be with my father. I brought my laptop with me so I could write while I was in his room. I never got a chance to use it. I was not in the room for more than an hour when he woke up and began to choke on the breathing tube.

I jumped to the side of my father's bed and tried to comfort him. Alarms from several devices sounded. "Dad, you have a breathing tube in your mouth, try to relax." He was in full-scale panic.

Spellman was on duty, raced into the room and assessed his difficulty. She brought a sedative with her, injected it into the IV and began to talk to him in soothing words. "Paul, you're in the hospital, and we had to put you on a ventilator to help you breathe. Just calm down," and she rubbed his shoulders, took his hand in hers, his chest no longer heaved and his vital signs began to settle down.

Spellman reached up and around and silenced alarms, reset devices and you could see my father's eyes lose their panicked darkness. He tried to speak, but the ventilator interfered.

I came alongside his bed and met his gaze. "You're okay, Dad." To the nurse I said, "Can we take out the breathing device?"

"No, we must follow procedures to do that. We will test to make sure he can breathe on his own, and we may have to wean him off the oxygen. He'll get used to the tube in a minute. We don't want him to stay on it any longer that he has to. She checked all the monitors and said, "His vitals look good." She took a penlight out of her pocket, flicked it on and asked my father to look at her and to follow the light with his eyes. He complied. "Excellent."

She smiled at me and nodded.

My father raised his arms and mimed writing on his hand. "Ms. Spellman, he wants to write something to us."

Father shook his head and pointed directly at me.

"I'll get a tablet and a pen." Then she left the room but the scent of hair spray and disinfectant hand soap lingered.

My father motioned for me to come closer. He grabbed my hand, and tears streamed down his cheeks. He continued to hold my hand tightly until the nurse returned with a clipboard and pen. He took the pad and pen and with his hand slightly shaking wrote, "I'm sorry about our fight." Tears still streamed on to the pillow.

I started to say that it was nothing, but before I could say anything, he tapped urgently on the clipboard and began to write again.

"God sent me back," he scrawled. Now he sobbed and could hardly write.

This was odd, for my father was not a religious man. His religious fervor over the years faded into a truce of inaction with God. He may have gone to mass occasionally, on Christmas and Easter, but beyond that, I found no evidence that he pursued God in any meaningful way.

"Dad, it's okay. It's okay."

He shook his head firmly and wrote, "No. Not okay. I want to see Billie. Please. Important."

"I'll call her later today and find out if she can come up?"

He shook his head again and scribbled, "Now, please." He underlined please three times and then wrote, "I don't want to die without telling her how sorry I am."

"I'll call her now."

He started to scratch on the clipboard again. "I'll pay for it, whatever it costs. But soon."

I walked out of the room into the hall leaving Nurse Spellman to minister to my father. I quick-stepped it to the end of the hall near a window to improve cellphone reception and called Billie.

She answered on the first ring, "Jack that's so weird, I was just getting ready to call you. . ."

"Billie, my father had a severe stroke early this morning. He's in intensive care and he just woke up from a coma. He wants to see you as soon as possible."

"What could he possibly want from me?" she said in an irritated tone.

"My guess would be your forgiveness. He said he didn't want to die until he told you he was sorry."

"After all the hateful things that man has done to me and now that he's dying, he wants me to make him feel better? That's bullshit, Jack. I'm not doing it. No way!"

"He said, God told him to come back and make it right."

"Well yippee skipee and with that I'm supposed to drop everything in my life and come up there immediately, so he can clear his conscience. Not going to happen, Jack."

"When I got back to Orlando, I confronted him about him throwing you out and we got into a terrible fight. I demanded that he come to see you and to apologize for everything he did to you. It was the last thing I said to him before I left his house. I haven't spoken to him in over six weeks. Billie, he needs to do this. You need to hear what he has to say. Would you do it for me, please?"

There was a long, awkward silence on the phone. All you could hear was his labored breathing.

"Would you do it for me, Billie?" I repeated.

292

Bill Cronin

"Alright! Alright! But, I'm not doing it for that selfish bastard, you understand me?

"Thank you, Billie."

"And I suppose you want me to come now?"

"Yes, please. As soon as possible."

"Well this is my day to deal with the bigots in my life. As soon as the judge granted an injunction, people have been combing through my trash, following me and talking to my neighbors. I'm certain it's Coats. It is too much of a coincidence."

"Have you contacted Pike about it?"

"I'll do that in the morning. I guess I can call her from Orlando."

More silence.

"I need to do some things around here and I'll head to the airport. Will you pick me up?"

I said, "I'll arrange for a ticket and will have it waiting for you at the ticket counter. And yes either I'll pick you up or I'll send a car for you."

I walked back into the room and Nurse Spellman had just finished up with my father. "Ah, Mr. McNamara." She hooked her hair over her ear, went to the sink and washed her hands.

"Is he okay?"

"Yes, remarkably so. It is rare for a stroke patient to come directly out of a coma to full consciousness. It happens, just not often. He's asleep now from the sedative I gave him, but all his vitals look good and brain activity looks nearly normal."

"I called my sister and she'll come to see him."

"Good, he seemed almost in a panic to see her."

"Thank you, for your help and forthrightness."

"That's what I'm here for. Let me know if you need anything," she said over her shoulder as she left the room.

I walked back into the hall and down by a window to call the airlines. There were no more flights leaving Key West that evening. I made a reservation for the first flight in the morning to fly from Key West to Orlando. I called Billie, gave her the flight information and assured her that I would meet her at the airport.

When I hung up with Billie, I had the oddest feeling. While I had referred to Billie as my sister, it was a term that had no personal meaning until now. It had just occurred to me that she was coming to see me and she would remain to spend time with Em and Ruby. I said to myself, "She's my sister." It became real to me. "My sister!"

I took my laptop out, but I could not get the "juice" to flow. I was worried about Father, even though he slept soundly. I could do nothing more for him, so I decided to head home, try to write some and then go get Billie in the morning.

On my way home, I called Em and filled her in on my father's status. She was overjoyed. She said as soon as I got home that she would go sit with my father during a portion of the night.

When I arrived home, Em took the car and returned to the hospital. Ruby wrapped herself up in a blanket and was nearly asleep in a chair.

"Hey, Darlin'," she said, as I walked into the living area. "How is your daddy?" She straightened in the chair as I sat down.

"He came out of his coma. He awakened and asked to see Billie. He said, God told him to make things right with her."

"Well if that isn't an answer to prayer, I don't know what is."

"How are you?" I asked as I leaned forward and took off my shoes.

"I'm afraid this hasn't been a very good day. I've just felt so weak and tired. And, I have no appetite. She shifted and scooted forward in her chair. "Could I ask you to get your recorder please and can we work on the story for a little while? God is telling me that my time is short."

"Of course, let me go get it." I went into my makeshift studio, found the recorder and came back into the room.

Ruby got up slowly and with effort walked to the kitchen. "I'm going to make some hot-chocolate. Want some?"

Ruby brought the water on the stove to a boil. She dressed up two cups and asked me to help her with them. Ruby labored with her cane into the living area and she slumped down into the chair. I placed her cup on a small table next to her along with the recorder set to record.

As soon as I sat down, she resumed her story. I sipped on my hot chocolate while she spun her tale about Awesome Banes.

29

Fulton

1938

Adel sat on the cypress bench with her back to the river to watch the sun go down behind the garage. It was Christmas Eve, and the air was unusually warm for this time in December and Adel was comfortable in a short-sleeved print blouse and shorts. Mosquitoes buzzed around her, but did not bother her and she thought how her life had changed for the better since Awesome came to work with John.

Trips to the beach for "time trials" were frequent and she and Awesome had developed a comfortable relationship. She felt that they were more than friends. She wanted him to kiss her again the way that he kissed her the first time. However, he seemed to hold his distance. She thought that it might be because of John, or because of the race issue. She was certain, though, that he felt for her and she was afraid to question him about it.

Millicent walked out of the back of the house and sat down opposite her on the bench with a plop. She pulled her long hair together with her hand and tossed it over her shoulder. She cradled her head in her hands and furled her brow.

"You look like you've lost your best friend," Adel didn't really care what daily, dramatic, attention getting issue Millicent faced.

"Oh, you have no idea." Millicent placed her face in the palms of her hands and began to cry; softly at first, then in deep sobs.

Adel stepped out of the picnic bench, walked around to Millicent's side, sat next to her and put her arm around her shoulder. Adel had never seen Millicent like this; this was not the normal crisis de' jour.

"What's this about, Millie?"

"I'm pregnant!" she yelled. She dropped her hands away from her face, turned her face toward Adel and tears cascaded down her cheeks. More softly, she said, "I can't believe, I'm pregnant."

"That bastard," anger swelled inside her. "I can't believe you let that animal get you pregnant!"

Millicent dropped her hands to the tabletop and clasped them together. "Buddy?" She looked at Adel through tears, which made her blue eyes even more vibrant. "It's not, Buddy." Then Millicent dropped her head and cried even more heavily. "Buddy and I never had sex, it's not him," she said through her sobs.

Adel was shocked. The way Millicent had fawned all over Buddy Hines, she was certain that they had been intimate. "Who then?"

"Nobody!" With her head still down, she spit the words out as though she had tasted something awful.

"Millie, I'm not stupid, who was it?"

"Awesome! Are you satisfied?" With her head still down Millicent turned her head and cut her eyes toward Adel. She looked almost demonic.

"Awesome?" Adel yelled. "AWESOME?" Adel felt as though her chest would explode. She jerked back away from Millicent and slid herself away from her on the bench. Her mind raced and weighed out the truthfulness of what she had just heard. "Not Awesome," she said aloud. The pieces of the puzzle that floated around in her memory began to gel into a coherent picture. She thought about Awesome's kiss and then his apparent disinterest and, Millicent's recent interest in Awesome, when she and Awesome were together. The fact that every other boy she ever had an interest in, Millicent tried to take them away.

What before was shock, now turned to humiliation and rage. She stood and backed away from the table. "You bitch! You selfish little bitch. You knew I loved Awesome and you couldn't stand it. You couldn't leave it alone, could you?"

Adel stood there and stared at the back of Millicent's head, hands balled into fists at her side, wanting to beat Millicent to a pulp.

Head still down, still sobbing Millicent said, "I didn't know how you felt about him. I swear." Millicent lifted her head, and turned on the bench and looked up to Adel. "Adel, you can't tell anyone. I beg you, please."

"Not only are you a little bitch, you're a lying bitch. You knew how I felt. You knew! Tell anyone? Do you think I care for one minute what happens to you. Did you even think of me for a minute when you slept with that little shit? Tell anyone? I'll climb the water tower in the middle of town and yell it at the tops of my lungs. I'll scream so loud they'll hear me in Tallahassee."

"Oh, Adel! NO. Please. You can't do that." Millicent pleaded as she stood up and approached Adel. "Buddy, will kill me."

"I hope he does . . . I can't believe this," Adel backed away from her supplicating sister. Then she turned and ran. She ran past the garage, past her puzzled father talking with a customer at the fuel pumps, down the road toward town. And then the tears came, she could hardly see through them as she ran in no particular direction but away from the betrayal that tore her heart apart.

30

January 5[th,]

On my way to the Orlando International Airport to pick Billie up, Em called and said that my father had awakened and they had some time to visit in the wee hours of the morning. She was in tears as she described the concern she had for him.

I had arranged with Billie to meet her at the curb at baggage claim. I called ahead for the arrival time – they had delayed the flight because of a mechanical issue in Key West. I slowed down on State Highway 528, turned into the airport and arrived at the same time the aircraft was due to land. Since it would take time for her to deplane and take the tram from B terminal to the main terminal, I circled the airport and made successive stops at baggage claim. On the third circuit, she stood at the curb waiting patiently for me.

She was dressed in jeans and a sweatshirt and had her handbag and jacket hanging from her arm and a small rolling carry-on that stood next to her. It was eight-forty-five a.m. and the flight was supposed to have landed at eight a.m.

I pushed the door open for her to get in. Instead, she opened the back door of the SUV, threw in her handbag, coat and carry-on, slammed the door and then hopped in the front.

She took a deep breath then said, "Hi Jackie." She leaned over the console between the front seats and kissed me on the cheek.

"Aren't you cold? It's forty-five degrees out."

"Nah, I'm fine. It was like sixty-five in the Keys when I left. I like cool weather. How's your dad?"

"I don't know. I haven't seen him since last night right after I talked to you on the phone. You okay with this?"

"No, I'm not. Candidly, every fiber in me is screaming not to do this. It took years of counseling to undo all the harm that man inflicted on me. You have no idea how much I hate him. How much I loathe the idea of doing this. I don't even know that once I'm in the room with that man if I can listen to a word he says. I'm doing this for you, Jackie. And if you knew how hard this was for me, you would appreciate how much I love you."

"I know how difficult it is, and I know it's a lot to ask."

"You don't understand that he destroyed me. By the time I was twenty, I felt worse than a worthless piece of crap. God, my own mother didn't even want me; wouldn't even stand up for me. I wanted to die. I had an enormous hole in me that I tried to fill with booze, drugs and sex. It wasn't until Alex came along that I felt like anyone gave a shit what happened to me. All those years, all that heartache, all the countless ways your mom and dad's collective rejection had impacted just about every corner of my world. Now I know it was all him. He wouldn't let my mom send for me. He prevented her from contacting me. He threw me out of your home in 1961 and he made certain that I could never see Mom until she was on her deathbed. Yes, this is very difficult for me."

"Did you ever think that if you forgive him it might be good for you? Do you think that letting all that anger go might make the time you have with Alex better?"

"I don't think so. If Alex fully understood why I came up here to be with you she would be livid. She despises him as much as I do. I don't know what she would do to him if she were in the same room with him." She wrung her hands and squirmed in her seat. "Jackie, I don't want to talk about this anymore. Let's just get to the hospital and get this over with."

With rush hours over, traffic on northbound South Orange Avenue was light and we made good time. The hospital was south of the downtown area, a collection of old and new buildings making up the medical center. We found a parking space around the corner from the main entrance and worked our way through the lobby, up the elevator and on to the ICU floor. I stopped by the nurse's station to see if Nurse Spellman was on the floor but it was her day off.

I walked into Father's room, but Billie hung back outside the door. I motioned for her to come and she did so as though she had entered a room filled with snakes. They had removed the respirator and tube, but not the other equipment.

"Dad, how are you doing?" I stood next to the bed.

He looked at me and then past me to Billie.

"Billie, come closer," He said, his voice hoarse and raspy no doubt from the tube.

My father's eyes looked more sunken since I had seen him several hours ago. His face was white, almost ashen. I vacated the spot where I stood to make room for Billie. She tentatively shuffled forward and took my place standing right next to the midsection of his bed. I moved to the foot.

My father looked at me, then at Billie. "I owe you a very long overdue apology. I was so selfish thinking only about what was best for me and I didn't give your welfare a single thought. I treated you horribly, Billie." He began to get tearful. "I was so stubborn and prideful I could never bring myself to call you or see you and tell you that I treated you dreadfully. I didn't want to die without setting things right."

Billie looked at me - eyes narrowed - then turned to my father and said, "You'll never, ever be able to set things right with me. Never! You destroyed me, made me feel worthless, unwanted and you cast me aside like a piece of human garbage, and you want to 'make things right?'"

With tears streaming down his cheek he said, "You have every right to be angry . . ."

Cutting my father off, she said, "Damn right I have every right to be angry," she began to cry tears of anger. She literally shook beside the bed.

"Jack, I died. I was separated from my body and found myself in the presence of God. He was a being like nothing I've seen or could possibly imagine." My father looked at Billie. "He never said a word, but he told me that I had unfinished business with you Billie and in his presence I was so ashamed at what I'd done to you. And then the next thing I know I woke up in this hospital bed." It became more difficult for him to speak. He was just on the verge of sobbing.

"I hope you rot in . . . ," and then something in her broke. Her face red with anger a moment ago, softened. Then both of them wept.

He regained some of his composure and said, "God told me that you were precious to him and that you will keep your restaurant. He wanted me to share that message with you. Billie, I've never felt so loved in his presence and that love humbled me to the bone. I was the one who felt like human garbage and He let me feel the anguish you've lived with your whole life because of me. I can't begin to tell you how sorry I am, and the deep regret I feel at this moment."

Billie reached out, took his hand and held it a long time before either of them spoke.

"I will not ask you to forgive me. I don't deserve your forgiveness. I just hope God will somehow show you the deep torment I feel inside."

"Yes, He is, Mr. McNamara."

"Then you know what I say is true."

"Yes." Billie still held his hand.

I saw the tension in his face, release. "Jack, I love you, son. Tell Emily how deeply I love her."

"I love you too, Dad." He locked eyes with mine for a few moments; he took a deep breath then closed his eyes.

I called for the nurse. She rushed into the room, looked at the monitors and said, "He's slipped back into a coma, again. You will all have to leave, I need to intubate him."

As we backed out of the room, I could see the nurse grab for the respirator and prepare to reinsert the breathing tube into his mouth.

Outside in the hall Billie said, "Jack that was something else. When I held his hand I could feel his pain and I'd no doubt that his regret was genuine."

The nurse came out and said, "His vitals aren't good. I paged the doctor. I suggest you wait in the ICU waiting area," and she pointed in the direction of the central hallway then went back into the room to tend to my father.

The lounge was a short distance down the hall. We sat together in the empty room and said nothing for a long time.

Billie broke the silence - there were still tears in her eyes. "This is so overwhelming. One moment all I could feel for that man was hatred. The next I'm standing there melting and I'm empathizing with your father's pain. The years of anger, pain and torture I've experienced at his hand were swept away. It was like God reached down and touched me in the very deepest part."

It was not ten minutes before the doctor came to the waiting room and introduced himself. "I'm so sorry to have to tell you this, but your father passed away a few moments ago. He suffered another massive stroke. This isn't that unusual to have a patient suffer multiple strokes. We did everything we could. Again, I'm very sorry. If there's anything we can do, please just ask."

The doctor reached for my hand and I said, "Thank you, doctor. Can we see him?"

"Certainly. I'll let the charge nurse know that you're coming. Take whatever time you need."

The doctor left the waiting room.

"Jack, do you really believe that God sent him back so he could say he was sorry to me?"

This is the second person in three days that asked me if I believed something about God. "Billie, I have no idea, but my father was certainly convinced of it. What do you think?"

"I don't think there's any question and I haven't given God a thought since I was a kid. There's no doubt that what I experienced holding his hand came from God. No doubt about it."

We went back to my father's room. They had removed the breathing tube and he lay there with his head slightly elevated as peaceful as I had ever seen him. If he died in anguish, there was no evidence of it on his face.

Initially, as I stood there with my arm around my sister, I could not help but run through the litany of abuses that my father had hurled upon her through the years. It seemed natural to list off all the things that he had done to Billie. As I stood there and looked at his face, none of that seemed to matter. There was one undeniable fact. I loved him. When it hit me that I would never talk to him again, my grievances seemed petty. Then both of us stood there in tears and consoled one another.

31

I called Em and shared the news of Father's passing. She cried and I tried to console her but I knew that would not be possible until I got home. Billie and I accessed the Interstate during rush hour, crawled through Winter Park, Maitland, Altamonte Springs, on to Deland, and turned toward New Smyrna Beach on SR44.

Billie repeated several times what a water-shed experience her time with my father had been for her spiritually.

"What did you take from your father's statement that I'd keep the restaurant?"

"I don't know, Billie."

"Did you tell him about the problems I've had with my landlord?"

"I haven't talked to my father since I returned from Key West and we'd that big blowout."

"Then how would he have known, Jack?"

"I don't see how he could have known."

"Exactly, so what do you make of his prediction?"

"Are you asking me if I think God sent a message to you through my father? Do I believe that you're going to keep your restaurant?"

"Yes that's exactly what I'm asking."

"I just don't know about the God thing. It is reasonable to assume that you'll get your restaurant because I think the law is on your side. Despite the flack you've gotten from your landlord, I have no doubt that you'll win."

"I have no doubt it came from God. Absolutely none."

I didn't know how to respond and silence ensued as we drove the rest of the way home.

It was dark when we pulled in the drive and Em burst through the front door crying and threw herself at me. "I just talked with him last night. He seemed fine. It was as if nothing had ever happened. Even Nurse Spellman remarked at how well he was doing. I'm so sorry, Jack. I know this has to be tough with all the other things going on in your life." She pulled away and surveyed my face for signs of a struggle.

"Surprisingly, Em, I'm okay."

"And this is, Billie?" Em closed the distance to Billie and gave her a hug. "I'm Em."

As we all made our way into the house, I explained the bedside confession my father made to Billie and her reaction. Ruby was already sitting on the couch in her bathrobe. It was apparent to me that her health had declined rapidly. She looked very tired.

"Well, I suwanee, if you aren't a sight. Come here child and give your Aunt Ruby a hug." Ruby tried to stand but fell back down onto the couch.

Billie said, "Ruby, don't exert yourself," then she moved down the couch, squatted and gently hugged her.

Billie sat on the couch with Ruby. Em and I sat in opposing club chairs.

Ruby said to me, "I'm so sorry about your daddy, Jack. I wish I could have been there with you when it happened, you poor thing."

Em said, "Yeah, Jack. Me, too. I'm glad Billie was there. I thought when you drove up, that I'll never see him again." She started crying again. "I really loved your father. How are you feeling about this?"

Em had read a book a year ago about depression and the importance of exploring ones feelings. Ever since she approached serious discussions that might affect me with "How are you feeling about _____?" Fill in the blank.

"I just wish we'd had more time. It just happened so suddenly. How am I feeling?" I wanted to say something smart like, 'How would you feel if your father died?' Instead, I answered, "I feel very sad. I loved him. For all his faults, I still loved him."

Then Ruby bowed her head and began to pray, "Father, I pray for Paul McNamara that he's with you this very moment in heaven. I pray that you use your enormous power to strengthen each of us in this moment of grief and sadness. I pray that you would show Paul great mercy and love and grant us comfort. I ask this in the name of Jesus. Amen"

316

I had already raised my head and Em, Billie and Adel were wiping tears away from their eyes.

"Ruby. Do you really think my father is in heaven?"

Before Ruby could answer, Billie said, "Aunt Ruby, the most amazing thing happened," and she proceeded to explain the message from God, and the deep change of heart that could only have come from God.

Of course, that set Ruby off on a mini-sermon.

"No one knows the mind of God. The bible teaches that unless you accept Jesus as Lord and Savior that you can't enter heaven. That happens differently for every person. It sounds to me like Jack's daddy had an intimate experience with God. We all face death at some point. It can come suddenly and rob us of an opportunity to acknowledge our relationship with God. God told me that I don't have much time, but I made my peace with Him long ago. And even then, there are still some loose ends that I need to tie up before He escorts me to Heaven."

With a captive audience, Ruby got to do what she has wanted to do since I picked her up from the hospital. Preach. She kept at it for nearly twenty minutes until she was exhausted from the effort. None of us had the heart to stop her.

Em looked at me with a look that said, "Do you believe that we have to sit through this?" Billie was enthralled and while she discussed her faith and the events of the day – what she felt God had done – Em and I inched out of the room and escaped to the porch.

The air smelled of salt and fish and the surf pounded on the shore. It was warmer tonight than it had been since we got here. We pulled a couple of errant chairs together and talked about the events of the day.

"Are you okay?" Em asked me, her face a silhouette against the light coming from the house.

"Actually, I am. I don't know why because when I first heard about his stroke I thought I'd come apart."

"Why do you think you're handling it so well?"

"When you left me, I reached down into my emotional tank and there was nothing there. Nothing. Now, I wouldn't say the tank was full, but I'm not running on empty. My writing is progressing and I feel better about myself. I'm optimistic about the future. I know deep down that I'm going to be okay."

"For now."

The implication was clear. I had to admit that I had had similar periods when I was not depressed and then fallen back into despair.

"That's fair, Em. For now."

"What makes you think it is different this time?"

"Because I finally got a grip on what caused it. I know now that my father was to blame for a lot of it. He had me convinced as a kid that I was a nutjob for wanting to write. He berated me and beat me up emotionally about it. He drove my mother crazy and nearly did the same thing to me. Subconsciously, I internalized all those messages he planted about being a failure and that I'd end up like Hemingway if I continued to pursue a writing career. When I unraveled it all, I began to see that I was allowing my father to control my life. My emotions were like a tape recorder. During a very vulnerable time in my adolescence, he recorded hateful things on that tape that I didn't start to replay until I was an adult. Before, I believed the messages as though they were mine. Now, I still hear those messages, I can still hear him say what a loser I was, but I now know that they don't belong to me; that I can ignore them. That I've built this marvelous career as a writer and I can be proud of what I've done, despite the damage my father tried to do to me. That's why I think it is different this time. I'm able for the first time to cut off the negative messages and listen to the truth."

There was silence. As I spoke to Em, I realized that I was free of it. Free of the cage in which my father had placed me. Em's demand to split the sheets was an opportunity for each of us to make new choices. It was at that moment, that I accepted that our marriage was irreconcilable. "Em, I'm okay with the divorce. I can see how I snuffed the love that you had for me. I have accepted the fact that it is over. I appreciate that we've been able to go through this without warfare, and that you've been so reasonable."

"You've been reasonable too, Jack. I know that you've had a lot thrown at you recently and candidly, your response has been commendable. I hope we can still be friends and work together."

I said, "At least for now."

I stood up, bent over, kissed her on the cheek and went inside.

Billie sat alone on the couch. "Ruby just went to bed. She wanted to see you before you went to bed."

"Y'all have a good talk?"

"Jackie, she's amazing. What a godly woman. Yes, we had a great talk. I wish I could stay longer. I could learn so much from her. She sure knows the Bible."

I left Billie in the living room. Ruby was in bed, propped up with pillows reading her worn leather covered bible. When I walked into the room, she tried to pull herself up, but quickly abandoned the effort. I pulled a chair over that Em brought in from the dining room and sat down next to her bed.

"Hey, Darlin'. I'm so sorry about your father and me adding to your burdens doesn't help, does it?"

"Nonsense. You're not a burden at all. I'm honored you're here. How are you feeling?"

"Not good, sweetheart. I don't have much time left."

"Don't say that. If you're not feeling well, the nurse is supposed to be here tomorrow. She'll know what to do." I remembered that earlier she had said God had told her that her time was short. "What has God told you, Ruby?" After I spoke, I regretted that my delivery sounded condescending and filled with disbelief.

"He told me a couple of days." I thought to myself that she wanted her own demise and used God to create the justification for it.

"And how does God communicate with you?" I did my best to hide my skepticism.

"I hear his voice as plainly as I hear yours. He talks to me all day long. It hasn't always been that way. I used to think that God was with me, you know like outside of me helping me. I saw a bumper sticker once that said 'God is my co-pilot.' That was pretty much how my relationship with God worked. I was the captain of my ship floating in oceans that He controlled. My ship went where I wanted it to go but He controlled the forces along the way that determined whether I would have a good journey or bad.

"Then one night, as I studied my bible, God showed me this verse." From memory she said "*Not that we are adequate in ourselves to consider anything as coming from ourselves but our adequacy is from God.* And after God hit me over the head with that verse I began to notice recurring statements in the New Testament that said that God lived in me."

She put emphasis on the word 'in.' "He told me that He wanted to be my strength and live his life through me."

She continued. "Then he showed me verses that talked about me being 'one' with Him. Ever since I was a kid old enough to carry this Bible, and all the years I studied it and read it repeatedly and I had never *seen* those verses. I saw them, yes, because I had read them many times. They didn't have any particular meaning, though. And when God opened my eyes to the fact that He lives in me, that we're one, that his thoughts are my thoughts and His life is my life . . . well, Darlin', it is an understatement to say that it changed me. That's what I want for you. That's what I want for Emily - Lord knows you both need it. He could fix your marriage if you both would let him."

As soon as she turned this from information sharing into a sermon, I felt very uncomfortable. I changed the subject. "Are you up to working on your story before you go to sleep?" She looked tired but her story had me hooked. I began to worry that we would not have enough time to finish.

"Yes, Darlin', but before we do, could I pray for you?"

"Oh, alright." The phrase was a cross between a question and a statement.

Ruby closed her eyes, palms placed down on the bible that lay in her lap. "Father, I pray that you would give Jack the faith to accept that you love him and want to have a relationship with him. Let him recognize that you're already in him and that all he has to do is believe it. This I ask in Jesus' name. Amen."

Now I felt very uncomfortable. I thought about Billie's statement earlier that Ruby was a godly woman and in my opinion a woman of faith, faith I wish I had. She made things sound so simple and in her world perhaps, they were.

I excused myself, went to retrieve the recorder and returned to her bedside. "Can I ask you a question, Ruby?"

"Sweetheart you can ask your Aunt Ruby about anything."

"What's the point of this story?"

"Does it need to have a point?" She paused a moment, licked her dry lips and continued. "This story has been in me for a long time. I just want to get it out of my mind before I die. Are you okay with that?"

"Yes, of course, Ruby."

32

Fulton

1938

Adel came home well after dark. She refused to talk to John and went straight to her room when he demanded to know where she had been. She tossed and turned unable to brush aside the betrayal, and the hatred she felt for her sister. She wanted to hurt her, to rip her heart out, as she had ripped out hers. She thought about telling John, but she knew John's heart was too big to let it bother him for long. Buddy. Now that would cause an explosion, she thought.

She got up early, walked to the Hines' estate and stood at the open gate waiting for nine o'clock. She walked down the long drive, dropped the knocker on the heavy wooden door three times and backed away waiting for a response. A black man answered the door. He asked whom she wanted and withdrew into the cavernous house. A minute later

Buddy Hines appeared rubbing his eyes, still in his pajamas.

"Adel, what are . . .?"

"Buddy, we need to talk." Adel paced back and forth on the stoop.

Buddy, opened the door wide enough to slip into the bright morning sunlight as if hiding Adel from the home's inhabitants. He pulled the door closed and stood with Adel shading his eyes with his hand.

Before he could speak, she blurted out, "Millicent is going to have a baby!" She stopped, then paced and turned to face him looking for a re-action.

"What . . . pregnant?" Buddy dropped the hand screening his eyes to his side as he processed this information. He looked up to the sky, to the ground then to some distant point beyond Adel. "That's not possible. There's no way."

"Well, I assure you she is." Adel held out the most important piece of information. She want-ed to see if the little snake had the gumption to ad-mit his lack of sexual prowess.

"Adel, that's impossible . . . unless . . ." Buddy put a hand to his brow and rubbed at his forehead, then looked at Adel with wide eyes. "Someone else?"

She nodded, watching Buddy's emotional ego light up like a roman candle.

"Who?" He lunged at Adel, grabbed her by the shoulders and shook her. "Who?" He yelled with enough strength that she feared he would hurt her. He towered over her and squeezed her as though the very act would propel the words out of her mouth. As soon as the name, "Awesome" slipped through her lips, she knew it wouldn't be Millicent who'd pay the price for her indiscretion. It would be Awesome.

Buddy let loose of Adel's shoulders and ground his right fist into the palm of his left hand as a chemist might grind compounds in a mortar with a pestle. "A Nigger? There's no way she'd have sex with a damn Nigger!" Now it was Buddy who paced from one end of the porch to the other, working his fist into his hand. He stopped. His green eyes were wide and the pupils almost in full dilation. "I don't believe it. You're lying."

"Buddy, she told me herself." Herself came out her . . . self. "When she told me she was pregnant you were the first person I thought of. I even asked her if it was you. She told me no." Adel could see deep in his eyes that she had touched a nerve, a very raw nerve.

"She wanted a Nigger over me?" Buddy swallowed hard several times, bit down on his lower lip, nodded at her a couple of times, then spun on the balls of his feet, opened the front door and slammed it behind him without a word, leaving her standing on the stoop alone.

Just as surely as an artilleryman could expect a report from a cannon once he lit the fuse, Adel expected an explosion from Buddy Hines. It was the when and how that she was uncertain about.

There was only one person left on her very short list of people with whom she would seek her revenge: John Barnes.

33

Fulton

1938

When Adel walked out of the Hines' driveway and left their estate, she turned toward home and the sweet taste of revenge turned sour in her mouth. She reminded herself that she had only been with John for four years and that he had treated her as his own. He was barely over the crippling grief of losing his wife Madara and the news of Millicent's pregnancy would hit him hard, not so much because of the pain that it would cause him, but she knew he would be worried sick about the damage it might do to Millicent.

By the time she turned onto the main road in Fulton and was a half-mile from Taggart's Livery, she began to think less of herself and more for John, and the enormous issues Millicent had to face. By the time she made it home, her resolve to blow this up in Millicent's face melted. She deeply regretted telling Buddy.

It was after ten a.m. when she walked by the garage, but the shop doors were locked up. A "closed" sign hung in the window of the door. John always opened at seven a.m. sharp. She circled the garage and entered the front door of the house. John and Millicent were sitting at the kitchen table. Millicent was crying, and from the condition of John's eyes, he no doubt had been crying, too.

Adel inched toward the table.

"Adel, I've been worried sick about you. Sit. We need to talk."

Adel pulled out a chair between John and Millicent and sat down. Millicent's face was white, eyes so red they looked painful. She looked at John who rubbed his hands together, as if he was washing hands caked with grease.

"Millicent told me about Awesome."

Adel felt like John was searching her face for a reaction. When there was none he continued, "I've made a horrible mistake and I need to fix it now before any more damage is done." John wiped his mouth with his palm and looked directly at Adel. "I just told Millicent what I'm about to tell you. Awesome is my son."

Adel could not believe what she had just heard. 'His son.' Her mind spun in an effort to make sense of it. In an instant, she saw the similarities between John and Awesome, the intense blue eyes, the sandy blonde hair the tall angular build, disposition and the shared mechanical genius.

John reached out and touched Adel on the forearm. "When Madara and I first got married we really struggled. We were just kids with more self-ishness than wisdom. Our adjustment to married life hadn't gone well, and Lydia Banes and I were friends. She's the illegitimate daughter of a colored woman and white man, an outcast just as surely as Awesome has been. She needed a friend and I turned to her in a moment of my own weakness."

The empathetic part of Adel struggled to understand the issues that faced the man who had adopted her and had taken her in. First was the enormity of his daughter's pregnancy at the hands of his own son. Then she considered the ramifications for the child. What kind of a world would it grow up in not only as a mixed-breed, but also as an in-bred child? Adel thought it would be hard for a child to fathom, grasp and understanding such issues, not to mention the external ridicule the child would be subject to if people in the community knew, especially from the likes of Buddy Hines.

What must be going through Millicent's mind now that John has told her that her lover is actually her brother? How could she – how would she live with such truth. Impossible issues faced everyone, including Awesome.

Adel asked, "Has anyone told Awesome yet?"

John answered her, "No, and I'm not sure I want him to know."

"He doesn't know he's your son, does he?" The impact of the secret hit her like a blast of cold air. "He was in the dark, too!"

"Lydia made me promise that he would never know." He looked at Millicent then to Adel. "When he came to work this morning I told him that we had a family emergency and that we might be closed for a couple of days."

"What're we going to do, Daddy?" Millicent looked at John then Adel bleary eyed. "What're we going to do? We can't let anyone know about this."

"Not until we figured out what our next steps are," John stood up from the table and stepped over to Millicent, bent over and put his arms around her and kissed her on the head. "Baby-girl I know you think this is your fault but it isn't. This is my fault. I never should have made such a promise to Lydia. I should have owned up to this long ago. This is my fault. How could you have known?"

"I've done something really stupid!" Adel said to both of them.

Millicent and John both looked up at her at the same time.

"I was so angry at you, Millicent; I wanted to hurt you as badly as you hurt me."

"You told Buddy, didn't you? That's where you went this morning wasn't it?"

Adel nodded then began to cry herself.

"You have no idea what you've done, Adel," John said, letting loose of Millicent, shaking his head in disbelief and looking up at the ceiling as though the solution to this mess might be written on the plaster there.

"I love Awesome. I was so angry at what you'd done." Adel glared at Millicent her anger eradicating the empathy she had been feeling moments ago. "Why did you do it? You knew how I felt about him." She yelled and cried at the same time.

Millicent looked back at her father, then at Adel. "I did it to hurt you."

"Why, what've I ever done to you?"

"What've you done to me? You're here. My life was perfect before you came here. You've ruined everything."

Adel was about to speak and John cut her off. "Millie," he sat in the chair next to her and turned to face her. "What has she ruined?"

"It wasn't six months after she showed up here Momma died. And you," she tilted her head in John's direction, "you treat her like she's your own child, for God's sake. She has stolen every friend I have and every boy that comes around here just loves that gooey-sweet personality of hers. It makes me sick. That's what she's ruined. I hate her! I wish you had never brought her here. And now she has ruined it with Buddy."

The only thing that surprised Adel about what Millicent had said was the intensity of her feelings. She knew that her adopted sister resented her; it found its way into every facet of their relationship. The fact that she would sleep with Awesome to express that resentment was a shock.

"I didn't ruin things with Buddy, you did, Mil, when you decided to sleep with Awesome. I'm very sorry that I told Buddy, but it has nothing to do with you. It is Awesome that I'm worried about and that it creates a problem for John." Adel pushed up from the table. "As for me being here, if y'all don't want me I can be out of here in ten minutes. I don't want to be anywhere where I'm not wanted. I mean it John, if my being here is a problem . . .

"Whoa, whoa . . . we're moving way to fast here. Please . . . please sit." He motioned for her to sit back down in her chair.

"Millie, do you really feel that way? Really?" John reached out and lifted his daughters chin with his forefinger.

"Yes," she barked. She jerked her chin away from John, looked at Adel for a moment and said, "No . . . I don't know." She stood and said, "No, I don't hate you, Adel. I did, and I've felt that way since you came, but this thing with Awesome made me realize how stupid this is. What I said to you was out of habit, what I used to feel. I don't feel that way anymore. And, who have I hurt with all of my bitterness. Not just the both of you, I've hurt myself the most." Millicent looked at her father, then at

Adel. "I'm very sorry. What I've done to you is horrible."

Adel knew that Millicent's words were sincere. The genuine contriteness was written in her eyes and Adel's anger faded.

"Will you forgive me?" Millicent reached out to her father and clasped his hand, then to Adel. "Will you both forgive me?"

Her father squeezed her hand, stood and put his arm around her.

Adel sat and looked at her hands folded on the table. The awkward silence extended for several uncomfortable moments. When she examined her heart, Adel understood the difficulty that Millicent had adjusting to an instant sister and no longer the only child. She comprehended Millicent's introverted personality, her difficulty making friends and how easily she had made them. Adel knew how frustrating it was to Millicent, because of her beauty, that people did not take her seriously and how easy it was for people to relate to her instead. Finally, she thought about how desperate Millicent had been concerning Adel's intrusion into her life that she would go to the lengths she had with Awesome.

"Yes, I forgive you. I'm sorry, too. I didn't really think about how difficult this has been for you since I came to live here. Now, what concerns me now is Awesome. Are you sure he doesn't know anything about this?"

"No, he has no idea." The tears were gone. "We have to get to Buddy before he does something stupid."

"I'll go back to his house and convince him that I was lying to him." Adel had no idea how she would do that.

"What if he doesn't believe you?" Millicent leaned forward and rested her arms on the table.

"I have to make him believe me." Adel said.

"Daddy, what am I going to do, if I have this baby . . .?"

Adel thought what a place for a father to be in, anything he does will hurt one of his children. If she keeps the child then Awesome will know it is his child. Then John will have to reveal to him that Awesome is his son. The stigma of a brother and sister having a child together would hang over the child like a plague. If Awesome had trouble growing up in a community as a mulatto child, what future awaits Millicent's child who would be the product of such a union.

What of Awesome? If he learned his hidden identity and that he had just produced a child with his sister, what then? If Millicent had the child and gave it up for adoption, even having the child here in Fulton would confirm to Buddy the truth of Millicent's infidelity to him, and raise questions regarding Awesome's involvement. Surely if the child had any Negro features, there would be no question of who the father was. The complications boggled Adel's thinking.

"We have to think about what's fair for the child. I can't imagine Awesome's child growing up in this town with this mistake hanging over its head," Millicent said.

John said, "I've watched Awesome grow up with the consequences of my indiscretion. No child should experience what Awesome experienced. This child's circumstances would be far worse." John began to walk slowly around Millicent and Adel sitting at the table. "Awesome can't know about this."

"John, we have to tell him. The secrecy, at least in this family, has to end. Awesome has a right to know."

"No, I can't let that happen," John said unconvincingly.

"But you said that none of this would have happened if you hadn't kept your relationship with Awesome secret."

"Daddy, I don't like it, but I agree with Adel. He needs to know."

John said, still pacing "Alright, I'll talk to him. But Adel, we need to find a way to convince Buddy that what you told him was not true."

"And, I can't stay here, Daddy." Millicent's voice was clear; her eyes determined. "What about Aunt Betty?" Millicent turned in her chair and looked up at her father.

"Michigan? You want to have the baby in Michigan?" Adel weighed the possibility of traveling that long of a distance.

"What else can I do, Adel?" she said. "I'm certainly not going to one of those places where they perform abortions. One of my friends in school got pregnant and she went to one and nearly bled to death from the procedure."

"Millie, I think that's a good idea," John said. "Are you sure this is what you want to do? Are you thinking about keeping the baby?

"I don't know. I just know I can't stay here," Millicent said.

"How am I going to convince Buddy that what I told him was not true? And will he believe me when he learns that Millicent has left town?"

John Barnes looked instantly older to Adel as though the weight of all of this had landed squarely on his shoulders. "You'll just have to be convincing, Adel, and pray that he believes you."

34

January 7th

Em was able to take care of my father's funeral arrangements. The only thing she asked me to do was sign documents since I was his only heir and executor of his estate. I had been able to write for a couple of days without interruption, the novel progressed on schedule and I liked what I had written.

Em came in to my makeshift studio. Before I could turn around to face her, she blurted out, "You won't believe this!" Em held a tri-folded document. "I just opened this. Your father handed this envelope to me and asked me to hold it in case he didn't make it. I put it in my handbag and with everything going on, I totally forgot it. It's a will of sorts."

"He already has a will. It has been more than a year since he went over it with me, so I don't remember all of it. I do remember that he put all of his possessions into a trust to avoid probate and made me the executor."

Em handed me the paper. I unfolded it. "Change to my Will" was hand written in block letters across the top. In cursive, my father had written the following:

"These are instructions to my son Jack, with regard to the division of my estate held within my trust. With the exception of real estate and my personal property, which Jack is to handle according to my existing will, all other assets, including stocks, bonds, life insurance benefits, securities, savings accounts and cash are to be divided equally between my son Jack, my deceased wife's daughter Billie St. John and Emily McNamara."

My father dated and signed the document the night before he passed and two other people, whose names I did not recognize, witnessed it. I looked at the back of the paper and it was blank.

"Do you realize the size of his financial estate?"

"I've no idea, Em. He never discussed it with me."

"Not counting life insurance, I'm guessing close to four-and-a-half million. Who would have guessed from the modest way he lived." Then, as though it occurred to Em that the new division of property would be a problem for me, she asked, "Are you okay with this?"

"I'm very pleased, actually. He loved you, Em. You were the daughter to him that he never had. You filled a hole in his life. He was lonely and you met that need. Am I okay? Yes. And Billie? This is incredible. It means that if she wins her suit, she can use her share to buy the restaurant. For me, it takes the pressure off to find a publisher. I think my father showed a lot of class in this change to the will. I'm proud of what he did."

"I can't wait until you call Billie, and share the news with her."

"As soon as I finish this next chapter I'll call her. How is the funeral coming?"

"I found his address book. There are approx- imately one-hundred names. I don't know whether they're friends, acquaintances or what. We should send notices to all of them immediately. The funeral is two days from now. I'm working with the funeral home to find him a spot at the National Cemetery in Bushnell, Florida, about an hour north of here. We should have it nailed down this morning. Full mili- tary honors."

"He would like that."

At nine am, I opened the door for Pamela Davis, the hospice nurse. She stood at the door in pink scrubs, her long light blonde hair pulled up onto her head into a bun."

"Good morning, Mr. McNamara."

"Come in. Come in, Ms. Davis."

"Pam," she smiled. She lifted up two bags, walked past me to the dining room and placed her bags on the table.

"Before you see Ruby, could we sit and talk a second?"

"Sure." She pulled out a chair and sat with me at the table. "What's up?"

Already sitting I said, "Ruby told me that God spoke to her and told her she only had a day or so to live. She has deteriorated since you were here just a few days ago. I'm worried about her."

"What worries you? Is it the fact that God spoke to her or her deterioration?" Her voice was soft and smooth.

"It worries me that she believes she hears voices from God and that she'll just give up and die."

"This isn't that uncommon. People of faith, especially as they face death, often report encounters with God. Some see God in visions where He's calling them home. Others see relatives in spiritual form and others talk with God. I used to be skeptical like you, but this job, seeing the miraculous things that God can do, has made a believer out of me."

"I'm worried that she has a death wish."

Her mouth broadened into a smile and quickly disappeared. "Let's talk this through. Your aunt is dying. She has a very aggressive form of cancer where, once contracted, it can turn on a patient quickly. Assuming for a second that you don't believe that she talks with God, she's drawing strength to face death from her faith. The longer she lives the more complications can arise from her cancer. Each of these complications has the potential to increase her pain dramatically. For example, it could spread to her bones. We have to accept the fact that Ruby will die soon and the best of all solutions is she finds a way to cope with what's ahead. It sounds to me like she's ready. She knows where she's going when she dies and she's dependent upon God to face it."

"Does God talk to you, too?"

"Yes, absolutely. This is a very difficult job, Jack. I deal with death every day. If I couldn't see God's work in and through my patients, I couldn't and wouldn't do this work. The stories my patients tell me about their near death experiences, and how frequently God permits some people to have just a little more time to settle unfinished business, are inspiring. My experiences with my patients have demonstrated repeatedly the depths of God's love: the fact that Heaven is real. Let me go in and visit with her and then we'll talk again."

Twenty minutes later, Pam opened the door to Ruby's room, came out to the living area and invited me to return to the dining table for a chat.

"Given the dramatic change in her condition from just a few days ago, I'd have to agree with Ruby that she has a day or so. She kept talking about you helping her with a story she wants you to write and that you were a writer. Wait a minute . . . McNamara, McNamara . . . of course. My ex-boyfriend used to read your books. He had quite a collection of them. She smiled and gave a fake-arrogant shake to her head. "I want you to know that I write some, too."

"What kind of writing do you do?" I said, happy to be on my turf.

"I'm writing a collection of my experiences with dying patients. So often when people move past the age of seventy they begin to depend on family for assistance. The elderly discover, like so many other things in this throw-away-society, they are discarded to fend for themselves or they are filed away in nursing homes. I love my older patients. Most have sharp minds, sharp wit and the most entertaining stories. They're still kids inside with bodies that are failing them. You wouldn't believe how much the old guys flirt and hit on me. None of them is serious of course; it's just playful fun. The knowledge and wisdom that flows out of these elders is inspiring. I love them and I want to preserve them forever in print."

Her enthusiasm showed in her expressive eyes, the way her pupils rhythmically contracted and expanded and how the color in her glacier blue eyes brightened. I said, "Sometimes when I think about leaving this earth the footprints we leave in the sand of life get so easily washed away. However, my books will endure. I hope that if I ever have children, I'll leave something of me behind for them to remember. I actually think about that with every book I write. So I get the idea for preserving a person's life in print."

"So you don't have children?" Pam asked.

"No. Em has some female issues that have prevented it. And now that she's divorcing me, the chances for children seem to be diminishing quickly."

"I don't have children either. I haven't met a man yet that I'd want to risk having a family with. I know this is personal, but from our first meeting my impression was that you and your wife were compatible. What happened? If that's too personal, please don't feel like you have to answer. People tell me that I'm too nosey."

When conversing with someone for the first time, it is amazing how often they talk about themselves, what they've done and what they're doing. Seldom do they ask about you. In the rare instances, when they do, it is even rarer you will engage in conversations at the deepest emotional levels. These people are the rare gems in life. You want to engage and appreciate them, for they could potentially become the supporting stones in your emotional foundation.

"No, not at all. I was crippled with depression the last two to three years. It got so bad that I couldn't write anymore. My career was in a nosedive, I had contractual commitments that I couldn't fulfill and I was emotionally dead inside. It really took a toll on Em. I made a business trip to New York and I returned early to find Em moving out. She'd finally had enough. I really don't blame her. Yes, we're compatible. Very compatible. The torch Em carried for me has been extinguished and she has finally convinced me that there's no way to rekindle that flame."

Her face softened and she transmitted an aura of empathy. "And you - are you still in love with her?"

"Yep, but I know that I don't do well in a stuck position. I know I need to move past it. It won't be easy. She's my editor and a manager of sorts and for the time-being we're attached at the hip."

"She's very beautiful and gracious. I can see the attraction." She looked at her wristwatch. "Hey I have to go. I'm running late and I've a full plate today. She stood, hoisted up her bags onto her shoulder. "Your Aunt is declining quickly. So I'll begin to look in on her every day. Toward the end, I'll be here with her full-time."

"I know that she'll be in good hands."

"Thank you, Jack. That's nice to hear."

I walked into Ruby's room and sat in the chair by her bed.

Ruby started to raise herself up but fell back in exhaustion. "Jackie, help me up will you, my body isn't cooperating. And would you hand me my robe, Darlin'."

I stood, walked to the door, pulled her robe off a hook, walked back to her bed, grabbed her hands and pulled her up to a sitting position.

"I want to go down to the beach and sit on the sand and feel it between my toes. I want to sit by the water one more time before I can't manage it. And you need to bring that recorder with you."

I found her slippers, placed them on her feet, helped her put on her robe and asked her to sit still while I went to find the recorder.

I walked out into the living area. Em had gotten up and flitted around the kitchen preparing for brunch.

"Good afternoon." I said as I approached the living area.

Em turned and smiled at me. "Ruby and I were up pretty late last night talking."

"Was she preaching?"

"You're such a skeptic, Jack. Of course she was. She needs to share the culmination of a lifetime of learning about God. It is very important to her. I'm learning a lot, actually."

"She wants to walk down to the beach and then sit. She wants to finish her story."

"I'm warning you, Jack. She wants to talk about your relationship with God. Please don't argue with her. You don't know how much she loves you and is concerned for your eternal welfare. Just let her talk. Listen to her. I mean really listen. It is sort of a dying wish. So . . . ."

"Okay, Em, I've got it. I'll be good."

"Do you want to hold brunch?"

"She seems intent on doing this now. I may need your help. I don't know that I have the strength to handle her alone especially going down the stairs off the dune to the beach."

Em went into Ruby's room and closed the door. When they came out, I was surprised to find Ruby had dressed in loose fitting shorts and a sleeveless top. Using her cane, and with great effort and help from Em, Ruby shuffled to one of the club chairs in the living room and fell backwards into the chair. As Ruby got her breath, Em brushed Ruby's hair and fussed with the collar to her blouse.

"Ruby, are you ready for this?"

"As ready as I'm ever going to be, Darlin'."

"Can you walk on your own?"

"Pull me up and we'll see."

I took Ruby's hands and pulled her to a wobbly but standing position. She tried her feet. She could hold her own weight but she could only manage to shuffle her feet about six inches at a time with the use of her cane and that with assistance from Em. The steps down from the porch were challenging. We had to lift her up to take the stairs down. Letting her set her own pace, we made incremental movement forty feet from the porch to the steps over the dune The wooden stairs down to the sand were weather-beaten and warped in spots, so Em and I lifted her up with our arms in hers and took it a step at a time to the beach below.

Her pace with the cane on the shifting sand below her feet slowed us to a near stop, and even though she was not complaining, her journey took every ounce of her strength as we inched along to the water's edge. Em backed away as Ruby and I stood barefoot in the surf that lapped on the hard white sand.

The sun was brilliant and reflected on the lightly chopped ocean. Ruby watched her feet as she dug her toes into the wet sand. She looked up at me and smiled.

"Darlin,' we need to find a place to sit. This is as far as this old carcass of mine is going to make it." Em joined me as Ruby gave us her full weight. "Whew, I hope I don't die right here," she said with a chuckle.

With cane in hand, Em and I flanked her; we all shuffled about ten feet from the water.

"I need to catch my breath. Can we sit here?" With that, she nearly collapsed as we lowered her to the sand.

"Are you okay, Ruby," Em asked her.

"Soon . . . as . . . I catch . . . my breath." She took in deep breaths and gradually she began to settle down. "I suwanee, I'm not sure I can do that again."

Em said to me, "We'll just carry her back, Jack." To Ruby, Em said, "Well, I'll leave you guys to it. If you want me to bring lunch let me know."

She trudged through the sand, up over the dune and then into the house.

"Look at those Pelicans, Jack. Aren't they amazing how they all fly in formation and just skim across the tops of the waves; how such an ugly bird can be so graceful in flight is beyond me." Ruby took in a deep sniff of the air. "There's nothing as unique as the smell of the ocean. It is as if you can smell the fish in the water. I'm so grateful you and Em brought me here. You've no idea of what this has meant to me."

"I'm pleased it worked out."

"Jackie, Darlin'. I want to talk to you about God. I know . . ." she held up a hand, "you're a hard sell. Very soon though, I won't be here anymore and this may be the last chance I have to share with you something that has been so precious to me. Would you humor your Aunt Ruby?"

"Yes, of course." I'd been sitting next to her and faced the ocean and I scooted around on the sand until I faced her."

Ruby's face was the color of old bleached out concrete, parchment thin and very drawn. Her hands trembled in her lap and the grimaces etched in her face announced the pain she was in as she sat unsupported on the sand. Unconsciously, she grabbed handfuls of sand, opened her hand and let the sand drift through her fingers.

"I've thought since we spoke last, of what I might say to you that would stick, that would plant a seed from which faith might grow. And, I realized this morning, that I can't do a thing to convince you that God really is in you, that all you have to do is see it, acknowledge it and yield to it. However, I want you to remember this. I see God in you. I've experienced His love and it made me a new person. I've never been happier than I am at this moment because He poured His love into me and it sustains me. My wish, my prayer and my hope is that you will see it, embrace it and claim it as your own.

"I'll say this and then I'll give it to God, for Him to work out in His own time. If you stood at the base of the dunes and looked west, you would never see the beauty of the ocean that lay behind you to the east. Because you don't see the ocean, doesn't mean that it isn't there. Facing west all you see is your old house. If you didn't turn around you would never see the grandeur of the ocean within your grasp.

"You don't have to budge an inch, just turn around, just look inside yourself, to see the richness and splendor of that which you already possess. I'm going to pray for you until I've no breath left with which to pester God to open your eyes."

355

She was already in tears and struggled with the last sentence. Ruby moved my heart by the sheer love of the gesture, her caring and boldness with which she confronted me. I had to admit to myself, as much as I wanted to have the faith she had, it just was not there. I believed that God existed, but I just could not summon the confidence to see God as Ruby did.

Ruby pulled some Kleenex from the pocket of her bathrobe and dabbed at her eyes. "I love you, Darlin' and I don't want you to forget it." More tears.

"I love you to. You're one of the most amazing women I've ever known. There's no way I'll ever forget you." I stood up on my knees, stretched out, put my arms around her and hugged her as gently as I could. She reciprocated with the fierceness of desperation as though she could communicate her godly message through her hug. I admitted to myself that this indeed had been a powerful moment.

Ruby composed herself. "We have a story to finish and this will be the last installment."

I pulled the recorder out of my pocket and she began.

35

Fulton

1938

An arctic front had swept across northern Florida and left in its wake sub-freezing temperatures and skies so clear you could reach out and pluck the stars from the sky. Adel and Awesome pulled onto the beach at low tide just before sunrise dressed in heavy jackets, heads covered with knitted caps and, except for their eyes, scarves covered their faces to protect them from the wind. Awesome had jettisoned the windshield in preparation for the race.

In just the space of a few minutes, the sky at the horizon changed from deep purple to dark pink, then orange and then yellow as the sun edged above the horizon. The cold still air and hard packed sand at low tide were ideal for racing. While John had done a fair job of stabilizing Awesome's car, Awesome told Adel he was still concerned about holding the car on straight line at high speeds and even with smooth sand and calm winds, the car's old suspension was problematic.

Adel was accustomed to Awesome's pre-race ritual. He liked to be on the beach ahead of the other contestants to evaluate the conditions and prepare mentally for the race. The barrel, a mile down the beach was already in place. Awesome angled the vehicle away from the water's edge, eased down the beach as he checked the smoothness of the sand and looked for any debris that might be on the beach to impede his run. He turned around the barrel and aimed back to the start finish line satisfied that the conditions could not be any more favorable.

Adel and Awesome had been silent from Taggart's to the beach and the cold weather clothing over their mouths discouraged conversation. Awesome rolled to a stop in an area twenty yards behind the start-finish line and turned off the engine. He got out of the car, took a small wrench out of his pocket and opened up the boxes on his exhausts, brushed off his hands and sat back in his car.

"Well, I guess all we can do is wait." He looked at Adel and blew warm breath into his uncovered hands.

"Who's coming?" Adel asked concerned about the competition and who might be a contender against Awesome.

"Everyone. This is a big deal this morning. Very big. My guess is there will be forty to fifty cars racing – maybe more."

Adel patted the '28 Ford on the dash and said, "You're going to do just fine. You always do, Awesome." She reached over and patted him on the arm. It had been two months since Millicent left Fulton to have Awesome's child and nearly as long since she sought out Buddy Hines to recant her story about Awesome.

Adel pulled the scarf away from her mouth, turned in her seat to face Awesome and said, "I know how painful the pregnancy with Millie has been, but you haven't said a word about it. Your silence is killing me."

Awesome pulled his scarf away and said, "I don't know what to say, Adel. I had no idea she was my half-sister. It's horrible and humiliating." He looked down at his hands folded in his lap.

"I just want to know if you loved her."

He looked up at her, "What difference does it make? What's done is done."

"It matters to me!" Her emotions swelled. The words almost came out in anger as her suppressed feelings worked their way to the surface.

"I still don't see why it's important."

"Are you blind? I love you, Awesome, that's why it's important. I've loved you since the day you came to work with Daddy. Surely you must know."

The waves lapped at the sand and the sun shown brilliantly above the horizon.

"No, I didn't love her. I very much regret what happened. But, no, I didn't love her." He lifted his eyes from his lap to look at her. "And yes, I know how you feel. But, Adel, it will never lead to anything good. Look at my mother and John. They had a relationship once and what has it gotten them? They can't be seen in public together. They can't have a relationship. What has it brought them? A child born in disgrace. I'm a disgrace! My mother told me after John exposed their secret that she was so in love with John that she could never think about marrying someone else. So she has lived her entire life, since I was born, alone - imprisoned in a love that can't be fulfilled."

"Awesome, you're not a disgrace."

Awesome sat straight up in his seat and turned toward her. "I'm not a disgrace? If I'm not a disgrace, then why did it take a crisis like Millicent getting pregnant for your daddy to acknowledge me as his son? If I'm not a disgrace, then why does Millicent have to give the child up for adoption? Why? Everyone is ashamed of me."

"John loves you, Awesome. I'm sure that whatever John did or didn't do he thought it was best for you."

"You mean he did what was best for him." His eyes narrowed. "He was ashamed of me. He didn't want a Nigger for a son." Awesome turned in his seat to face the steering wheel, the newly minted sun reflecting off the tears welled up in his eyes.

"You're not a Nigger, Awesome. What an awful word."

"Then what am I, Adel," he said still not looking at her. "Look at me, I'm a freak. I'm a bleached out Nigger."

Adel had never seen this side of Awesome Banes. He was always so positive and filled with optimism. "Awesome you're beautiful, inside and out. I'll not let you talk about yourself like that. You're intelligent, sensitive and one of the finest people I know."

Their conversation settled into silence. Seabirds danced around the foam of incoming surf. Pelicans skimmed the small waves looking for their first meal of the day.

"Do you love me, Awesome?"

"What kind of a question is that?" He still did not look at her.

"It's the most important question of my life. Do you love me?" Adel reached over and lightly touched his arm.

He turned his head, looked at her and said, "Yes."

The area around the start-finish line filled with modified and stock vehicles of every stripe. About ten minutes before the start of the races, Adel spotted Buddy Hines driving down onto the beach in his new '38 Ford convertible. He parked, walked up to the makeshift desk where race officials gathered, signed in and then he did a most curious thing. He looked to one side then another and then slipped a folded piece of paper to one of the officials.

There were very few rules on Jacksonville Beach for a barrel race. There were no classes or categories. Drivers knew the course; from a standing start, they raced a mile down the beach, slowed

362

to make a U-turn around the fifty-five gallon steel drum then raced back to the start-finish line.

Two cars would go down the track at a time. When one pair cleared the finish line, another pair would start. With each race, the losers were eliminated and winners paired again, until there was the final winner.

Awesome liked to be on the line first because, after a few heats, racers would chew up the sand at the start-finish and at the turn around the barrel. Officials determined the line-up for the race based on the sign in sheet on a first-come-first-served basis.

The starter raised his voice to get the attention of all the drivers and announced that they had paired Awesome Banes and Buddy Hines for the first heat. Normally such a violation of rules would have brought violent protests from the other drivers. However, all the drivers were familiar with the loathing that existed between them and said nothing.

Adel got out of the car and now understood the significance of the bribe she had witnessed. She watched Awesome make final preparations. Hines pulled his car close to the start-finish line, and a man – who must have been Hines' mechanic – got out of the passenger seat. While Buddy brooded, cutting glances at Adel and Awesome, his man re-moved his windshield, hood and discarded recently installed covers off his customized exhaust. The man then came around to the driver's side, got in, started the engine and moved the car to the start-finish line, revved the roaring engine a couple of times before shutting it down, apparently satisfied that all was in order.

Awesome got into his car, pushed his toe down on the starter switch and his machine screamed to life. He inched it forward to the line and turned off the engine. Drivers and spectators formed a human horseshoe around the pair while the starter yelled his explanation of how he would conduct the race.

Hines sidled close to Awesome within ear-shot of Adel and said, "Screwing that little piece of white-trash too?" he said with a grin.

Awesome was silent, but Adel could tell that he was seething.

"You think that little piece of shit car stands a chance?" Buddy looked over his shoulder at his man, and the mechanic smirked. The comment brought chuckles from the other drivers hovering around them, and 'oos' from some of the spectators.

Awesome looked at Adel, his eyes nearly slits and the muscles in his jaw bulging. Then he looked back at Buddy and said simply, "We'll see won't we?"

"Start 'em up," the starter yelled then gestured to Awesome to inch his way to the line then he repeated the process with Buddy. While Awesome's car burbled at idle, Hines revved his engine several times looking at Awesome as though he could wish him into Hell.

The starter motioned for the crowd to clear away from the back of the cars, then looked at each of the drivers, raised his arms, another visual check again then dropped his arms. As the drivers stomped the gas pedals to the floor there was a deafening explosion of exhaust, wheels digging into the sand then rooster tails of sand and smoke shot out from the back of the cars for fifty feet. The cars fishtailed for the first twenty-five yards while flames shot from the exhaust pipes with each change of the gears. Between the smoke and the sand pluming from the cars, Adel had a hard time discerning Awesome's progress against Buddy. As they approached the barrel, a mile down the beach there was no mistaking the two cars side swiped each other and Awesome's car cartwheeled in the sand and exploded in a mushroom of flames.

Adel stood on the running board of one of the driver's cars that sped down the beach to offer aid. Adel jumped from the running board of the car before it stopped but she knew, looking at the burning hunk of metal and enflamed tires, that there was no way Awesome could have survived such a vicious crash.

Adel remained at the crash site through the police investigation and the arrival of the coroner. The medical examiner removed Awesome's charred remains from the car, wrapped them in a canvas tarp and installed him in the coroner's sedan-delivery styled vehicle.

Despite Adel's repeated assertions to the police and anyone else who would listen that Hines deliberately caused the crash, everyone else wrote off the death of Awesome Banes as accidental. Awesome's self-characterization as a disgrace haunted her as no one, police, fire, or coroner gave much weight to the loss of a Negro. Even as the officials went through the motions of an "investigation," Buddy Hines preened and strutted about in abject narcissism, spinning his lies about how Awesome's car swerved into his path, complaining that officials should never have let Awesome bring such a disheveled vehicle onto the beach.

Several of the drivers offered her a ride home including Buddy Hines, which she vehement-

Bill Cronin

ly declined. When she refused Buddy's offer, he glared at her and said, now out of the range of anyone but Adel, "That little half-breed Nigger had it coming, Adel." Then Hines walked to his car, the mechanic waiting in the passenger seat, got behind the wheel and drove away.

36

Ruby indicated that that was the end of the story, cried and looked extremely tired.

Something had been nagging me ever since she began to tell me her story. I had felt that at every turn there was something more to this story than she told me.

"Ruby, this is your story, isn't it? This actually happened to you."

Ruby nodded without saying a word and feverishly wiped her eyes with the tissue trying to contain the rainfall.

"You're, Adel, aren't you?

Again a nod. She lifted her head looked at me through eyes that were red from crying and said. "I killed that sweet boy as if I'd forced Awesome off the track myself."

"Ruby you can't blame yourself for what Buddy Hines did."

"I knew exactly what I was doing when I told Buddy about Millicent's pregnancy. I wanted Buddy to hurt Awesome. Over the years, I've denied that was my motive. I told myself it was Millicent I wanted to hurt. But I confess now that it was Awesome."

"But you didn't want to kill him, did you?

"I don't know, Jackie. I've asked myself that question a million times. There's such a fine line between love and hate. Awesome hurt me. I loved him so and he betrayed me. When I walked to Buddy Hines' house, I was so angry I didn't know what I was thinking. I do know this: that sweet, handsome boy died because of what I did. If I'd kept my mouth shut, if I'd controlled my anger, he would be alive today."

I didn't know what to say but I ventured ahead blindly. "It seems to me that the God who loves you so much would have forgiven you for this, if in fact you did anything that was deserving of forgiveness."

"Jack, I have no doubt that Jesus has forgiven me. I haven't forgiven me. If I hadn't had Jesus in me, I don't know that I could have managed the pain of what I'd done to Awesome Banes. I've never loved anyone as intensely as I loved him. And I want your word about this, Jack."

"Alright."

"I want you to write this story and . . ."

"What else Ruby?"

"I want you to find Millicent. She never did come back to Fulton. She stayed in Michigan and raised her child. I don't even know whether she's alive or not. I never saw her again. Will you do this for your Aunt Ruby, Jackie?

"Yes," I said.

"Will you give me your word?"

"Yes, you have my word."

"Now, I need to get back to my bed and I don't think I've an ounce of strength left."

It was apparent she was in pain. I went to the house, employed Em's help. We went back to the beach and with significant effort Em and I carried Ruby back to the house and into her room. She was so exhausted that within minutes she was asleep.

370

Em and I retreated to the living room, she sat on a club chair and I plopped down on the end of the couch nearest to and across from Em.

"Ruby's story was a confession, Em, to something she did as a young girl; a death-bed confession." I had kept Em abreast of the story as it unfolded and she began to listen to the audio files evaluating the worthiness of her story for print. I filled her in on the last installment.

"That poor woman has been carrying that guilt around all these years. Maybe the act of telling her story to you will absolve her."

"She made me promise to write her story."

"You are, aren't you?"

"Em, of course."

"She also asked me to find Millicent. She told me that she stayed in Michigan and raised Awesome's child."

We fell into silence. I looked at this woman of rare beauty, who had the ability to care at such deep levels and I grieved.

"Em. I need to know something. I need to know if there's any chance that we can patch our marriage together. I'm willing to do anything. Talk to anyone. Whatever it takes."

"Jack, I'm astonished at your apparent re- covery. Given what has been thrown at you and all you're dealing with, I'm truly impressed. I have to be honest I thought there might be a chance, I want there to be a chance, but my love for you has changed. I love you but it is a different kind of love. I guess the only way to explain it is I don't feel one with you anymore. Something happened this past year, I can't explain it but you weren't my champi- on any longer. I became a parent in our relationship and it changed the way I saw you."

I started to rebut.

"Yes, we could get back together, but that wouldn't be fair to you. You would know, deep down, that it wasn't the same. So no, there's no chance. I wish it were different. It kills me that you're taking it so hard. It makes it even harder, knowing all the pressure you're under with your dad, taking care of Ruby and the book. I've never been through anything as difficult. I just know that it wouldn't work.

"I'm so grateful to your dad for sharing his estate with me. Under the circumstances, I wasn't sure how you would react. But you handled it with class and grace and I'm so proud of you."

"Thanks, Em. Well, I guess it's over. I wish it weren't so, but I love you enough that I wouldn't want you to be in a relationship that you didn't want. I wouldn't wish that on anyone."

"Will we be able to work together? I love my job, and thanks to your dad and our settlement, I'm set financially. So even if I only work part time and only work on your stuff I'd be very content."

"Let's see how it goes, Em. Things have been so crazy I really haven't had time to think about how things would go seeing you every day."

"I understand, Jack. As Ruby would sing, 'One day at a time, sweet Jesus.' Oh, I almost forgot my attorney called and said that the settlement agreement was ready for our signatures. He said your attorney has seen it and given it his blessing. How would you like to handle it?"

"You set the meeting up and I'll sign the papers."

She agreed.

In Florida, an uncontested divorce, according to my attorney, took only four to five weeks to go through the courts once filed.

We talked about my father's funeral and the eulogy she asked me to write and deliver. The funeral was a couple of days off and I had made good progress on my book, so, I was confident I would be ready and grateful Em was there to handle the details. This kind of thing was her forte, and she made it look easy.

It was a late start, but I returned to the bare-bones 'studio' and tried to lose myself in my book and the juice flowed. My writing progressed better than any book in recent memory. The pressure of the deadline in this and the last book gave me little time to embellish or expand, it forced me to write economically and concisely, the result of which was some of the best writing I had done in a while.

There were times that afternoon that my grief was overwhelming. I had three funerals to deal with. There was my father's funeral, Ruby's imminent funeral and the funeral for my marriage. At times, the weight of losing all three people I cared about and loved crushed me. Nevertheless, unlike the emotional burdens that led to my near brush with suicide, I was handling it. When it became too much, I cleared my mind confident that I could escape into my writing and live through the lives of the characters I created. I was thankful for the gift I was given. Thankful that writing has sustained me. I knew, confidently, that I was on the mend, perhaps even past the point of concern.

Just before dinner, my cellphone rang and it was Billie.

"Jack, I've got some marvelous news."

I had never heard my sister so excited. I hoped it was about the restaurant.

"Your father was right!"

"Would you calm down and tell me what's going on."

"Coats caved, he agreed to honor the contract. We close in a few days."

"How did it happen? Details, Billie, details."

"Cynthia Pike deposed all the workers at Sloppy Joe's who had heard Coats' rant about my being a lesbian, and then filed a discrimination suit seeking reimbursement of financial damages, attorney fees and punitive damages of two- million dollars. As soon as the judge ruled that the suit could advance through the courts and set a date for the hearing, Coats' lawyers called Cynthia and agreed to pay her fees, my losses, and offered one-hundred-thousand in punitive damages. She refused it and demanded two-hundred-fifty-thousand, which they quickly agreed to. Apparently, the case against Coats was so solid his attorneys convinced him to abandon his fight and agreed to sell the restaurant. Together with what your father left me and this award, I won't ever have to worry about my restaurant or anything else for that matter." She bubbled over the phone. In my mind's eye, I could see her toothy smile and the redness of her fair-skinned face.

"I'm so happy for you, Billie."

"Jody asked me if you could come to Key West. She would like to see you. She has something important to ask you."

"I can't come right now. Do you know what it's about?

"She was vague, something to do with a book. If you can't come, can I tell her to call you?"

"Yes, of course."

"Can she call you now? Would it be convenient?"

"Yes have her call."

We hung up and what came to mind was Jody's parting words the last night she and I had dinner. She expressed a desire to resume our relationship from when we were both kids and in love. She told me to resolve my marriage with Em and she would be waiting for me. I could remember in detail how desirable she was that night.

Just as I put my hands over the keyboard to start writing again, my cellphone rang.

"Jack."

"Hey, Jody."

"I have a confession to make I was sitting next to Billie when she called you. That's wonderful news about her restaurant."

"Phenomenal news."

"I miss you, Jack. I'd hoped Billie could convince you to come down for a day. I want to see you, but I have something I want to talk to you about."

"Billie mentioned something about a book."

"I want to tell my story. I want you to write a book about how and why my mother killed my father, and my brother and sisters. I want to talk about what happened to my life and what I went through."

"You mean like a documentary? Or a novel based on a true story."

"Either. Both. I don't know. We can talk about it. Is this something you would like to look at?

"Absolutely, Jody. My publisher fired me. We part company as soon as I finish this book in mid-February. I'd like to write about something different and establish a relationship with a publisher who'll let me stray from genre fiction. When I'm done, and I turn my book over to Em, yes, I'd like to talk with you about it."

"What about, Em? Have you two gotten back together again?"

"No, Jody. Quite the opposite. There's no chance of reconciliation. None."

"You sound disappointed." She sounded discouraged.

"Yes, I am." I refrained from telling her that I still loved Em. "But at the same time I know that I need to move forward. I'm done living in darkness and I'll never descend into that pit again. Never. So yes, I'm disappointed. But life goes on."

"You need to come to me as soon as you can. Find a spare day. I don't want you to wait for the middle of February. Bring your laptop stay with Billie or me. Finish your book here."

"I don't know, Jody. I have such a tight deadline to meet. Let me get past my father's funeral and I need to be here for my Aunt Ruby. She came to stay with me, and she only has a few days to live and I'll have to handle her affairs."

"Billie told me about your father, Jack. I'm so sorry. I'll pray for your Aunt. Billie says she's dying of cancer."

"Yes and she told me this extraordinary story, I want to share with you."

"I'm looking forward to it."

"I'll call in a few days and we can talk some more."

As I got off the phone with Jody, I thought all the pain that surrounded me, the death and dying and the pressure and stress created an enormous need for love. While I coped, and I handled it all, I needed to be close to someone, to be comforted. Even though Em was here with me, she had created a vacuum she was no longer able or willing to fill. At the same time, I was still emotionally bonded to Em. I felt I was betraying Em by entertaining a renewed relationship with Jody. I know it sounded irrational but that was how I felt.

I tried to write some more, but I had lost my juice for the day. I folded up the laptop and shifted my thoughts to what I would say at my father's funeral. Then Em popped into the room and said that Ruby was awake but restless. I wondered what the experience of dying would be like for Ruby. Inexplicably I found myself praying for her that God would take her and that she would not suffer.

37

January 8th

The night before, Em and I looked in on Ruby. She was propped up and asleep but her eyes moved rapidly under her eyelids. She pointed to the area in front of her bed, gestured and talked in unintelligible murmurs. This lasted for nearly ten minutes before she settled down into a deeper sleep.

I asked Pam about it when she arrived just before nine a.m. She wore baby-blue scrubs that made her blue eyes brighter if that were possible. She brought her bags into Ruby's room, came back out and joined Em and I at the dining table.

"It isn't uncommon for the dying to see friends and relatives and carry on full-blown conversations with them. Sometimes they talk to Jesus. You only hear one side of the conversation of course, but it happens more than you think. I'd like to think that they talk to people on the other side of death, people who are assuring them that they've nothing to fear. Some people find it very unsettling. I've come to understand it as heartening. I need to examine Ruby and then we can talk some more."

I followed her into Ruby's room. She pulled a stethoscope and blood pressure cuff out of her bag. She listened to her chest and bowels, took her blood pressure and temperature. She reached over Ruby, and tidied her covers, stood and looped the stethoscope around her neck. I backed out of the bedroom, turned and she followed me back to the table where Em waited.

"This is moving pretty quickly. Her vitals are weak and her breathing is much more shallow than yesterday. You can never be absolutely sure how and when the end will come, but I'd say later today, perhaps early tomorrow."

I asked Pam, "Would you like some coffee?"

Em had gotten up early this morning, showered, fixed her hair, and wore running shorts, white socks half way up her calves and a Florida Gators sweatshirt. Just as she was, she could adorn any fashion magazine cover and look at home.

"I'd love some. I had to race out of my apartment this morning, so I haven't had any."

"Black?"

"Yes, perfect."

She took a long look at Em, then me with a quizzical expression, saying with a gesture, "Are you nuts, this woman is a vision."

Em delivered coffee to Pam and I then sat at the table and asked Pam if she enjoyed her work.

Directed more to Em than to me she said, "I tried to explain to Jack yesterday that there's real beauty in the patients I come in contact with. Their outsides may be ravaged by age, but the insides are still beautiful. Sure, there are those who've been hit over the head by life, who are bitter and unpleasant, or those who've dealt with pain for a long time and have lost the ability to cope. For the most part, they all are sweet people doing the best they can with the process of growing old. I find that many of these people, like your Aunt, are some of the godliest folks I've ever met. There's no pretentiousness. It is faith without all the B.S. I guess what I'm saying is they're real, genuine and open – for the most part."

I looked at Em and I could tell that she was impressed with this gem of a woman.

"Well, guys I have to run some errands. We need some food and supplies." To Pam she asked, "Can I bring you anything?"

"No I'm fine."

To me she said, "I forgot to tell you. I called Tom Fowler a week or so ago, like you asked, to rebuild your dock and dispose of your boat. He called me this morning and said he finished yesterday afternoon."

"Thanks Em. Thank you for taking care of it."

Pam and I talked most of the morning and got to know each other. She was most interested in the process of writing and I found myself emptying my small fountain of knowledge and offered to help if I could. She was enchanting, vibrant and funny.

By four p.m., she checked Ruby's vitals and announced that she was close to death. Pam scurried around Ruby's bed and fussed with sheets that she had straightened ten times. She brushed imaginary hairs from Ruby's brow and then something most extraordinary occurred as Pam brushed her face. She began to smile broadly and tried to extend her hand in front of her. Then just as quickly, she lowered her arm to a resting position and the smile faded.

Em sat in the chair and I stood at the head of the bed. Over the next hour, her mouth slowly formed into an oval. I don't know whether it was because she was trying to get air, but shortly thereafter Pam reported that Ruby's legs and arms were cool. She said this was a sign that her organs were systematically shutting down and by five-thirty-eight, she pronounced Ruby dead.

Ruby had already told Em that she wanted to be cremated and did not want a service. She had asked that when she passed that she wanted the lyrics to an old Christian hymn, "Turn Your Eyes Upon Jesus," read over her before they took her body away. She said that all of her friends had passed, and only her sister Glory Jean was still alive.

Before Em called the funeral home, Pam, Em and I stood around her bed and Em read the words to the song.

O soul, are you weary and troubled?

No light in the darkness you see?

There's light for a look at the Savior,

And life more abundant and free!

Turn your eyes upon Jesus,

Look full in His wonderful face,

And the things of earth will grow strangely dim,

In the light of His glory and grace.

Through death into life everlasting

He passed, and we follow Him there;

O'er us sin no more hath dominion—

For more than conqu'rors we are!

His Word shall not fail you—He promised;

Believe Him, and all will be well:

Then go to a world that's dying,

His perfect salvation to tell!

38

The funeral home came for Ruby, and Pam scurried about and disposed of all the unused drugs left over from Ruby's care. She expressed her condolences to Em and I and then left. Em and I were exhausted. I needed the time to process Ruby's passing. I could not help but wonder if she had connected with Awesome Banes when she smiled so broadly and meekly reached out in front of her. Later, Em called Ruby's sister Glory Jean and let her know about Ruby's passing and they both cried on the phone.

Over the next day, I feverishly wrote, finished my eulogy for my father's funeral while Em packed up our things and prepared for us to return to Mr. Dora.

January 9th

On the morning of the funeral, we threaded our way from New Smyrna Beach to Mt. Dora. I showered and dusted off a suit I hadn't worn in ages. Em pulled her Miata into the drive, hopped into my black SUV and we headed to Saint James Cathedral in Orlando. It was the same church where I eulogized my mother nearly 20 years ago.

The Spanish architecture was every bit as appealing as I remembered. I traveled to Orlando often but I never occasioned by the church since my mother died.

As I returned to the cavernous cathedral, and participated in the High Mass celebrated by the priest, the loss of my father and the memory of my mother's death moved me deeply. I could not help feel a little lonely. I had always seen my father as an anchor in my life and I felt secure in the knowledge he was there. Now this icon was gone.

At the conclusion of the mass, the priest gestured me toward the massive pulpit to play my part.

I find myself often in front of groups at writer's conferences or in front of cameras for interviews, none of which made me as nervous as I was now. I feared getting through this in one piece. I settled in the pulpit, arranged my pre-written talk on the surface in front of me and lifted my eyes to folks loosely collected in the first four or five rows of this massive church. There were thirty people in attendance. Some I recognized, like his fishing buddies and some of the folks he worked with and many I did not know. As I scanned the gathering for familiar faces, I saw Billie seated in the second row dressed in black her rusted hair neatly combed and next to her Alex looked as comely as ever.

I spoke the rehearsed words and recounted Father's career in the Navy from which he took such pride. I shared his doting over my mother when she struggled with the cancer that took her life, and my own deep love for a man that I respected and from whom I drew strength. I held back my tears, delivered my talk and conveyed, as best I could, the qualities of the part of my father I loved. His sins, and the damage he had done to Billie, were no one's business but Billie's.

39

February 14, 1996

Earlier that day, I finished my novel for R&R. As was my custom, I had chilled a bottle of chardonnay, placed it in a bucket of ice, grabbed two glasses to take to the dock and to celebrate the end of the madness to complete my obligation to R&R by their deadline. Em called and was on her way to pick up the manuscript.

I admired the resurrected dock, the absence of my sunken boat, and the blue grays on the water while I waited for her to arrive. I positioned the bucket between two wrought iron chairs and set the glasses on the matching cocktail table. I sat for a while and basked in the completion of the book, when I heard steps on the dock.

She said to me, "Hi, Jack I'm so pleased for you. Congratulations."

I stood, walked over to her, gave her a hug. "Thanks, Em. I'm pleased you could share this with me. She sat down. I managed the cork out of the bottle and poured wine in two fluted glasses. We toasted, "To the next book."

Epilogue

One of the events over the past month that stuck with me that I could not push out of my mind were the words to the song that Ruby wanted read at her passing. "Turn your eyes upon Jesus. Look long in His lovely face. And the things of this world will grow strangely dim, in the light of His glory and grace." I found the hymn on ITunes, listened to Alan Jackson's rendition of the song and it moved me deeply as he sang it. While I resisted Ruby's intrusion into my personal beliefs, I had to admit to myself that she had made a profound impact on me. I was in awe of her simple faith and her courage facing death. Her love for me was genuine and without condition to the exclusion of herself. I admired this woman of character.

My father's deathbed confession to Billie and his claim that God told him to come back and make things right with her, found a home in me. I have always been skeptical of miracles, but if there ever was one, I was witness to it.

I had purchased a new pontoon boat and I had parked it at the end of my new dock. I felt better than I had felt in years. The sun was setting, the sky was on fire and the lights of Mount Dora to the east began to twinkle in the twilight. While uncertainties abounded concerning my future, I was at peace. As I stood at the end of the dock, looking down at my new boat, I knew that I would never return to the darkness of depression.

The End

If you liked this Book.

Reviews are critical. Many paid promotional sites require a minimum number of "reviews" before they will allow an independent author to advertise. Without these sites, independent authors like me have little or no hope of gaining an audience for their work. If you liked this book, please leave a review. Eloquent words are not necessary. Even a simple, "I liked this book," would be helpful. If you feel compelled to say more, you have my gratitude.

If you didn't like this book

My books are not for everyone. If you didn't care for the book, or you wish to make comments, reach out to me directly at billcroninwrite@gmail.com I welcome your input.

Keep up with Bill Cronin's novels, news and his views on writing and the craft of storytelling here http://billcroninwrite.com To receive updates and news on Bill Cronin's books, "like" his Facebook page at http://facebook.com/billcroninwrite

Other books by Bill Cronin

All available on Amazon-Kindle.

Dial Tone, 2012 http://amzn.to/1QJtbph

The Song of the Mockingbird, Book 1 Jack McNamara   Chronicles,   2013 http://amzn.to/1QJsbuK

The   Tainted   Lady,   2014 http://amzn.to/1QJsFRr

Letting Go, Book 3 Jack McNamara Chronicles, 2015 http://amzn.to/1JoybJr

Joe and the Governor, Book 4, Jack McNamara   Chronicles   2016 http://amzn.to/1UDXbxk

Bill Cronin

Letting Go

First Three Chapters.

Letting Go Chapter One

Key West - 1996

If a muse were a place, Key West would be mine. If you stripped away the hordes that descended upon the island from cruise-ships, the brashness of Duval Street, the carnival atmosphere on Mallory Square at sunset and those who searched for the hard-drinking ghost of Ernest Hemingway, a quaint island remained, whose laid-back atmosphere inspired creativity like no other place I knew.

Yes, Key West was a harlot. She applied gaudy makeup to appeal to the tourists searching for "Margaritaville" and those who wished to explore the lower keys on their hands and knees. Once she removed her carnival makeup, she was charming, an exceptional beauty and accepting of artists of any

i

creative stripe. Hemingway was emblematic of the Conch Republic. He drank and caroused to excess, but his artistic side enriched people worldwide. Key West inspired me as it had inspired Hemingway to write his most noteworthy novels. In my bleakest hour, when I couldn't write a single sentence, I found my literary footing here. I bound my emotional wounds and stitched together the tattered threads of my life.

My half-sister Billie, her partner, Alexandra and my childhood sweetheart, Jody Holland lived here. I was on the mend, thanks to them. Under the threat of a lawsuit by my ex-publisher, I had returned to Mount Dora and embarked on a writing marathon. I produced two novels in less than three months. In the midst of this herculean effort, my wife of eight years divorced me. When the court had finalized the papers and I had finished the novels, Jody invited me to return to Key West to rest and heal.

It was April and only a faint wisp of spring remained. In just a few weeks, oppressive humidity and heat would return. The snowbirds would withdraw beyond the Mason-Dixon Line. The change in seasons would return control of the Jewel of the Caribbean to the "Conchs," a nickname for those who call Key West home.

Hoping to hit the seven-mile bridge south of Marathon at sunrise, I left Mount Dora by car at two in the morning. I crested the bridge just as the sun breached the horizon and bled out purple, pink and orange on the calm aquamarine waters. At seven-thirty a.m., I called Billie and asked if she, Jody and I could meet at her restaurant at ten thirty for brunch. After I got off the phone, it occurred to me that Billie had always been the arbiter between Jody and me. Billie introduced us when we were fourteen years old. We attended the same swimming and diving classes in Hollywood, Florida. I was too shy to introduce myself to her. Billie mediated. Jody was my first love and the first girl I had ever kissed. Tragedy struck Jody's family and circumstances forced her to move away. After a separation of more than 30 years, Billie brought us together again just a few short months ago.

Seeing Jody was like walking back through a wrinkle in time. Her gracious, calm demeanor remained. She drew me into her warmth as she had so many years ago. When I was with Jody, it was like one continuous emotional embrace. Perhaps it was the softness in her light brown eyes; the way she scoured my face looking for emotional clues. She leaned in close when we talked and she was always touching me. She made every moment feel intimate. As much as I had loved Emily and others before her, I had never felt this way in the presence of anyone else.

The Mangrove was Billie's restaurant. On the eastern end of Duval Street near the lighthouse and close to Hemingway's house, it was a courtyard restaurant at the base of two enormous Banyan trees. The boughs of the trees provided shade to the entire property. An older remodeled two-story home housed the kitchen and interior seating. Paved in red used-brick and crammed with round teak tables shaded by green canvas umbrellas, the courtyard was appealing and casual. The bar, a long thin Victorian structure of white painted wood and stained teak, ran the length of the left side of the property. A white picket fence framed the corner lot so that the front and right sides of the courtyard were open to the streets.

I parked my car on Duval Street a few steps from the restaurant. From the host station, at the locked gated entrance, I caught the attention of one of the servers preparing for lunch.

"Hi, I'm Billie's brother. Could you please let her know I'm here?"

I peered over the gate and admired the ambiance of the courtyard as the server disappeared into the main building. The smell of sautéed onions, garlic and peppers filled the air.

"Hey, you," she said, with a tap on my shoulder.

"Hey, you." As I turned to face her, Jody extended her arms around my neck and enveloped me with a hug.

"I've missed you, Jack. I've been counting down the days." She moved away from me enough to kiss me on the cheek.

Jody was tall, athletic, tanned and wore her dirty blond hair straight back into a ponytail. The smile on her lips transmitted what the sunglasses hid – joy. She dressed in white shorts, orange sleeveless top and white, thong sandals.

"I've missed you, too." This time I initiated a hug of my own.

"Ahem." I heard Billie behind me. "Am I interrupting something?"

"I wish you were, Billie," Jody said, laughing, as she pushed away from me to greet Billie.

Billie unlocked the gate, and we took turns giving Billie a hug.

Billie said, "I'm so glad you're both here." To me, she said, "Jack, I'm so sorry about the divorce." To Jody, she said, "I'm amazed you could carve out the time from the gallery. Every time I go by there the place is so busy."

Jody said, "No ships in port. It's a Monday. Duval Street is a ghost town right now. I'll take all the breaks I can get."

"Let's go find a table and lock this gate. I don't want anyone to think we're open."

Billie turned and led us to the main building. Jody slipped an arm through mine as we followed behind. I had never been inside the main building. The front door opened into a foyer of sorts. Straight ahead were Dutch doors that led to a kitchen. To the left were bathrooms, and to the right, where the living room of the house would have been, was the dining room. To the rear, there was a private room. Billie led us to a table next to a picture window that looked out to the courtyard. The room was white, with white painted trim. Framed, colorful Key West scenes lit up the walls. Servers had placed multicolored gladioli on the tables.

"I made us something special for brunch. I'll put it in the oven." Billie backtracked to the foyer then disappeared into the kitchen.

I pulled Jody's chair out. Once she sat, I slid into the chair next to her.

"I had hoped you would've come sooner. I've been so worried about you, with your father and Aunt Ruby passing away, the divorce, and the mess with your publisher – well – I was just worried."

"I know, Jody, and I appreciate your invitation. If I had come before I finished the last novel, I wouldn't have been able to concentrate. I was making good progress and I needed to keep at it. Now, the pressure is off and you have my full attention."

Jody shifted in her chair to face me. The light from the plate glass window backlighted her hair and her light brown eyes. She put my hand in hers. "How have things gone with Emily? Billie told me you're worried about working with her."

"What did I say?" Billie asked, dressed in black slacks and a black long sleeve blouse. She raked her rusty colored hair with her fingers as she sat down in a huff.

Jody repeated her question for Billie's benefit."

I said, "I think it will work out. She's good at what she does, we work well together and I need her. After my publisher fired me, she and Lisa, my agent, have been searching for another publisher. Working with her is awkward at times, but, so far, we manage." What I hadn't said was the divorce was painful. It had wounded me. I had hoped coming to Key West would aid the healing process.

We caught each other up on events since my last visit. Billie announced a lease burning celebration now that she'd purchased the restaurant with her part of my father's estate. She wanted to wait to schedule the event until I could be there.

"Now that I have the funds, I want to upgrade the kitchen. It's small and out of date. I have a commercial kitchen designer working with my architect and our head chef to create a state-of-the-art facility. I want to elevate food quality and expand our menu to appeal to more sophisticated customers." There was excitement in Billie's tone and her passionate gestures hinted at the love she had for her business.

Jody's gallery, which featured an eclectic mixture of local art, was successful beyond Jody's expectations. She said, "The greatest challenge is keeping high-quality pieces in my gallery. I have a stable of artists who can't keep up with demand. I'm running ads in every town between here and Miami looking for talented artists and craftsman."

"That's a good problem to have, Jody."

Our server brought our food. All three plates were the same.

Billie explained, "This Mexican egg-casserole is a western omelet with a kick." There were three individual servings accompanied by sausage patties and cantaloupe slices cut into the shape of porpoise. The chef had divided the golden-brown crusted casserole into squares. As soon as the server delivered the food, another brought three Bloody Marys. "Something to start the day." Billie raised her glass. "To three healing souls."

While we ate, we chatted about how the cruise ships had changed Key West and brought a more sophisticated tourist to the island. Yes, Key West had a bawdy reputation to maintain, ala Sloppy Joes and The Hogs Breath Saloon. But, the ships brought more upscale patrons to the Southernmost City. They were willing to pay for an upmarket experience and both Jody and Billie hoped to appeal to this class of visitor.

After the second round of Bloody Marys, the servers cleared the dishes from the table. Jody looked at me then Billie. "I want to talk about my mother." Jody's forehead creased, and her shoulders slumped. "She wants to meet in person. I haven't seen her in thirty-five years. She says it is important. She hired a private-detective to track me down, of all things."

I asked her, "Did she call you?"

"An investigator delivered a letter to me three weeks ago. That's when I called you, Jack, about telling my story. To be honest, I've spent a lifetime trying to forget it.

Billie stretched across the table and patted Jody's hand. "What does the letter say, Darlin'?"

Jody pulled out a well-worn folded piece of paper from her shorts and handed it to Billie. After she read it, she passed it to me.

Dearest Jody,

For years, I have been working up the courage to reach out to you. Until now, I have bowed to your need for privacy and your need to forget about what happened. I just turned seventy-three. It occurred to me that opportunities to tell you how sorry I am face to face are dwindling. What I put you through and the trauma you suffered at my hand are unforgivable. Given the circumstances, I expect you to be skeptical of my expressions of love, which are true and deep. There is another side to the horror of our story, an explanation of how and why it happened. I would like the opportunity to tell you my side of the story before the opportunity is gone forever.

I would like to come see you. I would completely understand if you declined or don't respond. I think, though, what I have to share with you will sharpen your understanding of what happened and

x

why. I suspect that, deep down, you may want to know - at least I pray that's the case.

She signed it, "Helen." Below her signature were Helen's address and telephone number.

I folded up the fatigued paper and gave it back to Jody. "Are you going to meet with her?"

Jody moved the note from one hand to the other and then laid it on the table in front of her. "I don't know. She's right about one thing. There is much I don't know. First, my family protected me from any news about my mother. Then, I tried to bury it with drugs and alcohol. When I was in counseling, information about what happened could only come from my mother. I had no idea of where she was and I had no desire to dig it all up again."

I asked her, "How can I help?"

Jody reached out to me and took my hand in hers again. "I want you to help me find out what happened, Jack. I don't want to do it alone."

"Of course."

"I want to know what I'm getting myself in for before I agree to meet with my mother."

"I understand, Jody."

"Then you will help?"

"Yes, of course."

Billie said, "Jody, digging around in family closets can be painful. You sure you want that?"

"That's exactly why I want Jack's help. I'm not strong enough to face this alone. But I need to confront it. This is an open wound in my life that needs to heal."

Bill Cronin

Letting Go Chapter Two

Hollywood, Florida

July 1961

At five-thirty a.m., Mario Moretti couldn't sleep. The FBI had been investigating the Hollywood Police Department for corruption. Mario's Italian heritage and previous employment history with the New York Police Department, known for corruption issues of its own, made him an easy target for investigators. He was clean, but he understood why he was under suspicion. While Mario felt the PD command staff was above corruption, he knew many of the cops he worked with were not.

Kathy, his wife of twenty years, got out of bed, reached for a robe, slipped her arms in and straightened the thin garment around her.

"You're wide awake."

He said, "The FBI thing."

The day prior, an FBI agent cornered him at a local burger joint and threatened to subpoena him if he didn't cooperate with their investigation.

"What're you going to tell them?"

"No matter what I say, I'm screwed."

"Tell them you're clean, and that you refuse to comment on anything else."

"If I say that, I'm admitting that the department is on the take. Then they'll crush me to tell them what I know. If I refuse to tell them anything, then they'll assume that I'm dirty, too."

"Take your shower, and I'll fix some coffee. We'll figure something out," Kathy said over her shoulder as she aimed for the kitchen.

As Mario pulled clean underwear from his dresser, the phone in the kitchen rang. He sat on the mattress knowing the call was from the PD; no one else would call at this hour.

"It's the chief. He says it's urgent," Kathy stood at the doorway.

"Is he still on the phone?" He turned around to see the expression on her face. Kathy was forty-four and Mario thought she was still as attractive as the day he married her. Her braided black hair hung down to her waist and her narrow thin face showed concern.

"No. He just asked that you come to a crime scene immediately. I wrote down the address."

"Did he say what it's about?"

"Nope. He didn't sound good, though. Not his business-as-usual manner. He sounded upset. You get your shower, and I'll make some coffee."

Mario scrambled to get dressed. "No time. I'll get some coffee from the donut shop on Johnson Street later."

Kathy moved to her side of the bed and sat down. "You don't think the subpoena threat could be a fishing expedition do you? A way to sweat you for information."

Mario considered it. "I hadn't thought about that. I wouldn't put it past them."

"Then I wouldn't worry about it until you get served some paper. You don't have anything to worry about do you?"

Mario looked at her. The Italian evil eye, Kathy liked to call it.

"Well that came out wrong. That's not what I meant. I'm sorry. You know how cops are. When they go down the toilet, they like to flush everyone with them. I just don't want you caught in someone else's backwash."

Kathy had been a dispatcher on the job with him in NY. She'd witnessed corruption inquisitions launched by NYPD Internal Affairs. She knew, when the shit hit the fan in corruption sweeps, everyone caught their share.

"I'm good, Kathy. I wouldn't jeopardize what we have over a few lousy bucks."

"Aren't you at least going to shave?"

"I'll use the electric razor at work. This sounds pretty urgent."

Mario kissed Kathy, bent down and hugged her.

She said, "Don't forget Clarissa's birthday. Dinner and party at six-thirty."

"They grow up so fast." Mario couldn't believe Clarissa was fourteen today. "Before you know it all four of them will be grown up and on their own. Sorry to run."

"I know."

Due to the insane hours he worked, the chief had assigned Mario a city cruiser he drove home at night. When he got in the car, he flipped on the Motorola police-band radio mounted under the dash. All he heard were multiple ambulances dispatched to Pierce Street, the location Kathy had given him.

"What the hell's going on?" he said to himself.

When Mario turned onto Pierce Street, between the ocean and the Intracoastal Waterway, emergency lights from half the cars in the department washed every surface in red. Several ambulances helped to make the street impassable. Homes around the scene were lit up and residents huddled together at the curb observing the melee. Mario parked on the side of the road behind the chief's car and jogged to the subject house. As he approached the front door, a patrol officer bolted out and puked into the hedges. As Mario walked in, he met the chief as he came out.

"Phil, what's going on?"

Ignoring his question Chief Thompson said, "Good, you're here. I want you to take a look at this."

Mario followed the aging chief into the home. Lying face down, just inside the door, was a man dressed only in his underwear. Blood was draining from a wound in the middle of his forehead. Behind him, another patrol officer had placed a small, frail woman - in her late thirties - in handcuffs. A girl, Clarissa's age, stood behind her suffering from a wound to the right side of her head. Blood covered her pajamas, but she appeared to be all right. The woman in cuffs kept saying, "Oh God what have I done? I killed them. I killed them all."

Chief Thompson looked at Mario and said, "This is just the beginning. Come with me." He followed Thompson to the back of the house and turned into one room where medics had loaded the body of an infant girl onto a backboard. She'd been shot in the temple from what looked like a small caliber weapon. The smell of gunpowder filled the room.

There was a crib, from which the attendants had just removed the infant child, and two other twin beds occupied by children both of whom had been shot in the head. One boy about three or four and another older male about seven or eight lay on their beds in a pool of blood. One of the medical technicians said, referring to the infant, "She still has a pulse."

Another attendant huddled over the younger boy and said, "I don't know how, but this boy is still alive, too."

Phil walked over to the older boy, felt for a pulse at the neck and shook his head. "Let's get these kids to the hospital ASAP."

To Mario the chief said, "We aren't done." Phil led Mario out of the room as medics raced the surviving children to awaiting ambulances. In the next room, a female child lay on the floor with a gunshot wound to the temple. Attendants lifted a girl onto a gurney and covered the child's face. Blood covered both beds. The other bed must have belonged to the surviving girl.

"Find out what happened here, Mario. Drop everything you're doing. You're lead on this." The chief pulled a handkerchief from his pocket and wiped his eyes. "Sometimes I hate this job."

Mario followed the chief out of the bedroom and back to the living room where the handcuffed woman sat on the couch. "Mario, interview the girl while things are still fresh, then get her off to the hospital. Make sure the Identification Bureau scours the crime scene. Keep me posted." The chief left him standing in the living room. A medic bandaged the head of the older girl while the woman sat on the couch repeating that she'd 'killed them all.'

The child cried. Blood matted her blond hair. Blood and tears covered the right side of her face. Still standing, she rocked back and forth on bare feet. All Mario could think about was Clarissa as he watched the medic clean the wound above her ear. The attendant dashed into the kitchen, returned with a wet washcloth and cleaned her face. The young girl stared at him, still producing tears faster than the medic could wipe them away. Mario took a handkerchief from his pocket, handed it to the girl and she leapt into his arms and sobbed. He just held her and rocked her back and forth.

Mario told the patrol officer standing next to the handcuffed woman to take her to the station. That he would be there soon.

He looked down at the girl's bandaged head buried in his chest. "Come with me, sweetheart." He considered going out the front door, but thought better of parading the girl before gawkers on the street. The Florida room was empty of any evidence of carnage. Mario led the girl to a small wicker couch with green and red floral cushions. He eased her into a sitting position then sat next to her. She was taller than Clarissa but the same age. He wondered if they went to school together. He could see a crucifix hanging from the wall in the living room. They appeared to be Catholic, and Clarissa went to Little Flower School, a Catholic elementary school in town not far from the crime scene.

The girl sat with her hands in her lap, her head down and still crying. "What is your name, sweetheart?"

"Jody," she said without lifting her head.

Mario slipped his forefinger under her chin and lifted her face up. Her eyes were light brown. Her face tanned and her hair sun-bleached. The bandage the medic had wrapped around her forehead and ear stemmed the flow of blood. He wiped the tears from her cheeks. "Jody, I know this is hard, but can you tell me what happened?"

She sniffed back a runny nose. "I was asleep and heard this bang and then another right next to me but I couldn't wake up." Her eyes welled up, her mouth contorted and her shoulders heaved.

He hugged her and told her it would be okay, knowing it wouldn't. She regained a modicum of composure. "I kept hearing more explosions. When I woke up, I was bleeding and I saw Jeannie on the floor. There was blood everywhere. I ran to get my mom. Dad was lying on the living room floor and I found Mom sitting on the floor in their bedroom trying to put bullets in the gun. She'd shot everyone!" She looked up at me. "She told me, 'Go call the police.' I called the operator and asked her to call the police. Then I took the gun away from her. She was trying to kill herself! I put the gun on their dresser and just held her until the police came." She wiped her eyes again. "She tried to kill me!" She looked at me, then into the living room as medics loaded her father onto a gurney and removed the last body from the house.

Mario signaled for one of the patrol officers. "Call the station. Have Rodriguez get over here on the double. I want her to escort Jody to the hospital. And clear the crowd away from the front of the house. I want to take the girl out of here and I don't want a circus."

The girl asked Mario, "Can't you stay with me?"

"Jody, sweetheart, the doctors need to take a look at that wound on your head. You need stitches and I need to look after things here. Officer Rodriguez is a nice woman. She'll take good care of you. Would that be all right with you?"

She nodded.

"Do you have any family here in Holly-wood?"

"No. My Grammy and Poppy went back to Pennsylvania a couple of weeks ago. My aunt lives in Atlanta."

Mario got their names and he wrote them in his notebook. He escorted the girl through the house and out the front door. Officers had moved the curious back down the street behind barricades. He led Jody to Sergeant Rodriguez's pool car. The sergeant, who headed the dispatch unit, introduced herself to Jody, gave her a hug and opened the passenger door.

"After you take her to the hospital," he tore a page from his notebook and handed it to Rodriguez, "I want you to call her aunt and grandparents and let them know what happened. Make sure someone stays with the girl until she has family with her."

Mario, put his hand through the passenger window and touched Jody's cheek. "Doris will take you to the hospital and I'll be by to see you later to make sure you're okay."

Jody nodded, her cheeks still wet with tears. He watched her as the car pulled away. The sun broke on the horizon. Humidity clung to his skin in beads. A breeze blew off the ocean, a half a block away, as though this day were no different from the millions of days that had preceded it. As Mario watched the car stop and turn left on A1A, he knew this horrific day would change Jody's life in ways no one could predict.

Letting Go Chapter Three

Hollywood 1961

Mario stepped back toward the Holland home. The Identification Bureau had arrived and unpacked their equipment. Dressed in street clothes, their first step was to rope off the yard. The street dead-ended at the Broad Walk, a macadam strip that separated the beach sand from the homes and businesses that abutted it. To the west, at Mario's instruction, barricades blocked vehicular and pedestrian traffic several doors down from the Holland's home. The scene was secure.

To John Williams, the technician-in-charge, a short heavy set black man, Mario said, "Get a hold of yourself before you go in there." Even though medics had removed the bodies, the scene was gruesome.

Once in the house, Mario retraced his steps. From the blood patterns on the pillows and crib, Mrs. Holland had shot each of her children at close range in the head. The second oldest girl had crawled from the bed after her mother shot her and succumbed to her injuries on the floor.

From the position of the husband on the living room floor, the gunshots had awakened him and he came to investigate. Mrs. Holland intercepted her husband in the living room and shot him in the head.

In the master bedroom, the .22 caliber revolver Jody had wrestled from her mother lay on top of the dresser as she'd reported. Where Jody had said her mother had attempted to reload the handgun, an empty cartridge box lay on its side; .22 caliber shells covered the floor.

To the ID Unit, he pointed out the location of the father, and the second oldest daughter both found on the floor, and then the location of the other victims. "Find the six slugs and casings, John. Take plenty of pictures." Williams was as thorough a crime scene investigator as anyone from the NYPD. Meticulous, competent, patient and organized, he commanded the quiet respect of his team. "There is little doubt what happened. How it happened and why, those are the real questions," Mario said to Williams. "And when you're done, tag and bag the sheets and transport them to the coroner's office so that positive blood matches can be made." Although there were two children still alive when medics transported them to the hospital, Mario knew their gunshot wounds were so severe they wouldn't survive.

Satisfied Williams had the crime scene under control, Mario walked from the Holland home to his car. Except for his vehicle and the ID unit's van, all emergency vehicles, save one patrol car, had left the scene. One officer remained to keep onlookers away. He opened the door, sat behind the wheel and took a deep breath. The horror of what he'd just witnessed consumed him. "Lord, Jesus," he said and tried to remove the pictures of each of the blood-splattered children from his mind. "How could a mother do this to her children? How could she perform such a monstrous act?" he asked himself. The parallels between this family and his were stark. They were both apparently Catholic. He had four children under fourteen, the Hollands, five. Kathy and the woman they hauled off in cuffs were close in age. That this could happen to such innocent children was beyond Mario's experience.

Senseless violence had surrounded his childhood in Brooklyn. As an NYPD cop, gruesome murders had hardened him. By the time he'd made detective and began to investigate the murders that plagued the city, seeing dead bodies murdered in every conceivable fashion, was commonplace. Nothing in his past, nothing in this job or any other job he'd had in law enforcement, had prepared him for what he'd seen this morning. Nothing! All he thought about was his own children and how he would have felt if this had happened to them. He wrestled with his emotions. He pulled out his note pad and made detailed notes on the crime scene and other details that came to mind that he would need when he questioned the suspect.

Mario radioed ahead to have Mrs. Holland placed in an interrogation room. On his way in, he stopped at a donut shop for coffee, passing on food. At the station, several of the officers who were at the scene, huddled around the desk sergeant each sharing what they had seen and heard. He made his way to his desk in the detective bureau bullpen and asked bureau secretary, Mable McBride, to bring a recorder and steno pad with her and follow him to the interrogation room. When they entered the room, a uniformed officer stood guard and Mrs. Holland was still in restraints. She looked bird frail. There was no expression on her face. She sat quietly, eyes fixed on the blank grey wall in front of her.

To the officer, Mario said, "Why don't you wait outside. We can take it from here."

Constructed with soundproofing, the walls were painted battleship gray. Except for glass in the door, the room was windowless. A gray military surplus table and four chairs filled the space. The white linoleum tile was permanently soiled. A fluorescent light mounted to the cracked plastered ceiling added to the room's harsh appearance.

Helen Holland sat with her hands in her lap, with her back against the chair. Her face was expressionless. She hadn't moved since Mario came into the room. McBride placed the reel-to-reel recorder in the middle of the table and plugged it into a nearby receptacle. She placed a fresh tape on one reel, fished the new tape through the recording head and then strung the magnetic tape around the empty reel. She plugged a microphone into the machine and placed it in front of the suspect. She took a seat opposite Mrs. Holland, placed a spiral steno pad in front of her. Mario took a seat next to McBride. He thought Holland's eyes looked dead and black as charcoal. Mario signaled to McBride with a nod to turn on the recorder.

"For the record, the following statement is given by Helen Holland to detective Mario Moretti and police secretary Mable McBride on July 21, 1961 at," Mario looked at his watch, "eight a.m." McBride used shorthand to document the interview.

"Mrs. Holland, I'm Detective Mario Moretti of the Hollywood Police Department. This is Mrs. McBride. It is my duty to advise you of the seriousness of this case, and to question you about the events this morning. Before asking you any questions, I want to advise you that you may first consult with an attorney before you say anything. I also want to advise you that whatever you say may be held for or against you in a court of law. You don't have to tell me anything. Do you understand this?"

"Yes."

"What is your full name?"

"Helen Marie Holland."

"How old are you?"

"Thirty-eight."

"Where do you live?"

She gave Mario the correct address.

"Mrs. Holland, for the record would you describe for us what you did this morning?"

"I killed them all."

"By all, who do you mean?"

"My children and my husband."

"Do you believe that what you did was wrong?"

xxx

"Oh, yes. I know it was wrong. But, I didn't have a choice."

"Would you say that what you did was morally wrong?"

"Legally and morally wrong," she said.

"When did the thought of doing this first enter your mind?"

"A couple of weeks ago."

"Did you think how you were going to do it?"

"Yes, there was only one way."

"And what was that?"

"The gun."

"Let's go back to earlier this morning when this happened. Approximately what time was it when you decided that you were going to kill your family?"

"I've been trying for maybe two or three weeks."

"You kept thinking about it?"

"Yes."

"What time this morning did you finally decide that you were going to do it?"

"I've been trying to decide, and then I said, "I can't do it. I can't do it.""

"What time was it when you fired the first shot?"

"I don't know. It must have been close to five-thirty."

"At five-thirty this morning?"

"Yes."

"Had you slept at all?"

"No, not really. I don't sleep very much."

"Alright. Now, tell us what you did when you got up this morning. Tell us, step by step, exactly what happened."

"When I woke up, I laid there for a while thinking. My thoughts always came back that we can't go back and we can't go forward. We just don't belong here. We can't go on this way. The children don't have a mother or father. I can't take care of them. God won't take me back and let me live my life over again. I thought of Hell, like I always have. I thought, "Oh God, I can't go to Hell," but I know we're going to Hell. They can't live any longer. We just can't go on like this. It's been the same way every morning. Every morning, every morning, every day, every day and every night; and then I got up and smoked a couple of cigarettes and paced up and down the kitchen like I always do. I went in there and got the gun, and I put it under Jody's bed. Then I thought some more and smoked another cigarette and then went back and stood over her for a long time and said, "I can't, I can't, I just can't. And I said, "You have to. You're going to Hell anyway. You can't do anything about these kids anyway. They're all sick. They have no mother or father the way they should have. Thomas was a good father, but it takes a mother. And then, I just stood over her and over her again. I don't know how I pulled the trigger. I just don't know how. But I did. I know I did. And then, I said, "Oh God, Oh God" and I went around and killed Michael, Jeannie, Daniele and then the baby. And Thomas came running into the living room and I shot him. And I went into our bedroom and Jody came in. I thought she was dead, but anyway I tried to load the gun again, but the shells wouldn't go in. Something on the gun was jammed. Then I told her to call the police. I tried to load the gun again, but Jody grabbed it from me. Then the police came. That's all, I guess, but I'm sane."

Mario couldn't believe this diminutive woman recounted such a heinous crime without a shred of emotion. She spoke as matter-of-factly as one would describe rising in the morning, reading the morning newspaper and then going for a stroll. She sat with her hands folded in her lap.

"Mrs. Holland, just for the record, which one of your children did you shoot first?"

"Jody."

"How old is Jody?"

"Fourteen."

"The second?"

"In the order of their ages."

"I'm sorry?"

"I shot them from the oldest to the youngest."

"From the oldest to the youngest?"

"Yes."

"You said you went and got the gun. Where was the gun?"

"On the shelf in the closet of our room."

"The master bedroom?"

"Yes."

"And the bullets, they were there, too?"

"Yes, in a box with the gun."

"And whose gun was it?"

"My husband's."

"Where did you sleep last night?"

"Things have been a little messed up since I came home from the hospital. I slept in the baby's room."

"Hospital?"

"Yes, I was in the hospital for a couple of months."

"Why were you in the hospital?"

"I'm dead inside. I have no emotions."

"When did you begin to feel this way?"

"After I had the baby."

Mario looked down at his notes, "Robert?"

"Yes, when I came home I just wasn't right. I just couldn't manage. I couldn't sleep. I went back to the doctor that delivered the baby and he said I had a bad case of the baby-blues and sent me to some jerk psychiatrist. And he put me in the hospital."

"And how long were you in the hospital?"

"Twice."

"Twice?"

"The first time was for a few days. They said I needed to rest. But I knew I wasn't right. I was afraid to touch the baby. Afraid that I would hurt him."

"And who was the doctor that put you in the hospital?"

"Dunfree, in Fort Lauderdale."

"And what happened when you got out of the hospital the first time?"

"I tried to kill myself."

"Why?"

"I felt dead. I knew God hated me. I hated me. I was a horrible mother. I didn't want my baby or to be around anyone."

"Did you have thoughts of killing your family then?"

"Yes, but I couldn't do it. I just couldn't."

"How did you try to kill yourself?"

"I took some pills. But I couldn't even do that right."

Mario had interrogated murders of every description; they were all crazy to some extent. But it wasn't his job to make a determination of sanity. As obvious as her poor mental state was, his job was to get the facts, charge the defendant and, in the case of felony murder, turn the case over to the State Attorney for prosecution.

Mario asked her, "Did you ever try to talk with your husband about how you were feeling?"

"No, no one understood. Not even him. I had no feelings, no emotions. I can't talk to anyone about this because it doesn't make sense to anybody

but me, and I'm not crazy. Nobody can understand."

"Do you have any remorse?"

"No. I have no feelings. I lost them a long
time ago. I just know it was wrong."

"When did you lose your feelings?"

"When the baby was born."

"Are you sorry you did it?"

"I wish I hadn't, yes. But we couldn't go on.
I just wish that Jody hadn't taken the gun from me."

"Why do you say that?"

"I wanted to kill myself. That's the only way
we could all be together."

"How many bullets were in the gun?"

"Six or so, I guess."

"Did you load the gun yourself?"

"Yes."

"Where did you shoot the children, what parts of their body?"

"In the head."

"Why did you choose the head rather than some other part?"

"So they wouldn't suffer."

"How old were your children, Mrs. Holland?

"Fourteen, ten, eight, four and five months."

"And your husband, how old was he?"

"Forty-two."

"Mrs. Holland, why did you feel it necessary to kill your family?"

"We just couldn't live anymore."

"Why?"

"Because I couldn't be a mother. I couldn't take care of them. I'm a terrible mother."

"What made you think that?"

"Cause I have no emotions. I lost the children a long, long time ago."

"They were good children weren't they?"

"No, but it wasn't their fault. It was my fault because they didn't have a mother. I wanted to love them, but I couldn't."

"When did you stop loving them?"

"Now that I look back, I guess I never loved them, but I thought I did."

"Even that tiny five month old baby?"

"Yes, I'm dead inside."

"When did you first feel that none of you could go on living?"

"I've been thinking of it for the last month. I couldn't go and leave them here."

"You mean you couldn't commit suicide and leave them behind?"

"Yes. Since the baby was born, I was just not right. I knew that when I came out of delivery. I didn't want my baby, and didn't want to be with him. I had thoughts of dropping the baby out the window. I saw myself throwing him out the window of the hospital. I knew I was a horrible mother to think those things and didn't deserve to be a mother. It wasn't the children's fault they had no mother and no father. We just couldn't go on that way. So I tried to kill myself."

"Did you tell anyone that you wanted to kill your baby?"

"No, if I told them, they would take my babies away. I couldn't trust anyone. They would hurt my children. I couldn't let that happen."

"Did you want to kill your family, Mrs. Holland?"

"No, but I had no choice."

"Why did you feel you didn't have a choice?"

"I couldn't take care of them. No one could take care of them. We were going to Hell if I didn't do something. I couldn't leave them behind. I had to take them with me. We just couldn't go on the way it was."

"Is there anything you would like to say before we conclude this interview?"

"No."

"Has anyone mistreated you in any way?"

"I don't understand why everyone is trying to be so nice to me after what I did."

"For the record, this interview was concluded at . . .," he looked at his wristwatch, ". . . eight-twenty a.m."

Mario looked at McBride and signaled her to turn off the recorder.

"Mrs. Holland, I'm going to charge you with the murders of your family, and the attempted murder of your daughter, Jody. Do you understand?"

"Yes," she said without reaction.

"You will remain in the holding cell for a few hours until we can complete our paperwork. Then we will transfer you to the Broward County Jail. The State Attorney's office in Fort Lauderdale will handle your case after that. Do you have any questions?"

She shook her head.

"I'll have an officer come and escort you."

Mario opened the door and asked the officer to take Holland to a cell.

When the officer and Holland left the room Mario sat across from McBride, "What are your thoughts, McBride?"

"She's obviously sick."

"Anyone who deliberately shoots another is sick in my book, McBride. She planned the murders and she knew what she was doing. She even admitted it was wrong. This is no crime of passion. These were cold-blooded and calculated murders. She planned every detail; even killed those children in birth order. You should have seen those kids, McBride. It makes me sick to my stomach." Mario pushed himself away from the table, stood and began to pace the small, square room. "And she sits there," he points at her empty chair, "cool as a scotch on the rocks, not a stitch of remorse and says 'she's dead inside.' That little bitch took five innocent lives this morning. Five!" Mario couldn't erase the picture of the infant shot in the temple. "It was a massacre. And, the oldest girl? The irony is that the Holland bitch shoots her oldest girl and then the girl saves her life! The only good to come out of this is I'll get to see this monster fried in the electric chair."

Mario looked down at McBride and realized that the intensity of his anger had made her feel uncomfortable. He didn't care. He said. "I called the Sheriff's office earlier and asked them to assign a detective to the crime scene. Call the Sheriff's office and find out whom they've assigned, I want them to meet me at the Sheriff's office. Then call the State Attorney and try to get an appointment with Jonathan Richter after lunch. If they haven't heard what's going on, fill them in. Warn them about the press. And before you do anything, get Holland's shrink on the line. I want to talk with him as soon as you can arrange it."

"Alright. Anything else?"

"I'm worried about the girl, Jody. Call Rodriguez. I want to know that the Holland kid has family with her. What a nightmare for her. Post two officers at the hospital entrance with instructions to keep reporters outside. I don't want the press anywhere near that kid. Call the administrator of the hospital and make sure they're prepared for the press onslaught."

"Anything else."

"Pray for that little girl in Hollywood Hospital. She needs all the help she can get. Find out if I can stop and see her after I talk to the shrink."